ALSO BY ELIZABETH BERG

The Day I Ate Whatever I Wanted

Dream When You're Feeling Blue

The Handmaid and the Carpenter

We Are All Welcome Here

The Year of Pleasures

The Art of Mending

Say When

True to Form

Ordinary Life: Stories

Never Change

Open House

Escaping into the Open: The Art of Writing True

Until the Real Thing Comes Along

What We Keep

Joy School

The Pull of the Moon

Range of Motion

Talk Before Sleep

Durable Goods

Family Traditions

home safe

home safe

a novel

ELIZABETH BERG

RANDOM HOUSE   NEW YORK

Copyright © 2009 by Elizabeth Berg

Published in the United States by Random House, an imprint of The Random House Publishing Group, a division of Random House, Inc., New York.

RANDOM HOUSE and colophon are registered trademarks of Random House, Inc.

Library of Congress Cataloging-in-Publication Data

Berg, Elizabeth.
Home safe: a novel / Elizabeth Berg.
p.   cm.
ISBN 978-1-4000-6511-0
eBook ISBN 978-1-5883-6852-2
1. Widows—Fiction.   2. Mothers and daughters—Fiction.   3. Parent and adult child—Fiction.   4. Psychological fiction.   5. Domestic fiction.   I. Title.
PS3552.E6996H66 2009
813'.54—dc22   2008049247

Printed in the United States of America on acid-free paper

www.atrandom.com

2 4 6 8 9 7 5 3 1

First Edition

Book design by Susan Turner

for Jennifer Sarene Berg
and
Julie Marin Krintzman

home safe

One Saturday when she was nine years old, Helen Ames went into the basement, sat at the card table her mother used for folding laundry, and began writing. She wrote about the flimsy heads of dandelions gone to seed, about the voices of her parents drifting from their bedroom at night, about the nest of coins she once found in a field of grass; then, finally, about the drowning death of one of her fourth-grade classmates in a pond thick with algae. She had witnessed the attempted resuscitation, and certain images would not leave her: the boy's striped shirt, his waterlogged pants, the yellow-green gunk in his hair, the Davy Crockett watch on his wrist still ticking. From her vantage point, Helen could see the second hand going round and round, measuring something different, now, than the hours of a boy's life. She saw the mother—a head of closely cropped, dark hair that reminded Helen of a chickadee's cap—she saw that mother weeping, raging, wrapped in a blanket the medics had provided in an effort to stop her shaking. She saw the mother's friend weeping with her, saying over and over in a voice coarsened by grief, "You still have Sarah. You still have Sarah." Helen knew that what the mother would also have—equally, if not more—would be the loss of her son. For weeks, she had obsessed about the drowning, trying to understand the how and the why of it in order to dislodge the knot of pain it had created in her chest. Nothing helped, not her parents' explanations, not prayer, not the diversion of friends *and play. Nothing helped until the day she took a tablet and pen-cil into the basement and moved the event out of her and onto paper, where it was reshaped into a kind of simple equation: loss equaled the need to love again, more. With this, she was given peace.*

one

"MOM," HELEN'S DAUGHTER SAYS. "MOM. MOM. MOM. *DON'T.*"

Helen leans into the mirror to pick a clot of mascara off her lashes. This mascara is too old. She'll buy a new tube today, now that she intends to be a regular working woman, someone who, rather than making a thirty-foot commute from bedroom to study and working in her pajamas, actually dresses up and goes out of her house to be among other human beings. She'll buy some *antiaging* mascara, surely they've come up with that by now. What she really needs is an antiaging mirror.

"It's not cute, what you're doing," Tessa says. "It's not *funky* or *cool* or *fun.* You'll hate it."

Helen turns to face her. "How do you know? You're talking about yourself. Just because you didn't like working there doesn't mean I won't."

"Mom. Imagine yourself folding the same sweater one hundred times a day. Imagine saying, 'Welcome to Anthropologie!' to hostile customers who only want to be left alone."

"I hardly think they'll be hostile."

Tessa waves her hand as though flicking away the blackfly of her mother's ignorance. "You've never worked retail. You have no idea how rude people can be. Or how weird."

Helen refrains from answering, *Expect the worst, and you'll get it!* She applies a thin coat of coral-colored lipstick.

"Too yellow for your complexion," Tessa says. She is the beauty editor at an online magazine; she makes pronouncements like this with some regularity.

"You gave it to me!"

"I know, but it's too yellow for your complexion. Throw it out. I'll get you more red tones."

Helen looks at the tube. "I don't want to throw it out. I'll donate it somewhere."

"Mom. Mom. It's *used.*"

"Well, then, I'll give it to Grandma." Helen regards herself in the mirrror. She sees that Tessa is right about the color of the lipstick on her. She wipes it off and puts on a pinkish shade. Then she walks to the front hall closet to get her coat.

"This is going to be a complete waste of your time," Tessa says. One eyebrow is arched, and her head is tilted in the "I can't wait to say I told you so" position.

"The operative word being 'your.' "

"What?"

"It's *my* time. I can waste it if I want to. And anyway, it won't be a waste. I need a change of pacc."

Tessa puts on her coat. She does not button it, and Helen does not tell her to. As she is frequently reminded, her daughter is twenty-seven years old. Still, it's November and cold outside, an insinuating dampness in the air. Tessa does wrap her muffler securely around her throat, Helen is happy to see.

"You aren't going to listen to me no matter what I say," Tessa says. "You're going to go down there and apply and they'll hire you because they're desperate and then you'll see how disgusting it is to work with spoiled brats and then you'll quit."

"Well," Helen says. "It will be something to do. Won't it. Do you want a ride back downtown?"

Tessa wordlessly exits the house, letting the storm door fall shut instead of holding it open for her mother, who is close behind her. Helen figures the whole way downtown, Tessa will continue to punish her, and she considers for a moment telling her daughter to take the el home, but she won't. It's her *daughter*. She wonders how many times in her life she's told herself that.

There is silence until they are out of Oak Park and onto the Eisenhower, and then Helen looks over at Tessa, who is pointedly staring straight ahead.

"*Who's* spoiled?" she asks, and is gratified to see Tessa smile, then reach over and turn on the CD player. It's over.

Tessa selects Nicole Atkins's *Neptune City* and turns the volume up. Helen boosts the volume a bit more. On music she and her daughter agree completely. They have even gone to concerts together, and Tessa never seems to be embarrassed by the fact that she is there with her mother. Oftentimes, they will both hear something in a song, and turn to smile at each other like girlfriends. They feel music in the same way; it is a source of pride for Helen. Helen's best friend, Midge, has a daughter Tessa's age, and Amanda plays music that Midge says makes her feel like shooting herself, twice. But Tessa custom-mixes a CD for her mother every Christmas, selecting her own favorite songs of the moment, and it is always Helen's favorite gift.

Helen's husband, Dan, died suddenly eleven months and three days ago, dropping his coffee cup and sliding almost noiselessly out of his kitchen chair and onto the floor. Helen, who'd been standing at the sink, still feels guilty about yelling at him for breaking his cup before she turned to see him sprawled on his back, his eyes wide open and startled-looking. She believes the last thing Dan felt was surprise, and to her way of thinking, it wasn't a bad way to go. The bad part is he left her here without him, ignorant of . . . oh, everything.

People used to accuse her of being overly dependent on Dan, and it was true. "You give away your power," one friend told Helen. "You infantilize yourself." On that occasion, Helen looked down at her salad plate as though acknowledging culpability and feeling bad about it, but what she was thinking was, *Oh, shut up. It feels good to infantilize myself. You ought to try it. Might take an edge off.*

On that awful day when Helen realized her husband was dead, it nonetheless occurred to her to ask him what to do about the fact that he had just died. She had called the paramedics; she had tried CPR, now what should she do? When it came to her—slowly at first, then in a breath-snatching rush of feeling—that she could not ask him this or any other thing ever again, Helen ran to the bathroom to vomit. Then she ran back to kneel beside Dan, and called his name over and over again. And then she called Tessa, to ask her what to do.

As soon as Tessa heard her mother say her name, her voice dropped to a flat and foreboding pitch to ask, "What happened?" But she knew, she later told Helen, she knew right away that her dad had died. After Helen hung up the phone, she swept up the shards of broken china, including one that had cut Dan's hand. Then she put a Band-Aid over the wound on his little finger because although he was now clearly beyond needing her care, she was not beyond needing to care for him. She sat staring at the cuff of his sleeve, trying not to think, until the paramedics finally arrived and pronounced Dan dead. Helen thought, *Those words don't even go together, "your husband" and "dead."* And then she experienced the oddest sensation. It was of feeling herself ascend—her, not Dan. She felt as though she were leaving the planet and her own life, never to return. Because she was herself, but she was also Dan: they had merged their two personalities to create a shared one, that was what their marriage was, and she lived inside the marriage more than she lived inside herself. For her to lose Dan—especially so suddenly—was to step off a cliff where the falling seemed never to stop.

In addition to her greatest love, Helen has lost the person who handled the practical side of their life together. All this time later, Helen is still shaky on managing the simplest aspects of her finances, despite the fact that she has an accountant to ask questions of. She trusted Dan to take care of his own income and hers; she didn't want to know anything about what he was doing. Numbers had made her nervous since early on in elementary school, when her teacher had announced ominously that tomorrow they were going to start learning fractions, and the whole class had groaned. Helen remembers sitting in her plaid dress with the little bow at the neckline, laying her pencil down carefully in the desk trough and thinking, *Okay, that's it for me.* She'd been having trouble enough with what they were doing; long division made her jiggle her leg and yank at her bangs; she was not interested in being challenged further. Later she would learn about math anxiety and the things one might do to help oneself, but by that time it was irrelevant. She and Dan both were used to her making astonishing mistakes in the world of numbers: "It was four hundred and fifty dollars," she once told Dan about a refrigerator she had looked at and wanted to buy after theirs had broken. "Are you sure?" Dan asked. "Yes!" she said. "I remember exactly! Four hundred and fifty dollars." It was, in fact, four thousand, five hundred. "Oh," Helen said, when Dan came with her to the appliance store and showed her the price tag.

She didn't see her shortcomings as serious problems. What she believed was that each person brought to a marriage certain strengths and weaknesses; so each became naturally responsible for certain things. She rolled out the piecrusts and scheduled doctors appointments; Dan balanced the checkbook and managed their holdings at Morgan Stanley.

After her husband's death, Helen had left the investment firm's monthly statements sitting unopened on Dan's desk until a few days ago, when she mailed them to the accountant. She'll get around to looking at them when she's ready, if she needs to. She knows that whatever is there has been both wisely and conservatively invested and is earning a fair amount of interest; that much of what Dan told her she retained.

Mechanical repairs have become a more immediate problem. This morning, in fact, Tessa had taken the forty-five-minute el ride out to her mother's house to reset Helen's garbage disposal, adjust the flapper on her toilet, and replace a lightbulb in the ceiling of the front porch while Helen steadied the ladder, she was really very good at steadying ladders. Helen knows she should hire a handyman since she is unable or unwilling to learn about such things, but thus far, Tessa has not complained about helping her mother—in some ways, Helen feels it is her daughter's legacy.

"Do I have to do *everything*?" Dan used to say, kind of kidding and kind of not, and Helen would say, "Yes," and she was not kidding at all. She figured cooking and cleaning and the better part of child rearing were enough of a contribution, that and the money she made from writing, which was not insignificant. She contributed her *imagination* to the relationship, didn't that count for something? It may have been Dan who built the playhouse for their daughter, but it was Helen who had conceived of the idea for the design, complete with take-out window just off the kitchen, this because Tessa's ambitions at the time included having a drive-up pie shop.

Still, Helen had meant to help out a bit more at some point. She'd had glittering intentions to roll up her sleeves one day and become a citizen of the hands-on world, to acquaint herself with Dan's toolbox, with the way to change batteries and filters and fuses. She meant to learn to jump-start a car and change a tire. ("Well, why do we have Triple A?" Helen asked when Dan offered one day to show her these things. And Dan said, "What if Triple A doesn't come?" "When would *that* happen?" Helen asked. "Believe me, it happens," Dan said, and Helen said oh all right, she would learn but not today, she was wearing white pants today. On her way back into the house, she deadheaded some petunias in the garden, thinking, *See? I help!*)

The day for Helen's baptism into practicality had never come, in the way that most people never get around to cleaning the attic or garage, leaving their survivors to argue with their siblings over what stays and what goes. And so now she has made her daughter her fix-it man. She knows it's wrong, but she tells herself it is temporary. She'll be glad when she and Tessa go to visit her parents for Christmas. Then Tessa will get a break from being on call, for Helen's father is the consummate fix-it man: one of the first things he always does is ask if anyone has brought anything for him to repair. He's a specialist in stain removal, harbors some now illegal substance in his basement that works like a charm.

Last July, when Helen and Tessa came to visit, they took a walk around the neighborhood and Tessa asked her, "Mom? How come Grandma and Grandpa live in such a tiny house? Everything's so *tiny*."

"It wasn't so tiny when they bought it," Helen said. "People didn't used to have such big houses. Look around: all the houses in this neighborhood are tiny."

"I guess."

Carefully, then, Helen said, "I kind of like it. I've been thinking about downsizing, myself."

"What do you mean?"

"Just . . . You know, I think it might be nice to have a smaller place. Not so much to take care of. When Dad and I first got married, we lived in a really small one-bedroom apartment, and I loved how cozy it was. We lived above the landlady. Her name was Mrs. Assolino, and she had this really low and distinctive voice. She used to call us all the time, complaining about this thing or that: we were too noisy, or our blinds weren't pulled down evenly."

"*What?*" Tessa said.

"Oh yeah. When we moved in, she said"—and here Helen spoke in a low, gravelly voice—" 'This is my house, see? And I don't like the blinds to be uneven. It looks sloppy from the outside. So keep the blinds even.' We would try to remember, but we never did and then she would call us to complain and she could never get our name right. She would say, 'Hello, Mrs. James? I'm calling about the blinds. This is Mrs. Assolino.' As though it would be anyone else!"

Tessa was silent. Then she said, "You *love* our house."

"I know," Helen said. "Don't worry. I'm not doing anything yet. Just thinking about it."

"Was that apartment you guys lived in in San Francisco?"

"Right."

"Why didn't you stay there?"

"I didn't like it," Helen said, remembering the way she would sit at the window staring out at the piece of the ocean she could see, homesick for the Midwest, for the flatness of the land, the plainness of it. It was taxing to live in a place like San Francisco, where tourists crowded the sidewalks and exclaimed over the beauty, and the people who lived there were so *happy;* did everyone have to be so happy all the time?

"How could you not like it?" Tessa said. "I would love to live in San Francisco!"

"No, you wouldn't."

"You always do this. You can't decide for me what—"

"I know," Helen said. "I'm sorry."

Helen supposes downsizing might be inevitable, but she can't give it much thought now. There is, after all, a more pressing concern: she can no longer write. Bad enough that writing was the way she made her living; it was also her anchor, her lens, her abiding consolation. Next to Dan, it was her greatest love. Without her husband or the practice of laying out words on a page, she feels that she spends her days rattling around inside herself; that, whereas she used to be a whole and happy woman, now she is many pieces of battered self, slung together in a sack of skin.

In what she now thinks of as the olden days, she would leap out of bed, her mind watered, as she used to say, by the rich blankness of sleep. She would pour herself a cup of coffee, go and sit in her study in her pajamas and write for four to five hours, then get dressed and carry on with the rest of the day. That meant first scanning the newspaper, trying to focus on the stories about the better side of humanity, and reading the want ads for dogs, she liked particularly to see if there were any English mastiffs being offered. Dan was allergic to pet dander and they'd never had so much as a parakeet, but Helen grew up with dogs and missed them, their glad eyes, the way their paws smelled like corn chips.

After the paper, there was grocery shopping and laundry; expeditions about town to run errands; and always, always, always, people watching. Helen thought of observation as a kind of shopping, too: into her writer's basket would go snatches of conversation, the sheen of someone's long black hair, an exaggerated limp, the look that passed between lovers. Natural events that she witnessed—furious summer thunderstorms, the oblique flight of migrating birds, the cocooning of caterpillars, the formation of fuzzy stars of frost against her window—all these seemed rich with potential for metaphor. She would walk past a nursing home and see an imaginary Elwood Lansing, trembling hands resting on his knees, waiting for his five o'clock supper; she would see a couple arguing in a car and create lines of blistering dialogue for them both. She would walk along a narrow dirt path in the woods hearing things characters in whatever novel she was working on were saying to each other. Oftentimes, embarrassingly, she used to blurt lines of dialogue out loud. Once, a man turned around and said, "Well, hey. You, too."

These days, Helen looks around the places she goes to, and nothing seems worth noting, or even quite *there*. These days, she comes into her study, sits at the desk, starts up the computer, and drinks coffee while she tries to avoid looking at the blinking cursor, that electronic tapping foot. Sometimes she moves to her little white sofa to read from volumes of poetry she used to find inspiring, and sometimes she reads from her own previously published novels. Irrespective of what she reads, though, when she goes back to sit before the computer, there is the same stubborn emptiness, the same locked door. So she shuts the computer down and leaves the room, pulling the door firmly closed behind her. Her study, once bright with bouquets of flowers and Post-it notes and various ephemera meant to inspire whatever story she was working on (once she strung a clothesline across her office and hung vintage dresses on it, items her main character would wear), that study has now become a mausoleum. The framed book jackets on the wall and the gold trophy Dan gave her when she published her first book rebuke her; the three fetish stones she always believed brought her luck have been revealed as the false idols that they are; daily, they gather more dust.

Financially, she is fine: she and Dan created for themselves a nice nest egg. It is in other ways that she is not. "You still have Tessa," her mother told her shortly after Dan died, and Helen nodded, recalling the friend of the mother who lost her child on that day so long ago, the friend who offered the same words of consolation. But love for one child does not make up for the loss of another, and anyway, the love of a child is a very different thing from the love of a husband.

Naturally, she had expected great sorrow and disorientation after Dan's sudden death. But she had expected, too, that she would eventually get better, becoming one of those women whose well-managed grief endows them with an enlarged capacity for empathy and kindness and perspective, and with a newfound ability to manage things they never could manage before. Instead, in the time since Dan died, Helen's feeling of disconnection and helplessness has grown worse month by month, if not day by day. Now she thinks she has reached a kind of crisis point, and she is afraid.

Last time she and Midge had lunch, Helen tried to explain how she felt. She said, "Honest to God, Midge, I feel like I'm moments away from everything just . . . *imploding.* I can't even think, I'm not *thinking* right. I forget words, whole thoughts. I wake up at night and I don't know where I am. I mean, I know I'm at home, in my bed, but I don't know where I *am.*" She cleared her throat against the embarrassing tremulousness in her voice.

Midge waved a hand that held a heavily buttered piece of French bread. It was unsalted butter, and Midge had remedied that with characteristic gusto—when she shook the saltshaker, grains had flown so far as to land in Helen's lap. Now she spoke around her bite of bread to say, "Oh, well, *that.*"

"No, not that," Helen wanted to say. "*This.*" But what good would it do to try to explain? Midge was the kind of woman who had no problem knocking down walls in her house—herself. She knew how to upholster sofas, how to change the oil in her car. As a young woman, she had climbed mountains in a way that required driving spikes into rock, and run marathons, and gone through men like Kleenex until she finally found one who could stand up to her. Helen and she had agreed early on in their friendship that opposites really did attract, and anyway, they were alike in many ways, too—their love of food and cooking and gardens and books, of sappy movies, of old people and children, of trench coats and white orchids. So Helen shook salt on her bread and smiled and shrugged, as though she agreed with Midge that all this angst was really rather amusing, at least in daylight, in a pretty little French restaurant, sitting opposite your best friend. She tried to act like it was all to be expected, and, once expressed, was no longer anything to be afraid of—it was a boogeyman jerked out from under her bed, a bad dream whose power slowly dissipated with the turning on of the bedside lamp. It was just problem number 445.173 in some fat medical diagnosis book, something for which there was surely a pastel-colored pill that, if it didn't fix you, made you not care that you couldn't be fixed.

"What's Amanda up to?" Helen asked, but the lightness in her tone was glaringly false.

"Listen," Midge said, leaning over the table to speak quietly. "I don't mean to dismiss all you're going through. It's just that I don't always know what to say—or do—anymore. It's been al-most a year. I know you're still hurting, of course you are, but I would think that by now you would be starting to normalize, at least a little. You seem so *stuck,* sweetheart. Not that you're doing anything wrong! Grief takes many forms, it takes varying lengths of time to move through, there are all those stages; everybody knows that. But maybe you need to find a way to change chan-nels, you know?" She took a drink of iced tea, and it seemed to Helen that in this small act was evidence of the yawning differ-ence between them. Midge's husband would come home that night and sit around the living room with his shoes off. He would find a movie for them to see that weekend. Midge would go to sleep beside him and wake up beside him, and she, like most peo-ple, took all of this for granted.

Midge was not experiencing grief. When you were, you did not remark upon it and then sip your iced tea. If you spoke about your pain in any truthful way, you clenched your fists in your lap. You looked out the window to find something to distract you, to stop a flow of thoughts that would quickly overwhelm you. Or you laughed that thin laugh that is not laughter at all but tears, rerouted. So on that day when Helen had lunch with Midge, she decided not to talk about her problem anymore. She decided to fi-nally do something about it.

two

HELEN STANDS IN FRONT OF THE DOOR TO THE ANTHROPOLOGIE store on State Street. Does she really want to do this?

"Excuse me," someone behind her says, and Helen turns to see a woman who appears to be about her age. Helen smiles and steps aside, then follows the woman into the store. She sees the woman go immediately to the checkout counter. Helen stands at the front table examining various Christmas tree ornaments, but mostly watching the woman to see if she is possibly applying for a job herself. Yes—she's just been handed an application.

Now Helen decides against asking for a job here. It's as though the woman doing it before her is doing it *instead* of her. It's a sign. Or she'll take it as one. It's astonishing how her mind vacillates these days, how difficult it is for her to come to a decision with any semblance of resolve. Last night, trying to think of what to have for dinner, she stood before the open refrigerator for so long the milk got warm. Then she made chicken enchiladas that she didn't eat because by the time they were done she didn't want them anymore.

Well, as long as she's here, she'll look around and buy her daughter a little something, for coming out to help her today. Not clothes! No, she's been told a million times not to buy her daughter clothes, even from stores she knows Tessa loves. "I just like to pick out my own things, okay?" Tessa said, last time Helen gave her daughter a blouse. Helen said all right, she understood completely, and she did; she'd almost never liked the clothes her mother used to pick out for her. Still, Helen took the blouse out of the box that day and held it up to Tessa. "This would look great on you," she said. Nothing. "You should at *least* try it *on.*" Again, nothing. "Why don't you just try it on, and let me see how it looks?"

Finally Tessa exploded. "Mom! Mom! I want to pick out my *own clothes*. I appreciate your getting this for me, but I want to pick out my *own clothes*!"

"But do you like the color?" Helen asked.

Well. Never mind anything for Tessa. Maybe Helen will buy herself a candle for her office, she used to like lighting a candle while she worked. She used to like lighting a candle and then sitting down at the computer and letting her mind tell her a story, her fingers racing so fast across the keys she could hardly keep up. Occasionally she got complimentary letters from readers. Dan called it fan mail, and Helen would always say, "It's not *fan* mail, Dan!" but it was. It was! She used to be a scab-kneed little girl who put on her mother's bathrobe and high heels and pretended she was a writer waving to her fans. And then she actually got to have fans. She got to stand up and read what she wrote to people who came of their own volition to hear her words. Really, it was a miracle, her old life. She didn't know it then. Not the way she knows it now.

A lovely young woman with blond hair styled into high ponytails, wearing jeans and a ruffled dress, comes up to Helen. She has wide blue eyes like Tessa's. She seems to be in a very good mood. "Looking for anything special?" she asks gaily, and Helen wants to say, "Why, yes! I'm looking for a way to get my life back!" but instead she smiles and shakes her head no.

She looks at some of the sweaters—every now and then there's one that would look nice on someone her age. She finds a soft blue one that she thinks maybe her mother would like. She never would have thought to buy her mother anything from a store like this, but things are different now; she feels she knows her mother better. A few years ago, she asked Eleanor to write her autobiography for Helen's Christmas present, and her mother did: she set up a TV tray in the little den where she and Helen's father, Franklin, spent their evenings mostly ignoring the television in favor of reading, chatting with each other, and whistling to their parakeet, Iggy, in an attempt to distract him from what Helen's mother calls "romancing" his plastic ball. Helen saw the bird flailing away at it once, and, in an interesting reversal of roles, stood blushing before the cage while her parents chuckled.

When Helen requested her mother's life story, her mother wrote in a green spiral notebook for almost a month. After the first few evenings of this, Helen's father asked, "What are you *doing*, Eleanor?"

"I'm writing my life story," she said—or shouted, more likely; Helen's father was losing his hearing. He had hearing aids, but he kept them in his pocket.

"What are you doing *that* for?" Franklin said, and Helen's mother told him that their daughter had *requested* it. Her father sat still for a long moment, watching his wife write line after line in her neat Palmer script, and then he leaped up to get his own notebook. That Christmas, Helen received autobiographies from both her parents, and she told them in complete honesty that they were the best gifts she'd ever gotten: they helped her lift the stubborn scrim through which most children view their parents and see them instead as real people. There they were by the popcorn stand at the back of the dime store, meeting for the first time. There they were exchanging letters during the war years, getting married on an army base with a handsome first lieutenant serving as maid of honor, settling into a new house that still smelled of sawdust. Helen intends to one day provide Tessa with such a document, hoping against hope that her daughter's response won't be, "Mom. Why are you *giving* me this?"

On the sale rack, Helen finds a pair of pants and a sweater that she likes, as well as one that she is sure Tessa will like; she's sure of it, it is exactly her style. She won't give it to her. Instead, she'll wear it, and if Tessa admires it, *then* she'll give it to her. *There's more than one way to skin a cat,* she thinks, then wonders if anyone ever says that anymore. How many things in her past are now virtually unknown by people her daughter's age? Not long ago, on the phone with Tessa, she said, "Well, you never miss your water. . . ."

"What?" Tessa said.

"You never miss your *water.*"

"What are you talking about?"

Helen laughed, incredulous. " 'You never miss your water till your well runs dry?' "

"Okay," Tessa said. And then, "Who has *wells*?"

Helen goes to the dressing rooms at the back of the store to try on the clothes. When they don't work out (*Size 12, my eye,* Helen thinks, inspecting her butt in the mirror) the young woman who takes the clothes from her seems genuinely sorry, and asks if Helen would like help finding something else.

"Oh, no thanks," Helen says. "I don't really need anything. Well, not clothes, anyway."

"There are some great-smelling new candles out there," the woman tells her, and Helen says thank you, she'll look.

The woman is right, there are some wonderful-smelling candles, but Helen is not about to pay forty-eight dollars for the one she likes best. Why have candles all of a sudden become so popular, thereby making them so expensive? And why do the ones in nice stores seem so much more desirable than the ones at, oh, say, garage sales, when they are essentially or even literally the same thing? She takes her second choice, which also has a lovely scent but is less than half the price. Then, as long as she has saved herself so much money, she buys a candle for Tessa, too. Then one for her mother, and one for Midge.

As she waits in line to pay, Helen watches the people in the store. Mostly it's young women shopping, but there are some men sprawled out on sofas waiting for them—talking on cell phones or text-messaging, yawning, lazily checking out the other women. Here and there are women Helen's age: one looks at dishes, one is trying on a necklace featuring birds that Helen likes very much and wishes she'd seen first; she's sure the woman is going to buy it because she's shopping with a friend and friends always talk each other into buying things they don't need. If they're friends at all. She and Midge have made an art of it. When they are shopping together, Helen will come to Midge with some expensive article in hand, reveal the price tag, and Midge will say, "Get it. Life is short; we'll be bedridden soon. Get it," and Helen will buy it. Or Midge will say, "I love this, but I just don't need it," and Helen will say, "So?"

When it's Helen's turn to pay, the clerk says she herself bought the sweater Helen has selected for Tessa. "It's for my daughter," Helen says, and the clerk says, "Oh, she'll love it." She tells Helen confidentially that the candle she picked out burns a lot longer than the more expensive ones and now Helen feels *really* on the ball. On the ball. Does anyone say *that* anymore? And what does it mean, anyway? If you're on a ball, aren't you nervous about falling off? She imagines an elephant in a cartoon, wearing a hat and a ruffled collar, delicately balancing on top of a huge, striped ball. There is the ringmaster with his too sparse mustache, cracking—

"Ma'am?" the clerk says.

"Sorry," she says.

"I was just showing you this?" She points to a cleverly wrapped gift on the counter, and asks if Helen would like any of her purchases gift-wrapped. Helen says no, she wants to get home before the traffic starts, but she tells the clerk she appreciates the fact that the gift wrap is so charming. "I really like this store," she says, smiling.

"You know, we're hiring for the holidays," the clerk says.

"Well, I . . . Yes." Helen smiles, shrugs.

"Would you like an application?"

"Okay," Helen says, before she can stop herself. Christmas help is temporary. It's already November 15; she'll only work here for a few weeks. And never mind what Tessa said earlier; she would love it if she could use Helen's discount.

The woman hands her an application and Helen leans forward to ask quietly, "Do you like working here?"

The woman's face goes deadly serious and she says, "Oh. My. God. I *love* it. I came here from this other store? And this one is *so* much better? This is, like, the best job I ever had, ever."

Well, Helen thinks. There's *an endorsement.* She starts to fold up the application to put in her purse, but then she sees how easy it is, how brief, and she goes to sit on a sofa beside a young man to fill it out. When she has finished, she hands it back to the clerk, who says, "Our manager is interviewing today? If you'd like to wait?"

Helen goes back to the sofa where she filled out the application and sits down. The young man has left. She glances over at the housewares department, at the dishes, the aprons, the linens, the furniture. She likes everything she sees. Really, it might be fun to work here, she wouldn't be the only older person, she could have lunch with the other woman who applied today, they might become friends; she and Midge and the woman could all go out to lunch and talk about . . . What? What kinds of stories would come from here? Maybe all that will happen is that Helen will stand around folding and refolding sweaters, checking and rechecking her watch.

And now, she suddenly feels foolish, nearly angry. An "interview" on a sofa stationed in the middle of the store for a job working with infants! What a silly idea, to think that she should apply here. What should she do, put her gray hair in ponytails and wear stylish jeans under short-sleeved, ruffled dresses that reveal her arm fat? (Hoppy and Gene, Midge calls her swinging flesh, but Helen has not quite gotten to that level of acceptance.) Should Helen speak in declarative sentences that sound like questions? Should she go countless times into trashed dressing rooms to clean out piles of clothes someone threw on the floor? Discuss with her co-workers the relative merits of nose rings? She looks over at the checkout counter, where the girl who helped her is now busy with someone else, and walks quickly out of the store. Then, remembering the sweater she bought her daughter, she calls Tessa to see if she can stop by for a minute.

"Oh, Mom, I'm sorry, but I'm on deadline," Tessa says. "I can't stop working."

"That's okay," Helen says. "I just want to give you something. I have to get home. I don't even want to come in."

"What do you want to give me?" Tessa's voice is guarded. She has told her mother over and over not to bring her things, she appreciates the effort, but she just really doesn't need anything—her place is small, she's trying to reduce clutter, she doesn't need *anything*. Nonetheless almost every time Helen visits she brings something: a coffee mug, a book, leftovers from Helen's dinners (she has still not learned how to cook for one), striped paper clips, a little pack of Paris-themed stationery, bed socks. At first, Tessa took these things graciously; then she began to sigh when she took them; these days, she sends the things right back home with her mother. Still, every now and then something slips through, and so Helen keeps trying.

"I'm bringing you a *candle*," she tells Tessa now.

Silence.

"From *Anthropologie.*"

"Okay," Tessa says.

After she gets into her daughter's lobby, Helen takes off her coat and puts on the sweater, chatting with the doorman about the prospect of snow—a few inches have been forecast, but she and Walter agree that this means nothing. "Going up to see my girl?" Walter asks. He's an aging, rail-thin man, elegant in every way, and inordinately fond of Tessa. Once when she was on the way out, he commented on her wrinkled pants—this was when Tessa was between jobs and was on her way to an interview. "It doesn't matter," Tessa told him, but he crossed his arms and blocked her way to the door until she agreed to go back up and make herself presentable. It irks Helen that she is called controlling when Walter, who interferes in Tessa's life almost as much as she, is regarded with bemused affection. When Helen once complained about this to Walter, he said, "Now, now; you know you're not going to treat your family like your friends!"

In the shiny metal walls of the elevator, Helen regards herself: front, back, sides. Oh, this sweater is *darling,* its off-white crocheted trim on its round collar, its dusty pink color, its funky clear buttons with flowers painted on them. It is exactly the kind of thing Tessa would like.

She knocks on her daughter's door, and when Tessa opens it, she says, "Okay. So here it is." She hands her the candle, and Tessa sniffs it appreciatively. "Nice," she says. "Thanks, Mom."

Tessa looks cute. She's wearing pajama bottoms and a T-shirt, working in the same kind of outfit Helen used to work in, and her long blond hair is in a high ponytail. Helen is always trying to get her to curl her hair, but Tessa likes it straight.

"So, I'll see you later," Tessa says.

She has not noticed the sweater and so Helen puts down her packages and straightens the collar, buttons one of the adorable buttons. "Do you want to come over for dinner Wednesday?"

"Sure."

Helen pushes up one sleeve of the sweater. Then, slowly, the other.

"Okay, so I guess I'd better get back to work," Tessa says.

"I just bought this sweater!" Helen blurts it out, much too loudly—the sound all but echoes off the walls. Then, in the absurd way that people do, she repeats it, in a lower voice.

"Oh." Tessa nods.

"Do you like it?"

"It's cute. On you."

"Do you want it?"

Tessa leans her forehead against the doorjamb, closes her eyes.

"Okay," Helen says. "I'll see you."

After she retrieves her car, Helen makes her way down Michigan Avenue, where the traffic is not yet terrible. She moves easily past Millennium Park, thinks again about what it would be like to live in one of the condos across the street from here, sees herself as a well-dressed woman with a mastiff walking briskly toward her place, then decides, as she always does, that she must have her garden and the quiet of her neighborhood. Also she must have the young girls across her street who play outside on their lawn all summer. Last August she looked out her study window as the youngest, aged six, danced on the sidewalk in her bathing suit with a broom. She moved as gracefully as a young ballerina in her bare feet, her head thrown back, her face full of longing; it brought Helen such pleasure to watch her. Later, the girl sat on her front porch steps eating a Popsicle and shouting out "I grant you *three wishes*!" to every passerby, then giggling into her hand if they noticed her.

It brought back to Helen one of her favorite memories of Tessa as a little girl. The summer her daughter turned four, she played exclusively with boys, although she did, in a nod toward femininity, wear her pink tutu every single day. One afternoon that summer, she came banging in the front door, a line of three little boys behind her. Beneath her tutu she wore blue jeans and one of Dan's T-shirts. Naturally, it swam on her, but Tessa loved wearing her father's T-shirts because, as she once told Helen, they left room for things. "What things?" Helen asked, and Tessa whispered, "You can't *see* them."

On that day Tessa's feet were bare and muddy, and strands of hair, escaped from the ponytail she'd insisted on making herself, hung in her face. She carried a long stick under her arm and used it to point to a blueberry pie Helen had made earlier that morning and now was cooling on top of the stove. "*That's* what we're having for dinner," she announced, and the boys stared wordlessly, admiringly, really, Helen thought. Then Tessa slapped the stick against her thigh as though she were General Patton with his riding crop and said, "Let's go!" and they all filed back outside. Immediately afterward, Helen heard Tessa yell, "Mom! Mom! Hey, Mom!" When Helen came to the door, she said, "Do you want to play with us?" Helen smiled and declined, even though she wanted nothing more than to abandon her housework and go outside with that group of free little beings. She regrets to this day the fact that she didn't do it.

Helen drives slowly, looking at all the Christmas decorations this city so enthusiastically puts up, the little trains laden with gifts atop the subway entrances, the tiny white lights on red branches in the medians of the streets, the glitzy displays in the store windows, the red bows on the evergreen wreaths around the necks of the lions that flank the entrance to the Art Institute. She almost regrets that the traffic is moving as well as it is. But when she reaches the entrance to the freeway, she sees that she has waited too long to leave downtown after all; the cars are going no more than twenty-five miles an hour and she knows it will only get worse. She loosens the muffler around her neck, turns on the station that plays only Christmas carols, and starts to sing along. But then she is ambushed by the thought of the holiday without

Dan, and she turns on the CD that Tessa gave her last year and listens instead to Pink Martini, wishing she were drinking a clear white one.

A horn blares and a man next to her gives her the finger; she has strayed from her lane. "Sorry," she mouths, but the man misinterprets her, and from behind his closed window she can see him yelling so loud his neck cords stand out.

She slows down to let the man get ahead of her, and now the driver behind her begins to blare his horn. She blinks away tears and reflexively whispers, "Dan." She knows he would be able to make her laugh at this. It starts to snow, tiny flakes. She watches them drift down, touch her windshield and disappear. Here comes Joni Mitchell on the CD, singing, "I wish I had a river I could skate away on . . ." Just before her exit, Helen sees that she is even with the man who yelled at her. She taps her horn, and when he looks over at her she smiles gloriously and waves. He, having forgotten who she is, waves back, looking confused, but smiling.

three

AT THREE IN THE AFTERNOON, HELEN IS NAPPING WHEN SHE IS awakened by what sounds like footsteps on the stairs. She sits up quickly, leaving behind a dream of a snow tunnel, of being in a hollowed-out, white place tinted with blue, where she had hunkered down for warmth and found it. She listens; nothing, now. She lies back down, wondering whether or not to try to recapture sleep, that little blessing. She remembers red mittens in the dream, black boots, the clarity of those colors. She closes her eyes, but she's wide awake; she'll get up.

She goes to the bathroom and washes off her face, then looks at herself in the mirror. Her expression is as blank as her life these days. She feels as though mostly what she does is eat, sleep, and eliminate, eat, sleep, and eliminate, like some basic life-form one step up from a paramecium. At least paramecia get to have fringe-like cilia all around their bodies, which seem sort of lively and fun. It's been a very long time since Helen felt lively or fun.

Now she hears the noise again: *Is* it footsteps? Her pulse quickens, her breathing stops. "Dan?" she calls, her hand to her throat. He's not there; of course he's not there, but if the killer thinks a man is there, he might leave. Only last week, she read in the local paper about an intruder who was frightened away when the woman who was at home (in the bathroom, no less!) called out her husband's name. She moves to the top of the stairs. "Dan?" she says again, louder.

Nothing.

Oh, what to do? She stands still and then hears noise again, but now she sees that it is coming from outside and is not footsteps at all—it is a piece of equipment someone is using against the side of their house. The phone rings and she stares at it until the message machine picks up. She hears a man's voice and listens for a while without being able to identify who it is. How lovely to hear a man's voice in her house. Then she recognizes her accountant, going on about some discrepancy and asking her to call him back.

She doesn't want to call Steve Parker. She doesn't want to talk about finances. She wants a different message. What? What does she want to hear?

Nothing.

Well, not true. She would like to hear, "Helen? It's Dan. Don't tell I called you, it's not allowed." That is a message she would like to hear; that is a call she would like to take. Even if he could never call again, if he could just call once and say, "I'm all right, it turns out everything after death is just great. I'm here waiting, sweetheart; take your time, but I'm here waiting for you."

Late afternoon in November. If it were a song, it would be a sad one. What will she do tonight? Take a bath. Make herself a nice dinner. At the notion of this, her spirits lift in the smallest of ways, like an ancient dog lifting his head at the sound of the word "walk." Recipe books spread out on the kitchen table: myriad choices, all for something good. It's a welcome diversion.

She has a pork tenderloin. She has apples and potatoes. She has green beans. She is armed with groceries.

A few hours later, Helen sits at the head of the dining room table finishing the rather lavish meal she prepared: roast pork with cinnamon apple chutney, mashed sweet potatoes, green beans with crispy shallots. She made an apple crisp for dessert, but she's too full to eat it and doesn't really want it anyway; she just wanted to smell it baking.

When she carries the dishes into the kitchen, she notices the light on her phone blinking. It's not Steve; she erased his message when she came down to make dinner. Then she remembers that when the roast was in the oven, she brought the garbage out to the curb and stopped to talk to her next-door neighbor, Joanie—probably the call came in then. She presses the button and hears a young woman saying, "This is Amy Burken calling from Anthropologie? I understand you were in the store to fill out an application, but you had to leave before you could interview? I wondered if you'd be able to come to the store tomorrow at one. I'll assume you'll be there unless I hear otherwise."

Helen stands with her half-full plate in her hand, thinking. What would be so terrible about taking a job just for the holidays? The reality is that it's six-thirty in the evening and she's in her pajamas—again. It might do her a lot of good to get out of the house and be with people, despite the fact that they're nowhere near her age. In fact, working with mostly young people might show her that she has more in common with them than she thinks. They might really like her; she might become their pet. Their affection might impress Tessa. Never mind the negativity she was suddenly seized by in the store this afternoon. If nothing else, an outside job would get her mind off her inability to work at home.

Helen picks up the phone, hesitates, and then calls Tessa. When her daughter answers, she says, "I have an interview at Anthropologie tomorrow."

"Mom," Tessa says. "Mom. Mom."

"It's just for the holidays. Think of the discount!"

"Don't do it."

Helen watches the second hand moving around the face of the kitchen clock. Looks out the window and sees only her reflection. "Thanks for your support. I'll let you know what happens." She hangs up, then picks up the phone and hangs up again, harder. "What am I supposed to do?" she asks the phone. *"What am I supposed to do?"*

She starts to go upstairs, where she intends to read until she falls asleep, then remembers she's not brought in the mail yet. There are bills, catalogues, and a large envelope from her publisher, overkill for what it holds: one letter. Helen sits at the table to read it.

Dear Helen Ames,

You don't know me, but

A fan letter. Exactly what she needs right now. Helen puts the letter in her robe pocket. She'll look at it after she's read a few chapters in a novel she bought yesterday. These letters aren't coming so often as they used to, and God knows that unless she gets another book out soon, they'll stop altogether. What a relief it will be to read that letter and apply the psychic balm that is a stranger's approval.

four

"So!" THE MANAGER AT ANTHROPOLOGIE, NAMED SIMONE, SAYS. "Why don't we talk here?" She gestures to a sofa, the same one where Helen filled out the application, and she and Helen sit at either end. Simone is a very friendly type, wide-eyed, loud-spoken. She's about thirty years old, with a chic, asymmetrical haircut and the overly shiny hair that many people have these days. It is Helen's opinion that hair can be too shiny and teeth too white, but what does she know. Simone wears an outfit that might very well have come from the store: nubby black and white wool pants, a whimsically patterned top, a wrap cardigan sweater. "Thank you so *much* for coming down here!" she says, and Helen sees the flash of a tongue stud. A tongue stud! Right in the middle of her tongue! Don't popcorn kernels get stuck on there? Can she chew gum? Is it true that those things enhance one's sex life? Do you take them out for funerals? She wills herself to stop this, to pay attention, to act like an interested candidate, worthy of hiring.

"First off," Simone says, "I have to tell you that the woman who read your application knows your work? She told me that you were *ridiculously* overqualified. I know your name, but I haven't read your books. I think my mom has, though."

"Oh, uh-huh." Helen doesn't want to talk about her books. She wants to forget about the fact that she's a writer. Was. She sits up straighter to say, "In terms of the job, I guess I should tell you that I won't be here December twenty-first through the twenty-sixth. I should tell you that right away. I imagine that's prime time here, huh?"

"Well, I mean . . . *Yes.*"

"I'll be at my parents' house, I go to their house in Minnesota every year at that time. My daughter and I will be going. On the train, you know, it's nice to travel that way. Do you ever take a train when you travel?"

Simone shakes her head no.

"Well, *any*way," Helen says, "I wouldn't be able to work those days. And also . . . I'd prefer not to work the evening shift."

"I'm afraid we do require our part-time employees to work some evenings? And weekends."

"I see," Helen says.

"We only bend the rules for exceptional applicants?"

"Well," Helen says, laughing. She's not an exceptional applicant. The truth is, she's not overqualified, either; she's not even qualified. She's never worked retail, unless you count the time she was twelve years old and sold hot dogs on a golf course. All the way downtown this morning, she prayed she wouldn't have to learn how to work the register. Or lift anything heavy—she has occasional back problems. Or be the one to greet people at the door; she's too shy to do that, she'd stand there like an idiot, her hands clasped tightly together, feeling like she was failing an audition with every "Hi, welcome to Anthropologie!" Also, she does not want to work until closing because she doesn't want to have to stay late to restock the floor, which Tessa, when she called this morning, told her she would have to do. Tessa also said, "Mom. Mom. Try this. Out loud, say, 'Can I get you that in another size?' over and over. Seriously, can you see yourself doing that?" Tessa giggled quietly, not unkindly—Helen could tell she'd pulled the phone away from her mouth in an effort not to be heard.

No, was the answer. What Helen wanted was an imperative for getting out of her house so she could stop chewing on her paw, as Dan used to call it. "Take a walk!" he would tell her when she got a little tangled up inside herself—though he never saw her as bad as she is now. "Remember the world!" he would say. And she would get pissed off at him but also she would remember the world and take a walk and it helped. It helped to see leaves on trees, loaves of bread in the bakery window, mothers holding hands with toddlers on their way into the library, butterflies making their slow rounds of flower gardens.

It used to help Helen to iron, at such times, too; to lose herself in warm, cotton-scented labor, to have the satisfaction of starting and completing a task in one sitting, a task that was not weighted with anything else, but was instead its own simple, declarative self. Helen thinks menial labor is greatly underrated and could probably cure a number of ills. But ironing has not helped her, lately, nor has folding towels or alphabetizing spices or chopping vegetables or organizing closets or photo albums. She needs to be away from her house, her old routines. What she would really like to do at Anthropologie is sit at a little table and watch people.

She tells Simone, "I wonder if I could just . . . I guess what I'd like to do is work a couple of days a week, or, you know, even one day a week. That would be fine, one day a week. Doing something like gift wrapping. Just gift wrapping. Would that be a possibility?"

Simone shifts on the sofa. "Remember how you came down here and filled out an application and didn't stay for an interview?"

"Right, the traffic. I was trying to beat the traffic."

"Well, we hired so many people that day"—and here she leans in closer to Helen as though they are confidantes and nearly whispers—"we *over*hired. So . . . we kind of have a *problem*. We thought some people would drop off? They always do? But this time no one did. So we're actually . . . We really don't need any-one right now."

Helen feels a great lifting inside; a wonderful relief, mixed with a vague confusion. If they have enough people, why didn't they call her and tell her not to come? "I see." She stands, shoul-ders her purse, buttons her coat. "Well, thanks anyway."

"Of course," Simone says. "And thank you *so much* for com-ing down."

Helen walks quickly out of the store and down the sidewalk. She will go home and call Tessa and she will say, "I didn't get the job." Then she will call Midge and confess that she has appar-ently fallen a bit farther down the rabbit hole. Then she will read the letter she never got to last night. She fell asleep lying on top of her bedcovers, in her robe and slippers, her glasses on. When Dan was alive, he would find her like this sometimes, and he would gently remove her glasses, take off her slippers, and cover her with a quilt. Sometimes he awakened her with his ministrations, but she never let him know. She kept her eyes closed and waited for the little puff of air just before the quilt settled on her, waited for Dan's lips to press lightly against her forehead. Sometimes after he did that he would stand watching her sleep; she could feel it. The next time Tessa asks her mother why in the world she should ever get married, Helen will answer by telling her that.

It's cold in the house when Helen comes in, dark, too. She turns on lights in the kitchen and the living room, boosts the heat, and then sits at the table with her coat on. She stares into space, recall-ing the "interview" she had with Simone, and wonders again why the woman asked her to come in. It must have been that, soon after meeting Helen, she decided she didn't want to hire her. Helen really must get a grip on herself, and stop trying to get jobs she doesn't even want. Surely her need and desire to write will come back soon; in the meantime, why doesn't she simply enjoy the break? Why can't she sit at the breakfast table taking in the angle of the morning sun, the sight of birds at the feeder? Why can't she visit a coffee shop and eavesdrop for the simple pleasure of hearing another's syntax, vocabulary, accent, problems? Afternoon movies can be a wonderful diversion: why doesn't she walk over to the Lake Theatre, buy herself a heavily buttered popcorn, and lose herself in someone else's story? Because she wants to write her own stories, that's why. Because she misses having that elemental need satisfied. She feels like a junkie, jittery with need, unable to focus on anything but obtaining that fix, that fix, that fix.

Ah, well. She'll read the fan letter now and that will make her feel better, it will erase some of the indignity of the day. It will remind her that she is a respected author, with a lot to be grateful for, despite her present woes.

She takes off her coat and boots, and goes upstairs to pull the letter from the robe pocket. She perches on the edge of her bed to read it, but the room is cold—some draft has developed somewhere. She comes back downstairs and lays the letter on the kitchen table—she'll read it here, with a cup of hibiscus tea, how civilized, how very pleasant. She puts the kettle on and slides out the page. It's a short letter, only one paragraph, but many times Helen has gotten a letter brief in content yet full of feeling.

Dear Helen Ames,

You don't know me, but I've been wanting to write to you for a long time.

Usually when people start this way, they go on to say very specific and gratifying things about one of Helen's titles—or many titles. She reads on eagerly.

I can't tell you how surprised I am by the quality of your books. I was given the first by a friend who told me I really had to read it; it was your novel Telling Songs. *I did read it, and I must say I wondered about my friend when I'd finished—I enjoyed nothing about that mawkish and clumsily written book. But then I thought, Well, maybe it's a fluke; my friend—whom I normally admire—is so fond of you; and so I checked a few more of your books out of the library, only to find that I didn't like them, either. Who are you to have had these novels published? Your prose style is not "deceptively simple," as one reviewer wrote, but insipid. I feel compelled to write this to you because I am so frustrated by what passes for literature these days.*

Margot Langley

Against all better judgment, Helen reads the letter again. Then a third time. She smells it: nothing. Then she puts it on the table and folds her hands in her lap and stares straight ahead. When the teakettle whistles, she makes herself a cup of tea. A better woman would laugh at such a letter. Or be empowered by it; a better woman would think, *Oh yeah, well watch this!* and immediately turn out seven pages. Or she would show the letter to her friends, and they would rush to her defense, and that would make her feel better. Or she would stop reading the letter halfway through, throw it in the trash, and move on to something of worth.

Helen reads the thing yet again, then goes to get her stationery and writes:

Dear Margot Langley,

You ask who I am. That is a question I've been asking myself a lot lately. And the conclusion I have come to is this: not a writer. Not anymore. I hope this news will gladden your day, which will be in diametric opposition to what your letter did to mine.

She signs her name, and reads her letter again. Then she tears it up and throws it in the trash. The letter from Margot Langley, she keeps. She puts it in her kitchen junk drawer, beneath the rubber bands, the take-out menus, the extra keys and birthday cake candles. Even as she does this, she wishes she wouldn't. Bad enough that she will parse the attack over and over in her mind; must she also let the evidence live in her house? But for some reason, she feels she is not finished with it.

Later that evening, she eats a dinner of saltine crackers with peanut butter and great dollops of grape jelly. Then she puts on her pajamas and crawls into bed. She calls Tessa, who does not answer, and leaves her a message. "I didn't get the job at Anthropologie," she says. "Maybe you already heard and you're out celebrating." She pauses, and makes her voice more cheerful. "Hey!" she says. "I got your email with the video of that guy doing the Tim Gunn imitation. He sounds *just like him.*" Another pause, and then, "Want to see a movie tomorrow night? I could come downtown. We could go to a five o'clock in case you have plans for later on. . . . Let me know."

She hangs up, opens the novel she began last night, closes it, and lies staring out the windows into the dark. It is six-forty. Tomorrow morning she will call Midge and say, Help. I'm serious. Help me. She will not tell Tessa or Midge about the letter. She will not tell anyone. She closes her eyes and Margot Langley's words float back into her brain; she has the letter memorized.

She opens the novel again, reads one page, another. Then another. And finally, everything in her own life surrenders to the one being presented here. An uneasy pain thins, lifts, disappears. Dan once had a friend who died from metastatic cancer. Toward the end, Dan visited him with some frequency; and each time he would call before going, to see what his friend might want or need. Each time, his friend requested the same thing: books.

five

THE PHONE RINGS, WAKING HELEN UP. SHE PUTS HER HAND OVER her eyes against the strong sunlight coming through her bedroom window and lies still, listening to see who's calling. Steve Parker again. "I don't know if you got the message," he says, "but I really need to talk to you, Helen. Please call."

While he recites his number, she reaches for the phone, but then doesn't pick it up. She's got morning voice; it's after ten o'clock; she'd be embarrassed by her sloth. She'll call him later. She's beginning to be annoyed by his persistence. He's an accountant; can't he figure out whatever he's calling about by himself? What does she pay him for? What help can she possibly be? She feels herself getting angrier and then stops; she's blaming Steve for her husband still being dead. She looks over at the other side of the bed, reaches out to touch the uncreased pillowcase. Odd the way she looks every day to see if it is still so pristine. She knows it will be; yet she looks to see if it is. Sometimes she thinks coming to terms with Dan's death is like a log being rammed into a door.

Eventually, it will get through. Until then, she will awaken each day and the first thing she will do is look to his side of the bed.

She sits up and stretches, then casts about inside herself to see if today, if *today,* she feels a little bit like working, if she feels that *something* might be in her that would like to come out. Nope. The very notion of going into her study makes her stomach tense.

So. What to do. Call Midge, who was not home last night, and so Helen left a message about her experience at Anthropologie; she left what she thought was a very amusing message, considering.

But now Midge does not seem all that amused. "Listen," she says, after Helen asks if she got her message, "don't be offended, but I just have to say this. Anthropologie? You're almost sixty years old! Why would you want to work *there*? Why don't you stop being so self-obsessed and volunteer for some organization that really needs you? Give *back* a little."

Helen, wounded, sucks in a breath, clenches the phone tighter in her hand.

"I didn't mean that to be as harsh as it came out," Midge says. "This is tough love, okay?"

"I do give back! I give lots of money to all kinds of—"

"I don't mean checks in an envelope," Midge says. "I mean you should give of *yourself.* Volunteer to stack cans at a food pantry. Deliver Meals on Wheels. Walk dogs at a shelter. There are a million places to volunteer! Teach someone to read, for God's sake!"

"I can't do that," Helen says. "Every time I try to volunteer, they tell me they need a certain commitment, and when my life is *normal,* I *work* a lot, and I can't tell what day is going to be a really good writing day when I won't want to stop. And I also *travel* a lot for public speaking. I have a speaking gig in a few weeks, as a matter of fact. Though I'm thinking of canceling it."

"*Why?* "

"Because I'm a fraud, that's why."

"You're not a fraud," Midge says. "If you can't write for the time being, so what? Go out and live some life. That's what will give you the seeds to sow for the work you will come to do."

It occurs to Helen to ask Midge if she's having a Kumbaya moment. Instead, she looks out the window, where a bird has landed on a branch of a tree outside. The bird stares directly ahead, as though at her, cocking its head left, then right. *How about it? How about sowing some seeds?*

"Midge, it's . . . I *need* writing. Not the success, the success just makes me feel weird. *Grateful,* but weird. Writing to me is . . . It's not just the way I make my living. It's always been the place where I *put* things. It's my solace in a world that . . . God! It just seems like such a terrible world!"

"It *is* a terrible world," Midge says. "Also it is one of incalculable beauty. You know that."

"I have forgotten that," Helen says and hears the bitterness in her voice.

"That's why you have to do something to remember it."

"I have to go," Helen says.

"No, you don't. You're just pissed off."

Helen doesn't answer. She bites at her lip and watches the bird, who suddenly lifts off from the branch and flies away.

"Aren't you?"

"Well, I have to say, Midge, that you don't seem to be very supportive of the fact that I seem to be losing my mind! I really feel like I am!"

"Hmm," Midge says. "Now, why would I ever want to be supportive of you losing your mind?"

"Oh, you just . . . Look, I know you want me to be King Kong, but I'm *not* King Kong. I'm the princess and the pea, okay? I would feel the pea, I swear. I don't *want* to feel the pea, but I *would* feel it! Did you ever hear of Gregor Mendel? Some people—"

"Oh, stop using the theory of *genetics* as a rationalization.

Get dressed and meet me at the Museum of Contemporary Art in an hour," Midge says.

"How do you know I'm not dressed?"

"Took a wild guess. I would also wildly guess that you haven't washed your face or combed your hair. Or even looked at the newspaper, as usual."

"Okay, in fact I do look at the newspaper, and I usually elect not to read it. Why should I read it! It would only make me feel worse. Why don't they have a Pollyanna column, where the only news there is *good* news: humanitarian triumphs, small gestures of goodwill, recipes, who cares, just *one* place where you know you can go and read something and not feel *assaulted*?"

"Maybe you should write such a column," Midge says.

"Maybe you should remember that I *can't write*." Helen fumes quietly for a moment, then says, "Fine, I'll meet you at the museum. What's there?"

"An exhibit that's live people, and all they do is kiss."

Helen recalls a time she was sixteen and made a bet that she could kiss for ten minutes without stopping. She did it, she kissed a really cute boy she'd been very much attracted to, but the kiss lost all its passion after about thirty seconds and became an act roughly equivalent to cleaning out one's ears. Why in the world would a museum feature such an exhibit? She starts to ask Midge that, but then decides to find out for herself. Somewhere inside her weary brain, a little light flickers, then holds. "I'll see you there," she says.

Helen takes a long shower, using a great variety of the products she has available due to the largesse of her daughter. What Helen truly believes is that she could use 409 to wash herself and her hair and it would be fine, but in the area of beauty products she is a hypocrite. As she is in many areas of her life. She wonders sometimes how many people live lives congruent with their deepest beliefs. She wonders how many people go running off to seminars intent on changing their lives, then come home and fall back into the exact same patterns. Most people, she suspects. That's why those seminars make so much money, people keep failing to achieve their lofty ideals. And what about the people who teach those seminars? They're just as hypocritical as anyone else, Helen is sure of it. She thinks of her mother, telling her once that she didn't believe in therapy because psychiatrists were the craziest people of all. Helen herself has doubts about the efficacy of therapy: she tried it once, years ago. But she didn't like the way she would wake up on appointment days feeling perfectly fine and then have to dredge up some discontent so as to justify the time and expense. She quit after only three sessions, saying that the reason she was leaving was that she was moving. "Oh?" the therapist said. "Where to?" "Cleveland," Helen said, knowing nothing about the place and hoping the therapist didn't, either. Serene, that woman was called, unbelievably—Helen thought she must have given that name to herself on a mountaintop ceremony in California attended by other women therapists, all of them naked but for wildflower garlands, and *not ashamed*. It has always seemed to Helen that California is the place for outrageous acts of freedom, and only California. A bunch of naked therapists renaming themselves in Illinois? Never.

She steps out of the shower and wraps a bath towel around herself. What to wear? What effort such a decision now seems to require!

She selects a pair of black wool pants and a gray cashmere sweater. When she comes down into the kitchen to get her keys, she sees the red light blinking on the phone. Two messages; another call must have come in while she was in the shower. "Tessa," Helen says, out loud. She likes to predict who the calls are from and she is often right. This has scored her points with Tessa, who still sort of believes her mother is psychic. Helen does little to disabuse her daughter of this notion; she thinks it offers her a kind of power she would not have otherwise.

She is not psychic this time, though; the second call is from someone she doesn't know, saying she got Helen's number from Donna Barlow, a mutual friend who is also a writer, and that she wants to talk to Helen about teaching a very unique kind of writing workshop—Donna did it and just loved it, and thought Helen might enjoy it, too.

Helen doesn't teach. She doesn't teach because she has no idea in the world how she does what she does and therefore doesn't feel qualified to instruct others in the practice. For her, writing just happens. Or used to. Writing is like falling in love, she's often said. Or deciding what to have for lunch. Who knows how a person does that? And for heaven's sake, how can you instruct someone else in how to do it? "Think of walking," Helen has often said to audiences at book signings, speaking to people who asked the inevitable questions about the writing process. "Think of how you walk without thinking about it. That's how you need to write. If you thought about walking—the neuromuscular component, the speed at which you should move, what length your stride should be—you'd never get anywhere, right? You'd spend all your time thinking about *how* to get there." People would laugh and look at each other, but there were always some who crossed their arms in exasperation: she hadn't answered the *question*.

Helen looks at her watch, then quickly punches in the number to call the person who asked her about teaching, Nancy Weldon is her name. She'll let her know right away she's not interested, she'll get this out of the way.

"Helen Ames!" the woman, who apparently has caller ID, says. "How nice to talk to you! I just have to tell you, I really enjoy your books."

"Thank you," Helen says, and now feels bad about having to decline the woman's offer. Still, she speaks quickly, before the woman can say anything else. "Listen, I'm sorry, but I don't teach. It's not that I don't want to, it's that I can't. I'm a terrible teacher. Honestly. I tried it once and the people who came all but asked for their money back." A true story. Early on in her career, Helen was lured to an island to teach a group of very wealthy women. She thought the best thing to do would be to show how she found her own inspiration, and so she crafted a number of exercises for the women to do, and brought in objects she thought might be seen as evocative—an old silver hairbrush, a blackened frying pan, a love letter from the 1930s, a pair of men's shoes, a floppy-necked teddy bear, one dusty wing of a butterfly. One of the exercises was to use all of these objects in a short story, and Helen had to practically sit on her hands to keep from doing this exercise herself. Already she saw the man who would wear those shoes, the corn bread cooking in that skillet, the towheaded child weeping because he'd accidentally torn the wing off the butterfly.

But it seemed that all the women wanted to do was to read from work they'd already done and have Helen praise it. And so Helen sat stiffly, trying to think of kind and insightful things to say and finally agreeing to put in a good word with her agent for the work of the worst (and pushiest) writer, when in fact she had no intention of doing so. "I'm a terrible teacher," she says, again.

"Oh, I can't believe that's true," Nancy says, laughing.

"Believe it, believe it," Helen says. "Honestly, it's so very true."

"Well, let me tell you a little about this before you decide for sure, okay?"

I have *decided for sure,* Helen thinks, and feels herself getting angry. But she listens as the woman describes the kind of workshop she has in mind. Thus far, the people who would be in the group are an old man who lives in an assisted care residence, a middle-aged woman who works for an insurance company and lives downtown, a young woman who is mildly retarded and lives in a group home, a forty-five-year-old day-care worker from the West Side ghetto, a man from Evanston who does the news for one of the Latino television stations, and a twenty-year-old mechanic who lives in Lakeview. And they can add one or two more.

"Hmmm," Helen says.

"This is a kind of experiment," Nancy says. "It's something we've talked about a lot, how creative writing can help people understand one another's points of view. We wondered what would happen if you had a group of purposely disparate types, both from a literary and a sociological point of view. We've gotten a very nice grant from a humanities foundation so that we can try it for a year, and this is the second workshop, which would be starting the first Wednesday in January. It's once a week for six weeks, it ends with a really lovely celebration, and we can pay you—"

"I'm sorry," Helen says. "I'm sorry to interrupt you, but I've got to run and meet a friend downtown. I just wanted to let you know my answer right away."

"Would you just think about it?" Nancy says. "I'll understand if you don't want to do it, but would you just think about it? And let me make it easier: if you don't want to do it, you don't even have to call me back. I'll assume that if I don't hear from you by tomorrow night, you're not interested. Okay? I have other writers I can call, I know that Saundra Weller is dying to teach this workshop, but I just really think you'd be perfect for it. I think you'd enjoy it. We set the time to be in the late afternoon, from four until six, and from what I've read about you, you like to work in the early morning."

Right. When she was working. When she used to be a writer. But *Saundra Weller*! Helen can't stand her, with her endless self-promotion and her snotty attitude toward . . . well, toward Helen, for one thing. They were on a panel together at a book festival, and Saundra made no secret of the fact that she found Helen to be a vastly inferior writer. Oh, the way Saundra walks around with that tight smile! The way she gave Anne Jensen, a writer friend of Helen's whose lyrical prose raises the hair on the back of your neck, a scathingly bad review in *The New York Times Book Review*—the only bad one she got, incidentally, but so bad it made Anne weep for days. "I'll think about it," Helen says, more to get off the phone than anything—she wants to call Steve and go.

"I'm so glad," Nancy says. "Thank you!"

Helen hangs up, looks at the clock, decides to call Steve from the car. "What'd I forget now?" she asks, when he comes to the phone. She signals right and heads down Austin Boulevard toward the freeway.

"Helen," he says, "we need to talk. I'm wondering if we could get together, maybe this afternoon?"

"I'm on the way to meet a friend downtown. We're having lunch." No need to tell Steve about the kiss exhibit. He already finds Helen a little wacky, she knows this.

"This is very important."

"Well, is it . . ." Some sense of dread begins to blossom in Helen's stomach. "Is it bad?"

A pause, and then Steve says, "Are you aware of what your balance is at Morgan?"

Helen gestures to another driver, letting him pull out ahead of her. "I think it's just short of a million, actually." That was what Dan had told her last time they'd talked about it. They were fantasizing about what they'd do when Dan retired—he was thinking of taking an early retirement in two years. Helen had said she wanted a little one-level house in California with beautiful views and a garden full of flowers with intoxicating scents. He had said that what he would like to do was sail around the world. "You don't know how to sail!" Helen had said, and he'd said, "I've helped crew. I know a little. But that's part of the dream: we have a boat, we learn how to sail, and we go around the world. Wouldn't that be nice? We'd just sail around the world for the rest of our lives, living off our savings."

"Oh, no," Helen had said. "I can't help sail. It's too much like math. Plus there are all those cockamamie terms: 'starboard' and 'port.' 'Fore' and 'aft.' 'Coming about.' Why can't boat people just speak English? Plus we're too old to learn how to sail."

Dan had leaned back in his wicker chair—they were on the deck, in late summer, watching a spectacular sunset—and he'd said, "Helen. In the paper not long ago, there was a story about a woman who learned to sail when she was seventy-nine, because she wanted to learn how before she turned eighty. A guy named Geoffrey Hilton-Barber sailed single-handedly across the Indian Ocean, and he's *blind*. Not only can you sail; I predict that you will—not *help* sail, but sail all by yourself. I can *see* it. Honestly, I see it like a vision, you sailing somewhere you've never been but always wanted to go."

"I'd rather have the little house," Helen had said. "I really would. I want that more than anything, Dan." She'd told him she wanted a house respectful of nature and of human nature. She wanted whimsy and beauty and openness, she wanted a unique design that spoke to the people she and Dan were. She wanted many places to read, a stove with six burners and a griddle, oh, she had a million ideas, she actually had a folder marked "dream house" with ideas from magazines and ones she'd just made up.

"But, Helen," he'd said. "What if your roof was the sky? What if your view changed every day, every minute? What if you could be hunkered down below with a big fat novel and a quilt, while I fished for our dinner off the stern? If we were becalmed, we could take off our clothes and go swimming at night, and the phosphorescence would make it look like we were covered with stardust. I'm talking a big boat, Helen, where we'd have a galley with a dining banquette, and a chart room with a navigation table, and a stateroom big enough for a queen-size bed. And we wouldn't be on the boat all the time! We'd put in to ports of call and stay for as long as we wanted: Corsica. Tenerife. Lisbon. We could actually do that! And if you wanted to stay in a hotel some-times, we could do that, too."

"But . . . what about Tessa?"

"We'll come home a lot. And on her vacations, she could go places with us. Helen, think of it! We've worked hard for so many years, and now we can reap our reward. It wouldn't be forever. But before we check into the nursing home, let's do something that will give us such incredible memories. Let's go together around the world."

And she had said—oh, she remembers this now with such longing—she had said, "Wait. Isn't that a term for a sexual act, 'go around the world'?" It was the looseness of the day, it was the wine, it was how handsome Dan looked at that moment, his hair mussed, his face colored by the sun. He'd stood up and said, "Let's make it one." And then he'd taken her hand and led her inside.

Now Steve says, "Why don't you come in to the office? We need to talk."

Helen pulls over, puts on her hazard lights. "What is it," she says. Her voice is flat, nearly accusatory, and she regrets it. "Can you tell me what it is?" she asks, trying with some success to modulate herself.

"You want me to tell you now?"

"Yes. Tell me."

"I don't know if . . . All right, I will tell you now, but I want you to come in and see me, too. Will you do that?"

"I can't today. I could tomorrow, though. Ten o'clock?"

"That's fine. So . . . Look, I'm just sorry as hell to tell you this, Helen. Dan withdrew a large sum of money from this account a year ago."

"Well," Helen says, "he did that sometimes. He would pull money out of there and put it in our checking account sometimes. As much as fifty thousand once, when we were redoing the kitchen."

"Yes, I saw that," Steve says. "But this withdrawal was eight hundred and fifty thousand dollars."

She sits frozen, pressing the receiver of the phone hard against her ear.

"Helen? This is why I wanted you to come in. Are you all right?"

"This is a mistake," she manages.

"It appears not to be."

"I'm coming down there right now," Helen says, and Steve says he thinks that's best.

She pulls back out onto the road and calls Midge. "I can't come," she says. She is speaking oddly; it's as if her mouth won't open all the way.

"What's wrong?" Midge says. "What happened?"

When Helen tells her what the accountant said, Midge says, "Oh, honey. I'm sorry. Do you want me to come with you?"

"No," Helen says. "It's just a mistake. It has to be. He never said a word. It's a mistake. We'll go to the museum another day."

She snaps her phone shut, accelerates, then immediately slows down. What if she gets a ticket and has to pay some huge fine? What if she has to sell her house? What if Dan had another woman, another family, a gambling problem, he actually did gamble too much at one point in their marriage, that was part of the reason she went to the therapist.

She wipes tears off her face, sits up straighter, and tells herself to calm down, it might not be as bad as she thinks, it can't be as bad as she thinks, what will she do, what will she do, what will she do?

"Wow," Tessa says.

She and Helen are having an early dinner at Sepia, one of Tessa's favorite places, despite the fact that Helen now worries about spending so much money on one meal. Helen figured that if she was going to tell her daughter such unpleasant news, it might as well be in beautiful surroundings. She wondered whether it was ill-advised to tell her daughter at all; she didn't want to worry her. In the end, though, she decided it was better to tell her than not. So she has just revealed that Dan withdrew a very large sum of cash and she doesn't know why. She did not tell Tessa how much Dan took out, or how much is left. Nor did Tessa ask. Thus far, she seems more intrigued than worried or suspicious. She seems to be looking at this as a kind of fun mystery that will without question be solved.

"Are you okay?" she asks her mother. "You're not worried about money or anything, are you?"

"Oh, no."

Tessa's eyes widen. "Oh, my God. That's not why you applied at *Anthro,* is it?"

"No, that was just so I'd get out of the house a little bit."

Tessa takes another bite of her dessert. "You do *fine,* writing!"

"How do you know?"

"Dad told me what you get for your books."

"He did?"

"Yes. So you're okay, right?"

Helen attempts a smile. "Well . . . yes."

"Right?" Tessa asks again, looking more carefully at her mother.

Helen looks directly back at her. "Yes."

Tessa smiles. "Well, you always liked him to surprise you. You always liked that."

What Helen likes is that the question of infidelity—of any kind—has not crossed her daughter's mind.

six

HELEN LIES ON THE SOFA TAKING DEEP BREATHS IN AND LETTING them slowly out, staring at the ceiling. She has just gone through every room of the house, looking for some shred of evidence to indicate what Dan might have used the money for, and has come up with nothing. This after she called the yacht club, asking if Dan had been there, inquiring about a berth. No.

She regrets having given away his clothes: was there a piece of paper in a pocket, a key to something that she overlooked? When she went to the accountant, Steve asked her how it was that this was not a joint account, and she looked down at her lap and said it was because she trusted Dan completely, then looked up hotly as though she were going to have to defend him. But Steve made no accusations; instead, he kept assuring her that some answer would be found, Dan was not the kind of man to . . . An answer would be found. In the meantime, there was a little over fifty thousand left in the account. For some, this would be an enormous amount of money.

She swallowed, not knowing how to say that for her it did not seem so. Steve read her face and told her not to panic, she'd be fine. She made a nice salary with her books, she would continue to produce just as she always had, she'd be just fine. Yes, her retirement account was gone for the time being, but in terms of day-to-day living, she'd be fine. Politely, then, he asked when her next one was coming out. He wasn't a fan, Steve, he was the kind of person who would ask her what the title of the next one was, and she would tell him and he would raise his eyebrows and say, "Huh! I'll have to look for that!" She told him the next one would be out soon and when he asked what it was called, she said, "So far I'm coming up empty."

"Hmm. Interesting title."

"No," she said, laughing, despite everything. "I haven't *decided* what the title is."

"Oh!" he said. "Well. You will."

"Uh-huh," she said, and ever so quietly cleared her throat.

Helen gets up and rubs at her neck, her shoulders. It's late. She should go to bed. But she goes once more into Dan's office to look more carefully through every desk drawer. It is awful to do this, to see his penmanship, to recall the many times she sat in the chair in his office, chatting with him while he worked at the desk. There is a group of photographs on his desktop, family shots of the three of them, and a haiku that Tessa wrote in seventh grade. Helen framed it and gave it to Dan for his birthday.

Last night we had snow
Tattered pieces of white lace
Rode the winter winds

It had been a fierce storm; Helen remembers how Dan came home early from work, how Tessa exulted in the fact that school would be canceled the next day. Helen awoke around 2:00 A.M. and went to look out the bedroom window. It had stopped snowing and the tree branches were frosted down to the tiniest twig.

The sidewalks were covered with at least a foot of snow that glistened beneath the streetlights, and the street was covered, too; the plows had not yet been around.

She'd gently awakened Dan, asking him to get up and come for a walk with her. He refused and so she went alone. At first she was angry that he hadn't come with her, though she knew she had no right to be—Dan had to get up and go to work the next morning, and she should not have awakened him at all. But she trudged through the snow full of resentment for him not sharing this with her, and then her resentment was replaced with wonder, and she understood the specific kind of appreciation that comes to a person witnessing a thing of beauty alone, how the spectacle seems to sit whole inside the soul, undiminished by conversation, by any attempt at translation or persuasion. She stayed out for an hour, walking around a neighborhood transformed, and when she returned she very quietly fixed herself a cup of cocoa made with cream and topped with many marshmallows, and then she sat in the living room to drink it, only one small light burning. When she heard the sound of the snowplow, she watched with some regret as it turned the street back to normal. And then she tiptoed back upstairs and slid into a bed that had been kept warm in her absence. She felt Dan pull her close to him, heard him murmur into the back of her neck that he loved her, then fall immediately back to sleep. She and Midge talked sometimes about moments when you understood your great luck, when you experienced gratitude as a body-wide, physical sensation; that had been one of those moments.

She turns out the light in Dan's study and goes upstairs.

In the morning, Helen makes coffee and then sits at the kitchen table listing her minimum monthly payments. Not *too* bad. Then she sees that she has forgotten annual tax bills, and adds that on. And car maintenance. And home insurance. She adds those on.

Then she picks up the phone to call Nancy Weldon to say she'd like to accept the job teaching.

"Well, I am thrilled," Nancy says. "But not really surprised. I have to tell you, I knew you'd come around."

"Did you," Helen says. Outside, birds have congregated around the bread crumbs she sprinkled on the ground for them. It's all sparrows, a dusty, mud-brown sea of them. She has always thought of sparrows as scrappy little city birds who descend en masse to gobble up the offerings, and she used to resent them, fearing they would leave nothing for the beautiful birds who might happen by, the cardinals and the goldfinches, the blue jays, whose deep blue feathers more than made up for their terrible personalities. Now, she identifies somehow with the sparrows, and intends later to put out suet for them, fresh from the butcher.

"I just knew it," Nancy says. "I figured you'd think about the people who were in the workshop and your curiosity would get the best of you."

"Something like that," Helen says.

"So, we'd like to give you complete freedom for the way you teach the classes. The only thing we ask is that at the end of the workshop, each participant shares something they've written with an audience at our ceremony—as I think I told you, we have a little ceremony at the conclusion of the classes. The students' families and friends come, and we have a stipend for bringing in some professionals—an agent and an editor, usually. We've been lucky with that so far—we've gotten some really good people."

"Great," Helen says. "So I'll come to the library for the first class, and where do I go?"

"It will be one of the study rooms upstairs," Nancy says. "We haven't quite decided which one yet, but we'll let you know at least a week beforehand. I'll send the information with the contract."

"Looking forward to it," Helen says. It sticks in her throat a bit, yet she finds she really means it. At last, a way to get out of the house that carries with it some familiarity and legitimacy. And income. She recalls a time when she was ten years old and made pot holders on a loom, then went door-to-door selling them—ten cents for the small ones, twenty-five cents for the large. An unshaven man wearing a soiled bathrobe bought out her entire remaining inventory, and for years she clung to the belief that he was very wealthy. Never mind the ramshackle appearance of his one-story home—peeling paint, a dying lawn—Helen just knew that he had sacks of money in the basement with dollar signs stenciled on them, Scrooge McDuck style.

"I'll be really glad to finally meet you," Nancy says, and her voice is warm and sincere.

"Me, too," Helen says.

She hangs up the phone, leans against the kitchen counter, and thinks about what besides milk and suet she needs at the grocery store. She feels a pleasurable stirring of something she cannot quite identify, but then does: it's the idea that she will now write something. Even if it's only exercises for a writing class, she can step out of here into *there*.

seven

"WELL. HAPPY DECEMBER SEVENTEENTH!" HELEN SAYS. SHE IS
standing at a podium before an audience of two hundred, orga-
nized by the friends of this particular library. Most times when
Helen does these things, she prepares a few words of general introduction, then reads from her work. This time, the woman in
charge asked her to speak only. "After all, we can all read by our-
selves," she said. "We look upon this as an opportunity for our
patrons to get to *know* you."

Helen understands the impulse; she has felt it herself. Once,
she and Dan took a driving trip in Maine and they found the
house where one of Helen's favorite authors, E. B. White, used to
live. They sat parked outside it for some time, Helen imagining
the life that used to go on there. She wondered what the kitchen
looked like, the bedroom, the library, surely there was a massive-
size library. "I wish we could walk around the grounds," she said.

Dan shrugged. "Let's ask."

"We can't do that!" Helen said, and Dan said why not, all the new owners could say was no, nothing would *happen*.

Helen sat still, thinking.

"Want me to go ask?" Dan said.

"Yes. No!"

"I'll just see if anyone's home." He went up the walk and knocked on the front door. When it opened, Dan spoke to someone and pointed at the car. Helen waved—at whom, she had no idea; she couldn't see who stood inside.

Dan came back to the car, beaming. The woman who lived there was most accommodating when she heard Helen was a writer (though she'd never heard of Helen, he reluctantly admitted) and she told Dan that he and Helen could go ahead and look around all they liked. She even told Dan how to get down to E. B. White's writing shed by the water, trusting them to be there alone. When Helen walked into that little shed with its slab of wooden desk and bare floors and open window that framed the blue waters of the bay, she burst into tears. She cried for the beautiful words White had written, and she cried because he was dead, and she cried for the privilege of being in this space, where he had looked out this very window and smoked and thought and written lines full of such humor, intelligence, and heart. "Sit down," Dan said quietly, pointing to the bench where White had sat, and Helen wanted to smack him. Sit there! Sit *there*! "No," she said. "No, it would be . . ." She walked to the window and looked out at the water, then turned around. "I just . . ."

"I know," Dan said.

"What he offered the world, still offers the world, is so important."

"I know," Dan said again.

She wanted to talk about White's essay "Death of a Pig." She wanted to see if they could find the dusty path that Fred, White's beloved dachshund, traveled alongside his master when they buried that pig; she wanted to invoke the names of the characters in *Charlotte's Web* and feel inside herself some of the wonder the author must have felt looking out at these acres of beautiful land, where geese lowered their long necks to hiss out warnings, and grandchildren ran, shouting; where his wife Katharine's well-considered gardens grew, where he must have struggled to come to terms with a diagnosis of Alzheimer's. What sad irony, that a man so gifted with language would, at the end of his life, end up without the facility for it.

As she stood in White's work space that day, it occurred to her that she was grasping at straws when it came to really understanding anything about the man; you could read his work, even biographies about him, and imagine a certain kind of person; but the reality of him would forever be a mystery. She thought this was probably true of anyone who made any kind of art: the work did not necessarily represent the person. She thinks it was Margaret Atwood who said that wanting to meet a writer because you like their work was like wanting to meet a duck because you like pâté.

So when the librarian, Doris McCann was her name, told Helen that her patrons wanted to know her, she understood completely. She just didn't know if she could comply.

She straightens before her the paper where last night she scrawled some prompts to help guide what she would say. But now, to her dismay, she finds that they make no sense whatsoever. She has no idea what "river" means, or "broken lamp." She sees the word "roses" and seizes gratefully upon it. "When my first novel was accepted for publication," she tells the audience, "my best friend sent me twelve long-stemmed pink roses with a card that said, 'This is the stuff of your dreams.' And it was." She smiles, and some of the women in the audience smile back. She looks at her notes again, feeling long moments go by, feeling perspiration start under her arms. She scratches her forehead, pushes back her hair. "Yikes, I really need a haircut," she says.

Now the women simply stare, one with her eyebrows knit, her

arms crossed tightly. Helen sees one woman elbow the woman next to her. She has seen this before, but that was when it was something positive, when it was one friend telling another she was having a good time. It does not mean that now.

"But *that's* not what we're here to talk about!" Helen says gaily, and she sees Doris, sitting at the end of the front row, nervously smile and turn ever so slightly in her seat, looking to see how the audience is doing. Well. Helen can tell her.

"You know, I was asked not to read," Helen says, finally, and it comes out far too defensively. She leans closer to the microphone to say, "Which is *okay,* it's *okay,*" and there is a terrible squeal of feedback. Helen steps back. She clears her throat, looks again at her useless notes. What in the hell is "refrigerator repair man"?

She looks out at the audience again and presses her palm against her sternum, as though trying to resuscitate herself. "I apologize," she says, finally, and now her hands move to clasp each other on the lectern before her. *Calm down.* She breathes in deeply, lets it out. *Just talk. Just say something.* "Usually I read from my work, my novels, I guess you know I've written some novels." She holds up the latest one, which she brought along as a kind of talisman. "But anyway, I usually read from them as a way to . . . Well, as a way to show my art, I guess. Though that sounds pretentious to me, as I say it: show my *art*. It sounds like . . . Well, but what I do is, I read and then I take questions. I don't usually just . . . *talk*. About myself, I mean. I must confess, in fact, that I feel very nervous talking only about myself. I think most writers are shy people who hide behind others, who want to talk not about themselves but about other people. Of course, they *are* actually talking about themselves when they talk about other people . . ."

And now there is nothing. White space inside of her. White noise around her. There is nothing she can think of to say.

"I wonder if . . . I think I *am* just going to go ahead and read a little, just a couple pages of my latest novel, to show you something about how writers work. Well, how I work, anyway." Helen opens her book to the prologue, then looks up to say, "There is a tarot card called the King of Wands, and it represents a man who appears to be terrifying, really fierce; but on the inside, he's a real softie. This novel is about a man like that." She reads the opening pages of *The King of Wands,* about ten minutes' worth of material. Then she closes the book, and smiles. "So, I think that might show you how a character's voice can take the lead in crafting a story. Just a sample, there, of how that works."

It is so quiet. Helen clears her throat. "How about if we move to questions? Are there any questions?" Last time Helen did an event, they had to cut questions off after half an hour. She prays for that now.

No one raises a hand. What feels like a year passes while Helen stares at a spot on the back wall. When someone does finally raise her hand, Helen practically yelps, saying, *"Yes?"*

"Where do you get your ideas?" the woman asks.

I don't, lately, Helen wants to say. I don't have any ideas. Do you? What she does say is, "Well, they're all around. You know. Life. Ideas are all around; the real question is, Where *aren't* ideas? I mean, there's a story you can imagine about two random people in an elevator, isn't there? One person in an elevator. An elevator! And then the rest is . . . Well, it's alchemy. That's what you hope for. And rarely achieve. It's hard to achieve what you mean to, to get to where you think you're going to go, when you first start a book. And in some ways, the more success you have, the harder it gets. You begin writing in fresh air and sunshine; with each book, you suffer more pollution. Sales figures, reviews . . . your own . . . your own . . ." She clears her throat, looks around the room at the audience. She sees a kind of polite bewilderment.

Another woman, seated in the back, raises her hand, and Helen nods gratefully at her.

"This isn't a question," the woman says, "it's just a comment.

I just wanted to tell you that I loved *Telling Songs* and I gave it to all my friends for Christmas last year. It's a beautiful book. And also I wanted to let you know I have to leave early; I didn't want you to think I was leaving in the middle of your talk. So thank you."

"Thank *you*!" Helen says, and watches as the woman gathers up her purse, her coat, the program with Helen's bio. She wants to beg her to stay, to come and stand on the stage with her.

Another woman raises her hand. "Could you tell us something personal about yourself? Something that nobody else knows?"

Helen has no idea how to respond. "You first," she says, finally, and laughs, though no one else does. They all wait. Finally, she says, "Well . . . why would I *do* that?" Now she has completely alienated them, she can feel it. She speaks quickly, saying, "Okay, here: I have a very clean house, but my refrigerator shelves are awful. Plus I have a little crush on Donald Trump, I don't know why."

Oh, God, not a sound. They are taking her too seriously, she has come off so strangely she can't even kid around. They think she's odd, they don't like her, and they are disappointed. They have set aside time to come here, and for what? This is the talk that would let them get to know the author?

Helen stands there, increasingly dry-mouthed, then says, "I'm sorry. I don't know what you want of me." She feels very close to tears. She shifts her weight, looks down again at her useless notes. She looks out at the crowd and a great weariness comes over her. She thinks for a moment about simply walking offstage, but then says, "I don't see how you can get to know a person from a lecture. I guess I think if you want to know an author, you should read her books. Because that's the part . . . That's the personal part, even if it isn't real. You know? That *thing* you try to get at, so you can . . .

"I'm afraid that's all I can say. Unless there are any more questions. Or comments. Anyone have anything they'd like to say? About anything?"

No one does.

"Well, then . . . Thank you." Helen moves off the stage to a light smattering of applause, the sound of which is easily overwhelmed by the low murmur of conversation.

Doris McCann is standing backstage, a tight smile frozen on her face. She offers Helen a white envelope. Her payment.

"That's all right," Helen says. "I'm so sorry. I haven't been feeling well."

"I'm sorry to hear that," Doris says, but her tone says, *Then why didn't you call and cancel?*

Helen starts to explain, then does not. Why say this has never happened before when that might only make her hostess feel worse? There is nothing to say; the damage is done. It's like a disastrous first date: Midge once went out with the captain of the football team in high school and farted as she was getting into his car, him behind her gallantly holding the door open—and that was the end of *that*. Doris will tell Helen's lecture agent about this performance, or lack thereof, how could she not? *Why* should she not? Helen's track record, which thus far has been so good, will be spoiled.

Doris offers the check again. "Go ahead and take it. We did sign a contract. You did appear. Maybe you could just sign some books?"

"Of course."

"Well, then . . ." Doris puts the envelope into the outside pocket of Helen's purse. "Let's go and do that."

They go back into the auditorium, where there are four people in line, and the last one asks Helen quietly, "Are you all right?"

"Thank you for asking," Helen says. "I'll be fine."

After the room empties, Doris says. "Well, I'll buy one. Could you sign it to my mother? Her name is Phyllis. She liked you."

She seems not to notice the slip: *liked.*

Helen pulls out her pen, signs the book, and hands it to Doris. "Thank you. I hope she enjoys it."

"Oh, sure," Doris says. She scratches her ear. Smiles.

"Again, I apologize for—"

"It's all right. These things happen."

"You know, I wonder if—Maybe I could try again another time." She'll share with them the story about telling her father as a little girl that she was going to be a writer someday and how at first he had laughed but then had said, "I believe you." She'll explain how important it is to have someone believe in you, how important it is to nourish dreams, especially your own. She'll tell them that she used to pull books behind her in a wagon when she played outside, they were her favorite toy, and that all one summer, after her parents made her turn out the light, she read under her covers by fireflies in a jar. She'll talk about the time she was twelve years old and got so sunburned she couldn't wear clothes and had to lie in bed with only a sheet over her for four days and it was then that she read *Gone with the Wind* for the first time. And then she went on to read it eight more times. Oh, she can think of a lot of things to say, now! That the impetus for one of her best-loved novels was a sentence in a conversation she overheard in a gynecologist's office. "There'd be no charge for my coming back, of course," she tells Doris.

"Well, that's very nice of you. But you know, we schedule so far in advance . . ."

"I see," Helen says.

They leave the empty auditorium, their footsteps echoing. At the doorway that leads to the parking lot, Helen shakes hands with Doris, and heads out into the parking lot. A raw wind blows, and Helen shivers in it.

When she gets to the car, she calls Midge. Who is not home. "Well," she says to the message machine, "you were kind of wrong about how I'd do."

She wishes Doris had taken back the check. She doesn't want it. But she needs it.

The next morning is December 18, the anniversary of Dan's death. Helen comes into the kitchen early and turns on the light. She makes coffee, waits for it to brew, drinks some, then puts her cup in the sink to rinse it out. She turns on the water, speaks above the noise to say, "Damnit, Dan! I just *bought* that cup!" She stands there for a long moment, the water running, her hands clenching the edge of the sink. Then she turns around and looks at the spot where he fell. Behind her, the water runs and runs. She turns it off, then goes to sit at the kitchen table, still staring at that spot on the floor. She moves to Dan's chair. She opens her hand as though a cup is falling out of it, then slides onto the floor, adjusts her body to look the way his did. She is looking in the direction of the sink, right where she was just standing. He would have seen her ankles, the hem of her robe. He would have seen how the cabinets looked immense from there, the ceiling so far away. He would have heard her speaking. He would have seen her turn around and start toward him. He would have known she was coming to save him.

She gets up off the floor and stands there. Outside, the sunrise completes itself, trades its rose colors for gold, and bars of light stripe the kitchen table. She hears the sound of birds, and she goes to the window to watch them eat.

eight

At eleven-thirty in the morning, Helen is at her desk, trying to think of exercises for the first writing class. Her phone rings and she answers immediately, grateful for the distraction. But there is no one there. "Hello?" she says again. There is silence, then a gentle hang-up. *A caller who keeps hanging up? A call that changed your life? A misunderstanding that occurs when you think you're talking on the phone to one person but in fact it's someone else?* She taps her fingers against the desk, arranges again the red roses she brought home from the grocery store this morning. *The first time you got flowers, or gave them? Your first dance? Your first date?* No, no, and no. She looks carefully around her study, as though an idea will come floating down from the ceiling like Groucho's duck.

Exasperated, Helen calls her friend Jessica Miller for ideas; Jessica is a writer who has taught a thousand workshops. "Well, I have an exercise I always use for the first class," Jessica says. "It gets the juices flowing right away, and it helps people in the group get to know one another. I just say, 'Write one page telling me who you are.' And then I give them twenty minutes. I use a timer, by the way; there's something about that *ding!* that's pretty un-equivocal."

"That's a big assignment!"

"Yes, but restricting it to one page and giving them so little time keeps them focused on just getting something down on the page. There's no time to listen to that critical voice in their heads, no time to judge, no time to even plan anything. Tell them there doesn't have to be any rhyme or reason, that you're not looking for a completely finished piece, just an interesting fragment that feels true to them, maybe even scary. To feel a little scared, to take a risk when you write, is a good thing, and they need to learn that, right away. What you want is for them to trust the process, you know?"

Helen thanks her friend, and for a moment after she hangs up, she considers attempting the exercise herself. But no, here comes the same feeling she gets when she thinks about trying to write anything these days: a great weariness, a flat sorrow. Perhaps she will use the exercise for her class, though, despite the fact that she wanted very much to come up with an idea of her own. Her phone rings again, and again when she answers it, there is a hang-up. She feels a sudden sense of dread. Her father has been having health problems, and now she imagines her mother sitting at the edge of her bed, the phone in her hand, unable to say the words she needs to. Full of fear, Helen calls her parents' number. When her mother answers, she says, "It's me. Did you just try to call?"

"No," her mother says. "But I'm glad to hear from you. How are you?"

"I'm fine," Helen says. "But Dad, is Dad okay?"

Eleanor laughs. "You're not going to believe this. He's off playing pinochle. Then he's going bowling."

"Are you kidding?" Two days ago, her father had refused to get out of bed and had told his wife he'd be staying there. He'd asked her to inquire about hospice care. Eleanor had said he was being overdramatic, and Helen privately thought her mother was being insensitive. But it turns out that her mother was probably right.

Still, *"Bowling?"* Helen asks. The man isn't exactly a tower of strength.

"Well, he won't bowl, himself. He's going to watch Ed Silverman and Tom Larson and that other character, whatever his name is."

"Ernie Sanchez?"

"That's it." Her mother sighs. "Your aunt Caroline says we should rename your father Lazarus."

Helen hears the call-waiting signal, tells her mother they'll speak later, and hits the flash button. Silence, then yet another hang-up.

Helen jerks the phone away from her ear and slams it down. Why didn't she get caller ID when it was offered to her? She enters *69, and a recording tells her she can't access the call. Then her cell phone rings, and she answers it, only to be met with another hang-up. This time, though, she has the number, and she calls it back.

A man answers, saying mildly, "Tom Ellis."

"Yes, I'm . . . *Who* is this?"

"Tom *Ellis,*" the man says, and Helen writes his name down.

"Do you keep calling me and hanging up?" she asks.

"Who is *this*?"

"It's . . . Mrs. Ames."

There is a long silence, and then the man says, "Could you tell me where I might find Dan? I've been trying to reach him for a while."

She draws in a steadying breath. "But who *are* you?"

"I need to talk to Dan," he says. "Would you ask him to call Tom Ellis? It's just a business matter."

No. Not now. She is not going to tell some irritating stranger that her husband has died. She hangs up and then sits staring out the window.

Focus. Work. She turns to her computer and types, (*1*) *Introduce self, include brief history of career.* (*2*) *Explain class will introduce themselves to each other by doing exercise "Who are you?" Then they'll read aloud and critique each other. Gently.* She stops typing. What if they don't want to share their work out loud? Under step number one, she inserts, *Explain concept of workshop.* There. But what will she do while they're writing? She rubs her forehead, looks at the roses, rearranges them once more. When the phone rings, she looks at it as though it is a bull snake, then slowly picks it up.

"*What.*"

"Whoa!" Midge says.

"Oh. It's you."

"Last time I checked. What's your problem?"

"Somebody keeps calling and hanging up."

"Are you hungry? Because I need to go to Wendy's."

Helen is not hungry. She ate a late breakfast. And she really needs to get this work done. But she tells Midge she'll meet her in fifteen minutes. For one thing, she wants to switch problems. Instead of worrying about writing exercises or her father, she'll worry again about where the money went, now that it's fairly certain that Dan didn't buy a boat. She'll brainstorm with Midge about various possibilities. Conversations about this problem are easier since the first "I'm sorry but let's just get this out of the way" one. The one where Midge asked about prostitutes and mistresses and gambling and hidden drug habits and second families. "What do you think he *was*?" Helen asked Midge. "A politician?" They'd gotten a little laugh out of that. A little one.

It remains a painful mystery why Dan withdrew such a large

sum of money, in cash, from their account. For Helen, the biggest problem is not how she will manage financially. She can always sell the house. She has proven that she *can* get a job. No, what bothers her most is her sudden inability to feel certain about who Dan was. It makes her sad; it makes her feel foolish; it makes her frustrated—to the point of tears one day, to pounding rage the next—to understand that she might never know for sure where that money went. Only Tessa is stalwart in her belief that nothing underhanded could possibly have happened. Tessa still sees Dan exactly the way she saw him before, and Helen does nothing to take away from that—let the girl have her father in the only way she can. But for Helen, it's different. She sits sometimes studying photos of Dan, looking for something she didn't see before. She imagines them making love, wondering if, when he closed his eyes, it was in pleasure or to hide something. She re-creates conversations, trying to retroactively find clues; she regrets that she was never the kind of wife to check receipts, mileage, to look for lipstick on collars, for heaven's sake. Mostly, she is bitter that in his death Dan has managed to present her with a problem on top of a problem: in addition to recovering from his loss, she now must also find an answer to this puzzle.

One of the things she and Dan used to argue about, one of the things that drove him crazy, was the way she would sometimes refuse to work things through and pretend instead that everything was fine. And now that is precisely what she decides to do; she puts the money problem in the subbasement of her mind. She will not discuss it or any other problem with Midge. Instead she will celebrate with her the merits of naked burgers at Wendy's— yet another thing she and Midge agree on, that a good burger needs nothing but salt. And a vanilla shake. In the car, she turns up the radio, taps her fingers against the steering wheel in rhythm to the sound.

Just before she gets to Wendy's, Helen sees a shoe in the middle of the street, a man's dress shoe. Could some sort of writing

exercise be made of this? Something about all an article of clothing can suggest? A pair of dusty tap shoes? A blue negligee? A box
of monogrammed men's handkerchiefs, never opened? *Stop,* she
tells herself. Before the group meets, she will have a plan in place.
She will. She hopes.

nine

HELEN LEAPS OUT OF THE SHOWER, PULLS HER NIGHTGOWN ON over her hastily dried body, and races to the ringing phone. Too late. Whoever it was hung up. It wouldn't be any of the boat dealerships she's most recently called; they would leave a message. She's got only one more call out; then she'll be back to square one: What did Dan do with that money?

She makes a pot of coffee, pours herself a cup, and goes upstairs to her study. She'll try to write something. Both her agent and her editor have told her not to worry about when she gets the next book out, both have suggested that someone as prolific as she *deserves* a hiatus, but they don't know about her money problems—she was embarrassed to tell them, and until she learns more, she doesn't know *what* to tell them. They also don't know the extreme difficulty Helen is having writing; she doesn't want to admit it to them and make the problem that much more real. "Take your time," each has said kindly, but with a breeziness that suggests they're confident something will soon emerge, a confidence Helen does not share. She feels like a patient in a hospital, being visited by people who stand back a little too far and glow with good health.

She'll try a stream-of-consciousness piece just for fun, and see what happens. *Before,* Helen types, then stares at the word so long it transforms itself into an ideogram: it is a stout governess, pushing a pram. *Before. Before . . .* Helen sighs, takes a sip of the cooling coffee, turns to look out the window. The winter sky is colored pale apricot; the day has just begun, and she's already stuck. Back to that familiar place of no place at all.

She hears the sound of air brakes, and here comes the garbage truck rounding the corner. Once again she has forgotten to put out the trash—she has two weeks' worth in the garage and despite the cold, it's beginning to stink. She rushes downstairs and bundles newspapers into paper bags, carries them and the kitchen trash out to the bins, then rolls them to the curb. She arrives just as the truck is pulling away from the house next door, the house that comes after hers. "Hey!" she yells at the truck. She pulls her coat tighter around her nightgown, and runs in her slippers after the truck, praying she won't fall on the icy sidewalk. *"Hey!"* The truck stops and a man pokes his head out the window. "Can you back up?" she yells. "Can you come back and get my trash?" Loud beeps sound as the truck slowly backs up. Helen holds up her hand and yells thank you. The man waves back, and he is frowning. It is not anger, it is concern. Well, she is in her nightgown, her hair wild about her head. Her coat is flapping open, hanging off one shoulder, now. Her slippers are full of snow. Also, apparently, she is crying—she can feel the wetness on her face. She runs back to the house, tries the door, and finds it locked. *"No!"* she wails, but then remembers the spare key hidden on the porch. When she finds it beneath a planter, it seems to her to be a miracle all out of proportion and she nearly weeps again. She is aware that, not so very long ago, all of this would have been funny, a good story.

Inside the house, she changes from wet slippers to bed socks, and returns to her study. On the computer screen, she looks at the one word she has typed. *Before.* In her mind, she sees a jewelry case, absent of wares. Its wooden corners are nicked, the glass scratched. These flaws are all there is to focus on, now that the cabinet is empty. The image widens, and she sees everything so clearly, the maroon carpet of the store, worn nearly silver in places that were heavily trafficked. The dusty plate-glass window, yellow sun pushing through to the display space, empty but for dead flies. The outline on the walls of the merchandise that used to hang there. She can smell the air, the ironed smell of an over-heated room. Keys to cabinets lie on top of the empty cases. There is a door at the back of the store, slightly ajar. Behind it, a small bathroom, the toilet ruined by rust, a few paper towels still on the roll, at the edge of the little sink a thin bar of soap cracked with age and turned up at the ends like a potato chip. A small, high window with bars behind it. Why bars? Why a jewelry store? In any case, the image doesn't inspire her. It sits in her brain and then it fades away, and then there is only the sound of a ticking clock, a passing car.

She sits with her hands in her lap. Rubs the back of her neck. Picks up a fetish stone, the bear with the turquoise chip on his back, and holds it until it is warm in her hand, then puts it back in its place. Sits still again. A row of icicles hangs outside her study window and she counts them: twenty-seven. This seems an excessive number to her. Her neighbor's house does not have such icicles. She remembers that she never got around to having the gutters cleaned. After two hours of accomplishing nothing, she turns her computer off.

She will dress. Then she will make a grocery list. There is laundry to do, baking for the visit to her parents. Later in the afternoon, she will attempt some exercises for her writing class. The phone rings, and she seizes the receiver, says hello.

A man clears his throat, then says, "Helen? Mrs. Ames?"

She clutches at the top of her nightgown, squeezes the fabric in her fist. What. What *now*?

"Yes?"

"This is Tom Ellis, and I just found out . . . I have just learned of Dan's death."

She draws in a steadying breath.

After a moment, the man says, "Hello? Are you still there?"

"Yes."

"Mrs. Ames, I had some business dealings with your husband, and I need to talk to you. Is there somewhere we can meet?"

"You can't come here," she says automatically.

"That's all right. I'm in town; I'm staying at the InterContinental. I'll meet you anywhere you like."

Should she? She supposes she has to. She supposes she's about to find out what happened to the money. She hopes she doesn't owe more. "Your hotel restaurant," she says. "Noon? How will I recognize you?"

"I'll wait by the entrance," he says. "And I'll definitely know you." He adds hastily, "Don't worry. It's just that I've seen your picture."

But she is worried, of course she is; she's afraid, and she starts to call Midge to see if she'll go with her, then hangs up. She's not sure why it is suddenly so clear to her that she must go alone.

She dresses quickly, aware of the fact that she is happy for an excuse to get dressed. She has so often expressed her gratitude at being able to work at home and in her pajamas; but as it happens, there is a downside. One can deteriorate a little, under such conditions. One can put off getting dressed; then, as long as one has done that, one can put off brushing one's teeth, combing one's hair. On the days when Helen leaps immediately into the shower and dresses for the day, she always feels better, yet she rarely does this. *Why?* she wonders. Is it a person's natural inclination to be so lazy? Or is it just her? And *is* it laziness, or rather a kind of protection of the dream state, a state to which you are tangentially linked by virtue of the fact that you are wearing the clothes you slept in? Helen would like to know the percentage of people who work at home and jump out of bed and get dressed just as they would for an outside job, versus the number of people who, like her, stumble into their workplaces wearing mismatched pajamas, contemplating what to do first.

She selects a black skirt and a white Anne Fontaine blouse to wear, a black blazer. She puts on pearl studs, her pearl necklace, trying not to remember her fortieth birthday, when Dan presented her with these things at their favorite French restaurant, over dessert. *"Dan!"* she'd said, when she opened the box from Tiffany. "Helen," he'd said back, simply, and kissed the middle knuckle of her right hand.

She puts on very little makeup: a bit of concealer under her eyes, mascara, a light pink lipstick. She has the odd feeling that she is preparing for a blind date, and ruefully reminds herself that such is hardly the case.

She pays bills before leaving the house; she'll drop them in the mailbox by the post office on her way downtown. She has a fear of paying bills late or incorrectly. She writes checks slowly, in silence, and tries to pay bills the day after she receives them. "So you make a *mistake,* paying bills," Midge said, when Helen confessed this to her friend. "So it gets there late, or it's the wrong amount. What do you think is going to happen? Worst-case scenario, okay? What do you think is going to *happen?*"

Helen thought for a moment, then said, "Jail?"

Midge, always the voice of reason and practicality, has suggested that with Helen's number phobia, it would be good for her to have someone else handle her finances entirely, just as Dan used to do for her. It wouldn't cost her all that much and then she could spare herself the agony she puts herself through. But Helen resists the idea—she can't imagine trusting anyone the way she did Dan. She tells herself that in time, as she grows used to managing money, she will relax about it. Her plan now is to take a class, just as soon as the right one comes along. "Managing Your Personal Finances" does not appeal. "Soothing Advice Plus Chocolate for Women Who Would Prefer Doing Almost Anything Else to Managing Their Finances" does.

Helen drives downtown and arrives fifteen minutes early at the InterContinental. She decides to get a glass of wine before going to meet Tom Ellis—she can use a little bolstering up—and she finds an end seat at the little bar next to the entrance of the restaurant. At the other end of the bar is a man reading a newspaper, and Helen studies him, wondering if he's the man she's meeting. He's tall, dressed in dark slacks and a pin-striped blue and white shirt, open at the neck; and from what Helen can see, he appears to be nice-looking. He looks up then, smiles in Helen's direction, and she smiles back. He *is* nice-looking, in fact; he reminds her of a boyfriend she had in college who used to tell everyone—in truth—that he had been runner-up for the most handsome boy in seventh grade. It was meant to be a charming and only slightly ironic icebreaker when he met women, and it worked, especially when he produced the aging page of the yearbook that he carried in his wallet of a cute kid with a longish crew cut, whose expression told you that he thought the world was a swell place. This man has the same qualities: a kind of all-American look, the kind of handsome you feel comfortable with rather than intimidated by: even features, warm brown eyes, thick blond hair, longish. "Helen?" he says, and she swallows, nods. The man gets up and comes to sit beside her, offers her his hand. "Tom Ellis." From here, she can see that he's older than he looks; he has graying temples and many lines around his eyes. He's tan, clearly he's not from here. She supposes he might have gotten his tan in a booth, but the tan seems too real, and anyway, he doesn't seem the type.

"I want to say first that I'm so sorry about your husband."

"Thank you."

"I feel like I knew Dan pretty well—even though we only met face-to-face a couple of times."

"Who *are* you?" Helen asks.

He starts to answer, then says, "Tell you what. Let me buy you some lunch. I think this is going to be a long conversation."

They move to the restaurant, and are seated by the window. Despite the nature of this meeting, Helen regrets the brightness of the light. She looks old, sitting here, she knows it. Oh, who cares? When will she stop worrying about how she looks? Maybe never. She listened once to an NPR story about a woman who was ninety-three and on a diet. Ninety-three!

She lays the napkin on her lap, accepts the menu from a bored-looking waiter. It is Helen's habit to try to engage every waiter she meets—something that used to drive Dan crazy, and still aggravates Tessa. "Mom," she said, last time this happened. "You don't need to make *friends* of everyone!" When Helen said she wasn't making friends, she was just interested in their lives, in who they were, Tessa said, "You don't have to be *interested* in everyone, either!" It stung, hearing this, and Helen wondered if she was foolish, if it was annoying to be with someone who liked to engage in conversation with virtually anyone who came along. But then in her mind she defended herself, deciding it was a necessary quality for doing the work that she did. *Something* interesting was in everyone; her obligation and her delight was to unearth it. Her purpose, even.

But this waiter does not respond to her usual overtures: a smile, a greeting, a comment on the weather, an inquiry into what *he* really likes to eat here. "It's all good," he says, and there is in his statement an air of impatience that draws Helen's eyes from him and onto the menu. "I'll have the Caesar salad," she says, and snaps the menu closed in a way meant to convey her disappointment at his unwillingness to cooperate, as she sees it.

"The same," Tom says, and Helen senses that he's not looked at the menu at all, because he has been studying her.

"You look a little different from the picture," he says, and before Helen can ask, adds, "Dan showed me a picture of you that he kept in his wallet."

"Oh, God," Helen says. "The one on the porch? With the dog?" They'd been visiting friends at a cabin in Vermont—this was a good five years ago—and Dan had snapped a photo of Helen on the front porch with her arm around their friends' Great Dane. She had just come out of the shower and her hair was flat and wet, her face lacking any makeup.

"That's the one."

"Yes, and the dog looks infinitely better than I. I don't know why Dan liked that picture so much."

"You look . . . friendly," Tom says.

"As opposed to now?" She's a bit insulted.

"You look scared now."

"Well." She takes a piece of bread that she doesn't want, butters it, cuts it in half. Then she looks over at Tom and shrugs.

He leans forward, speaks quietly. "Why don't I start by telling you how Dan and I met?"

She nods.

"I was here in Chicago, meeting with a guy Dan worked with. We all went out to lunch, and Dan saw pictures of the house I remodeled for his friend in Santa Rosa. He hired me on the spot to do one for you."

"What are you talking about?"

Tom makes a widening gesture with his hands. "He hired me to do a house for you. He wanted it to be a surprise, and he gave me the money and told me never to call him at home."

"How much money?" Helen asks quickly.

"Eight hundred and fifty thousand," Tom says, and Helen thinks, *At least he's honest.*

"I have about twenty-five thousand left over, which I'll give to you."

"But how . . . ?"

"He got a post office box for me to send him photos and progress reports. He said if he ever had any problems with what I was doing, he'd let me know, but otherwise just proceed. I thought it was odd that I never heard from him, but then I decided he was just a very busy man, and that he was happy with everything. He had come out early on and seen the land and the original structure and the blueprints for the renovation. I figured that when we had the walk-through, he'd let me know if anything needed to be done. And so now . . . it's built. It's finished. Has been for a month. I couldn't reach him, and so I called you—he had given me your cell phone number just in case of emergency. After you hung up on me, I did a little more research, and found out that Dan had died."

She can't think of what to say. Inside her, Dan has just died again.

"He said it was your retirement home. And he had me build it according to very specific directions. The bedroom, for example, is . . . Well, it's just *bed*. But there's—"

"A refrigerator in the wall?" Helen asks. "And a big TV? And a few drawers built into the wall? And a bunch of bookshelves?"

"Right. So this was your idea, I assume? As well as a bedroom-size closet?"

She shakes her head. "I can't believe this. I told him once what my fantasy house would be, but it was just . . . Well, it was a fantasy! I never expected that he'd *build* it, that we'd live there. I thought, in fact, that we might end up living on a boat. That was *his* fantasy."

"He told me that," Tom says, smiling, and moves his hands to let the waiter put down the salad. He takes a bite immediately. "Sorry, I'm just starving. I skipped breakfast, and didn't have much of a dinner last night."

"That's fine," Helen says. You can have mine, too, she wants to tell him. What little appetite she had, she has lost.

She watches Tom take a few more bites, then says, "So this house is in Santa Rosa?"

"It's in Mill Valley, over the bridge from San Francisco."

"I know where Mill Valley is."

"It's a great place," he says. "I have to tell you. The kitchen is a masterpiece."

"Six-burner stove?" Helen asks.

"You've got a six-burner stove with a griddle at the center. Burr elm contrasted with pale elm cabinets. There's—"

"How much do you think I can get for it? Can I get my money back?"

Tom sits back in his seat. "You want to *sell* it? Wow." He stares at her, says again, "Wow. I didn't expect that. I thought you'd . . ."

"What? What did you think?"

"You want the whole scenario?"

A couple is seated next to them—a man and a woman, serious-faced, each with an open laptop—and Tom lowers his voice. "You want me to tell you exactly how I imagined it would play out?"

Helen nods.

"Okay, I thought you'd start crying. You know, happy tears. And then I thought you'd ask a million questions, which I was going to be reluctant to answer. Because you've got to see this place. You've just got to see it. You might think you know how it looks, because he designed it to your specifications. But the tree house—"

"What tree house? That wasn't my idea. I never said anything about a tree house."

"Well, you got one. With wide-tread stairs for climbing up into it. He said he wanted you to be eighty and still able to get up there. It's quite a tree house, not the kind of thing you usually think of when you hear the word."

This is beginning to be unbearable. "You know, I . . ." She smiles, pushes her plate forward. "I wonder if we . . . How long are you here for?"

"Going home tomorrow."

"Where do you live?"

"Mill Valley. Not that far from your place. I was looking forward to being neighbors with you." His voice softens. "I only met with Dan those two times, but I really connected with him. He was a hell of a guy."

"Yes, he was."

"Hell of a guy."

"Yes."

"I'm so sorry. Again."

She feels herself beginning to tear up. "I'm going to need some time to think about all this. I wonder if we could talk in a few days."

He reaches into his pocket, pulls out a card, and slides it across the table to her. It's a handsome card, simply designed, a sepia print on a cream-colored background. She puts it in her purse. "I'll call you. I think for now, I just need to go."

"I understand."

"Do you want my salad?"

"That's okay. But there's one more thing I need to tell you."

She sits back in her chair, stops trying to find the arm of her coat.

"I'm sorry, but you'll need to start paying the bills for electricity, for—"

"You have twenty-five thousand dollars, right?"

"Right. *You* do."

"Can't you use that to pay expenses until I decide what to do?"

"I guess I could handle that for you for a while."

"I could pay you to do it," Helen says.

"You don't have to. I'll take care of it for now. But you'll have to decide pretty quickly what—"

"I know. I will. Right now, I just need a little time."

"Of course."

She gets up and starts to walk away, then turns back. "Do you have pictures with you? Any pictures of the house?"

Tom shakes his head. "He was adamant that the first time you saw that house was when you were there. He was actually going to blindfold you a few blocks away and uncover your eyes when you were smack-dab in the middle of the kitchen. I thought it was right. Kind of romantic. You can't capture it in pictures, anyway. You just can't."

"What's the address?" she asks.

"It's a post office box. It's a little road, unpaved, very few houses on it. Very private, and really beautiful."

And now she does start to cry. She manages a pinched "Thank you," and rushes out to get her car and go home, she wants so much right now to be home.

When she pulls into the driveway, she rests her head against the steering wheel. Then she comes into the house, and, without taking off her coat or her boots, heads upstairs to her bedroom. In the very back of her closet, she moves aside shoe boxes that have been stacked up to hide another box. There it is, the Christmas gift she bought for Dan and received in the mail two days before he died. As part of the gift, she had promised herself not to tell anyone else about it, not Tessa, not even Midge. Dan had a man's typically ambivalent feeling toward the relationship his wife enjoyed with her best friend: glad she had such a treasured confidante, but a bit worried about the content of all they shared. She thought it would please Dan that this gift was something only the two of them knew about. It had pleased her.

On the day the gift was delivered, she immediately hid it in her closet until she could wrap it—she'd intended to put it in a much bigger box, so that he'd never be able to guess what was in it. She has not seen it since the day she put it here; she had, in fact, forgotten about it.

She unfolds the paperwork lying on top of the Bubble Wrap: *World War II Navy Mark II Sextant, manufactured by David*

White, 1943, Original GI Issue. Precision ground lenses, brass gears and fittings, stainless steel screws. Very fine and precise navigational instrument.

She pulls the antique out of the box and holds it in her hands, moves the horizon mirror forward and back, studies the half-moon-shaped graduated arc, the telescopic lens. She imagines how pleased Dan would have been to receive this, how he would have looked at it, then up at her; again at it, then up at her. He would have understood that she had gotten it as a way of telling him to go ahead and buy the boat. Not for nothing had he read aloud to her William Steig's *Amos & Boris,* the children's book about a mouse who sets off to sea. Dan had brought the book home the day after he and Helen had shared with each other their retirement fantasies, and he had read it to her that night, in bed. Helen had particularly liked the passage about Amos, the mouse sailor, lying on his boat's deck and looking up at a night sky crowded with stars. At that moment, Amos was more aware than ever of his tiny size against the vastness surrounding him, but he also came to understand his essential part in and of it. For Helen, the scene suggested a metaphysical kind of anchoring that one longs for and rarely achieves, a respite from a primary loneliness as common to humans as blood and bones. So although Dan had read the book to her as a last-ditch attempt at persuasion, she took it as a conversion experience.

meet a fucking psychopath who ends up murdering me in my bed, and not because I invited him to be *in* it!"

"Okay," Helen says. "That's just—"

"I will not do it and I don't want you to *ask* me about it again, ever! Just *stop!*"

"Fine. Don't do it. Stay single and end up a bitter old woman whose only love is some matted, ancient cat. Who stinks. And who snakes around your ankles every morning in that creepy way they have, begging for cat food that also stinks. Food covered with used foil that you will wash off and use yet again. And that's all that will be in your fridge except juice that you use to mix with your Metamucil."

"Mom. I think you're describing *your* fears about *yourself.*"

Helen considers this. Tessa is possibly right. But she tells her daughter, "No. I wasn't alone. I had a great love. And a great marriage."

Tessa puts her carton down on the coffee table, leans back against the cushions. She pulls a handful of hair up close to her eyes, checking for split ends. "How did you and Dad meet, anyway?"

Helen smiles, remembering. "Didn't we ever tell you? It was at a party. I hadn't wanted to go, I had a big pimple on my chin, but my roommate talked me into it. It was a really crowded party but I saw your dad right away, he was leaning against the refrigerator, talking to someone. He was wearing one of those fisherman knit sweaters, an off-white, and he looked so handsome. I didn't talk to him until I'd been there for almost an hour and went to the refrigerator for a beer. He was still standing there, and I remember thinking it was so odd that he hadn't moved. But anyway, I'd been having a discussion in the living room with a bunch of people who thought the idea of life on other planets was ridiculous. And I thought it was ridiculous to think that we were alone in the universe. I asked your dad if he believed there was life on other planets, and he said of course and then we just started talk-

ten

"GOOD EVENING," TESSA'S DOORMAN SAYS.

"Hi, Walter. Is Tessa home?"

"Surprise visit?"

"Yes."

"She just got home. She got a new pair of boots today. That young woman has *style*. Of course, I'm the one who told her about them. They were in *Vogue*. Would you like to see?"

"Maybe later. I need to go and talk to Tessa."

Helen rides the elevator up, thinking of how she might tell her daughter what she has learned. All afternoon, she pondered whether or not she should tell her at all. Maybe she should just sell the place without looking at it, why make it more complicated? In the end, she decided to come and talk to Tessa face-to-face.

When her daughter opens the door, Helen speaks before Tessa can. "I know, I didn't call. But I have to talk to you about something."

"What happened? Did something happen?"

"It's not bad. It's . . . odd."

Tessa steps back from the door so that her mother can come in. "I just got some Chinese," she says.

"Enough?" Helen asks, and Tessa says of course.

While they eat straight from the cartons, Helen tells her daughter about the house. She tells her, too, that she's thinking of selling the place, sight unseen.

"How can you say that?" Tessa asks.

"Because we're not going to move there, so why spend the time and money looking at it? I like living here. I don't want to live somewhere else."

"I could live somewhere else."

"No, you couldn't." Helen grabs a broccoli spear, puts it in her mouth, and sucks off the sauce.

Tessa gives her a look.

"Well, all right, yes, you could; but do you really think it's a good idea?"

"Of course it's a good idea! What better time? I can work anywhere, why not there? I've always wanted to live there." Then, before Helen can protest, Tessa adds, "I don't tell you everything, you know."

"I know. Of course I know. Some things are private—and should be. But where you'd like to live, that's not private!"

"In fact, sometimes it is." Tessa puts down her carton of kung pao chicken and leans back, untucks her shirt from her jeans. She looks over at her mother. "You know?"

"Okay, Tessa."

"Don't get all peeved."

"I'm not."

Tessa makes a grunting sound, the equivalent of *"Right."*

"I'm not! I'm just surprised, that's all. I mean, when did this *California* thing start?"

"February seventeenth, 2004," Tessa says. "Four-thirty-seven

in the afternoon. A gray day, a storm predicted that never materialized."

"Okay," Helen says. "All right."

"Mom. Mom. Aren't you even curious to see the house? Aren't you *dying* to see it? Dad had it *built* for you! It's your *dream* house!"

What Helen wants to say is, "Yes, and that's why it's not appropriate for us to live there together. It wasn't for you and me! It was for me and Dad, and Dad is gone and now there's no reason for that house!" What she does say is, "Fine, we'll go and see it." Some miniature version of herself that lives at the center of her brain throws up her hands. When Tessa asks when they can go, Helen says after Christmas, after she teaches her first class. They'll go then.

"Promise?" Tessa says.

Helen nods.

They return to eating, listlessly now, and when they've finished, Tessa says she has to go; she's meeting a friend.

"Who?" Helen asks.

"A *friend*."

"A date?"

"No. Not a *date*."

"You know, I wish you'd just consider Internet dating. People are too busy to meet any other way! I read this article about a couple who just got married, and neither of them ever thought they'd use Internet dating services, but—"

"Mom! Mom! Mom! I said I'm not *doing* it. What I meant when I said I'm not doing it is that *I'm not doing it!*"

Helen bizarrely interprets her daughter's strong refusal as possible interest (she was just scared! And why not! It *was* scary!) and blithely continues. "Oh, try it just once. What could happen?"

"What could happen?" Tessa says, her eyes big, round pools of blue. "What could *happen*? Well, let's see. For one, I could

ing and he . . . he asked me out." Actually Dan had spent that night with her in her little apartment, but there was no need for Tessa to know that. How to explain the sexual freedom of the sixties to a daughter you want to be fiercely discerning? In the morning, Dan had put on the glasses he had refused to wear at the party (that was why he'd stayed at the refrigerator. Everyone came to the refrigerator eventually and then he could see them close up). But he'd put on his glasses and pointed to her pimple and said, "Ouch!" and Helen had felt so happy because it hadn't offended her but made her laugh; and it had put them on the fast track for being comfortable with each other. As they were, ever after. Always comfortable in a way that Dan described as *home safe.*

Then Helen remembers. She *has* told Tessa this story, and Dan did, too. In fact, Dan told Tessa about them spending the night together, carefully emphasizing that it was *another time.* Tessa just wanted to hear it again.

Helen and Tessa clean up after dinner, and then Tessa sees that it has begun to snow, and tells her mother she'd better get going.

In the elevator on the way down to the lobby, Helen regrets having told Tessa about the house. Look what she's started now. If Tessa sees the house in California and wants to move there, Helen will have to move there, too. Because although Tessa can be without Helen, she can't be without Tessa. She knows it's wrong. She knows it.

She drives slowly down streets that have already gotten slippery. At a stoplight she sits waiting for the green, unwilling to look at the car next to her, at the park across the way, at the shops on the street, their windows full of wares. She looks only at the light, waiting for it to change.

eleven

It's Saturday, ten-thirty, and it's possible that Tessa is still asleep—she sometimes works late into the night. But Helen needs to talk to her about their trip to Minnesota tomorrow; she wants to be sure Tessa remembers to bring the cosmetics samples she's been collecting for her grandmother, who is more thrilled by samples than by the real deal. She always claims they put better product in the samples, hoping to persuade people to buy; then they water down the big sizes. Just like Coca-Cola, she says, Coca-Cola puts the same amount of syrup in the little bottles of Coke as they do in the big ones. Helen and Tessa once did side-by-side comparisons with Helen's mom and admitted she might be right: the Coke in the little bottles did seem to taste better.

Helen's mother, an otherwise intelligent woman, also seems to fully believe every claim cosmetics people make. When Helen once said, "Come on, Mom, do you really think *cream* can get rid of *cellulite*?" her mother looked over her glasses and said, "The people who make this stuff are *scientists*, Helen." And when

Helen said, "Mom. Angelina *Jolie* has cellulite!" (though she did not know for a fact that this was accurate and in truth doubted the veracity of her claim even as she said it; Angelina Jolie was clearly not human but was instead some marvel of bioengineering meant to make sure women kept feeling bad about themselves), her mother drew herself up to say, "If Angelina Jolie has cellulite, it's because she doesn't have time to do what they *say* to get *rid* of it. Really, nobody does. But if she did what they said, she would not have cellulite." Then she asked Helen, "Where *is* Angie's cellulite?" and Helen looked away and mumbled something about how she was hungry, did anyone else want a sandwich.

Helen dials Tessa's number and her daughter answers groggily.

"It's me," Helen says.

"Mom. Mom. It's *Saturday morning.*"

"You're not up?"

"Oh, my God."

"Sorry," Helen says.

"I'll call you back."

Helen unloads the groceries she's brought home: supplies for the cranberry chocolate biscotti she's making to honor a request from her dad, for the Russian tea cakes and shortbread she's making for her mother. She thinks about what their reaction will be when they hear about the house; she hasn't told them yet and still wonders if she should. But she certainly could use the comfort and advice they might offer.

She is measuring out flour when the phone rings. Helen answers it, saying triumphantly, "See? You're not asleep!"

"Pardon?" an unfamiliar voice says.

". . . Who's this?" Helen asks.

"It's Saundra Weller. I'm calling because I understand you've been asked to teach a workshop at the library in January?"

You can't have it. "Yes, I have been. I will be."

"Well, I am, too, and I wondered if you'd like to get together sometime and talk about what we might offer these people."

"I didn't know there was another instructor," Helen says.

"There wasn't meant to be. But there was such an enthusiastic response this time. I *told* Nancy that would happen. Word spreads, and you know how *everybody's* a *writer.* Anyway, she said she'd asked you to lead a workshop; I'm sure she assumed I wouldn't really be interested and it's true that I'm terribly busy. But now she needs another instructor and I find I actually *am* interested. One needs, occasionally, to give back."

Helen pulls out the sugar canister, goes to the cupboard for red and green sprinkles, banishes an encroaching memory of how much Dan loved these cookies, how he used to eat them for breakfast. "You know, I'm kind of swamped right now," she tells Saundra. "I have to make—"

"I'm only trying to make sure the classes are good," Saundra says. "Just because they're free doesn't mean they should be substandard. So I thought we should get together and compare notes for what we intend to do."

Helen hesitates, then says, "I'm confused. Are we teaching together?"

"Oh, heavens no. No. I'm just saying that I think these people should be well taught, even if they're . . . Well, let's just say they're not exactly MFA candidates, okay? And I know you've not done much teaching, and—"

"Yes, I have," Helen says. *Don't ask where.*

"Where?"

"On . . . this . . . It was a special retreat. For writers. Who I taught." *Whom! Whom I taught!*

"Oh? Well, I understood that—"

"Who did you 'understand' it from?"

"Nancy Weldon told me you hadn't done this kind of thing before."

"Did she ask you to help me?"

"Well, she . . . didn't exactly have to."

"I see. Well, no thanks." Helen opens the bag of walnuts, pops a few into her mouth, chews a bit harder than she needs to. Into the mouthpiece.

"Well, I must say you seem *offended*. I apologize if I said anything that made it seem . . . if I offended you in any way."

"It's okay," Helen says. "I'd just like to do this on my own."

"All right," Saundra says lightly. "I just wanted to make the offer. So . . . How are you otherwise? You've another book coming out next year, I imagine?" Oh, with what ill-disguised weariness she offers this last.

Nope. Not another book. Not another anything. "I *do*," Helen says.

"I'll have to look for it. My, you are nothing if not prolific."

"Yeah," Helen says. "Well, listen, thanks a lot for the offer. And the same to you, by the way!"

"The same . . . ?"

"If you need help, just let me know."

Silence, and Helen can all but see Saundra's look of incredulousness. She imagines her dressed in black, looking chic and beautiful. Saundra is a remarkably beautiful woman: blond, green-eyed, ultrathin, bone structure to die for. "I'll see you soon," Saundra says, finally, and hangs up.

Helen goes defiantly to her cookbook shelf. Where is that recipe for pumpkin flan. It's really hard. You have to know what you're doing to make it.

Helen has finished with all the baking when Tessa calls back. It's five o'clock and dark outside.

"You just got up?" Helen asks.

"No. I forgot to call you back."

"Thank you."

"Mom. I have ten thousand things to do. I haven't even started packing. How cold is it in Minnesota?"

"Freezing. Don't forget to pack the cosmetics samples for Grandma."

"I *know.*"

Helen frowns at the phone. "Are you crabby?"

"*No,* I am not *crabby.*"

Helen could argue that point. But she doesn't want to argue. She wants to lie down. And she wants to go to her parents' house and be taken care of. Also, she wants to go there and take care of them. "Well, I'm just trying to help you not forget anything," she says. "You always forget something."

"So do you," Tessa says. "Last time you forgot your *glasses.* And you had to wear your *contacts* all the time and you kept *bitching* about it."

"Good-bye, my little darling, my sweet angel daughter, light of my life."

"I'll see you at Union Station," Tessa says. "Wear a red rose so I know who you *are.*"

twelve

HELEN WEARS A RED ROSE, A FRAYED VELVET ONE THAT USED TO go on a vintage hat, pinned to her coat lapel when she goes to the train station. When she sees her daughter at the entrance to the Great Hall, she waves exuberantly and shouts, "*Tessa!* Over here!"

Embarrassed, Tessa puts her head down and comes over. "I *saw* you."

"Did you bring the samples?"

"Yes, I brought the samples. Did you bring your glasses?"

"Ah, jeez." Helen sees them in her mind, lying next to her bathroom sink, so that she'd be sure to remember to pack them.

There is an echoing announcement that it is time for boarding, and they make the long walk down the narrow concrete strip to their car. As always, Helen is thrilled by the immensity of the train, by the sight of the uniformed conductors helping people up the big metal steps, by the loud hissing and clanking sounds, by the idea of travel—all these people *going* somewhere. Walking ahead of them is a family with two small children, a boy and a girl, and each rolls their own small suitcase dutifully behind. Helen wonders what's in there: stuffed animals and toys, coloring books and games? Or is it their clothes and pajamas, stacks of folded underwear? The first time Helen saw little children pulling suitcases she felt sorry for them and wondered why their parents didn't pack for them, and carry the children's things in their own bags. Why make the children lug suitcases behind them and often carry backpacks besides? But then she became aware of the pride in the children's faces, the way that they seemed to *want* to do this. It was a good idea, she decided, to foster this sense of *can-do* early on in life. Maybe if she'd been made to carry her own suitcase as a child, she'd know how to fix her own toilet flapper now.

After she and Tessa get seated inside their roomette, Helen says, "Want some wine?"

Tessa smiles. "Sure."

"Cheese? Chocolate?"

"Mom."

"*What?*"

"Maybe *later*? Like, after we've left the *station*?"

"I have little sandwiches, too."

"Mom. Mom."

"I didn't *offer* them to you. I'm just saying we *have* them. Then, later, when you're riding along and you get hungry—and you *will* get hungry—you'll know what we *have*."

"We have a *dining* car."

Just then, as though confirming Tessa's point, the conductor pokes his head inside their room and says, "Ladies? What time would you like to have dinner?"

Tessa raises an eyebrow at her mother.

"You choose," Helen tells her, then rushes to add, "I always like the first sitting. Then they still have everything, and you can be done with dinner and have the rest of the trip to just relax. Your dad and I always got the first sitting. But you choose whatever you want."

Tessa looks at the conductor, rolls her eyes.

"Okay!" he says. "First sitting!" He's cute, the conductor, and Helen can tell he finds Tessa attractive, though who wouldn't? But he's not for Tessa. Tessa needs someone else. Soon. What if it takes her a long time to get pregnant? What if she wants more than one child?

Helen pours Tessa and herself a glass of wine each and waits for the thrilling lurch of the train as their trip begins, waits for Chicago to slide past and into the distance. Then, as the sun starts sinking in the sky, the train will make its way through open land and into and out of little towns and cities. Once, she was traveling alone to St. Paul and when the train arrived in Milwaukee, she heard a woman say to her husband, "Milwaukee. What do they have here?"

"Beer," the man said. "That's about it."

Helen loves Milwaukee: its fine art museum; the excellent theaters; the Italian grocery on Brady Street. Glorioso's has not only killer salami but a black "complexion" soap that all the old lady customers swear by—it is kept behind the counter like contraband. There are exquisite galleries and stores in the newly restored Third Ward, and the lakefront is full of homes worthy of openmouthed admiration. She politely interrupted the couple to tell them all that, and they told her to buzz off.

Helen settles back into her seat, stares out the window. She always feels so cozy on a train, so privileged. She sometimes likes to imagine the engine having a face, as in children's books, and at such times sees the lead car chugging cheerfully along, calling out greetings to the deer in the fields, to the tall pine trees, to the white-faced cliffs along the Mississippi, to the stars that, toward the end of the trip, will come out and shine high above them.

. . .

Helen startles awake, unsticks her mouth from itself, and checks her watch. About forty-five minutes away from the elegant city of St. Paul, her birthplace and in so many respects still home. It's not yet time to awaken Tessa, who has been sleeping soundly since after dinner. Tessa works hard, and she is chronically behind on sleep. Helen is glad they will have time to relax, to unwind and enjoy themselves. Her father has a nightly martini with Tessa, her mother listens with great interest to any stories Tessa wants to share about work, about friends, even, to Helen's chagrin or plea-sure (or sometimes, oddly, both), about Helen.

Tessa never displays with Helen's parents the kind of short-temperedness she often shows her mother; instead, she is patient, kind, always loving. In some respects, Tessa has made Helen love her parents more, because of the easy way they reveal themselves to their granddaughter. "Did you know Grandma had a boyfriend in high school with really curly blond hair who went on to play professional football?" Tessa has asked her. "Did you know Grandpa had a pet mouse that lived in a cage he built out of sticks and his dad drowned it in the toilet?"

Helen reaches over and pulls Tessa's blanket up to her chin, and hopes that no announcements will come on over the loud-speaker and wake her up. She hopes the conductor will not knock loudly at the closed door, asking if they need anything. Not that this has ever happened, except on one notable occasion. Helen nearly laughs out loud, recalling it now. A couple of years ago, when she and Dan were taking a vacation trip to Boston, she had been sitting opposite her husband in a roomette such as this, and she began feeling a bit amorous. She watched her handsome hus-band reading, his tortoiseshell glasses slid partway down his nose, and grew more and more aroused. Finally, "Dan?" she said. He held up a finger, read to the end of the sentence, then looked up. "Would you like a little train sex?" she asked. And Dan blushed—oh, it was so dear, the man blushed. "Would you?" she asked, giggling. She flung herself at him and started passionately kissing him, feeling him up generally, then quite specifically. They laughed at first, but they were both very turned on. Helen had just unzipped Dan's pants when there was a sharp rap on the door. Helen leaped back into her seat, Dan zipped up and opened the door. "Yes?" he asked the conductor, and his voice was high and nervous and unnatural. Like Woody Allen's, she told him later.

"You need your trash emptied?" the conductor asked. He was an older, angry-looking man, nothing like the cute and undoubtedly liberal conductor they have on this train. He looked suspiciously at Dan, then Helen.

"I believe it's empty," Dan said, and pulled out the little trash can to show him.

"All right, then," the conductor said, and moved on down the aisle. Across the way, Helen met the eyes of a middle-aged, stout woman, who was furiously knitting. Helen fluttered her fingers at her, and the woman turned away.

"She told on us," Helen whispered to Dan, pointing at the woman and then sliding their door closed.

"I know," Dan whispered back, and then they couldn't help it; they started laughing.

"*Yes?*" Helen said, imitating Dan. "*Yes,* Mr. Conductor?"

They laughed and laughed, and later that night they finished what they had started and then some. Helen stares out the window into the blackness. Every now and then, there is a house with a light on. She strains to see the people there, and across what seems a vast distance, she wishes them all well.

thirteen

"WHAT HAPPENED HERE?" HELEN'S FATHER, FRANKLIN, ASKS Tessa. "You've grown about three feet, haven't you?"

Tessa smiles and points to her boots. "They're high."

"But you've grown, too!"

"I think I've stopped growing, Grandpa."

Franklin studies Tessa's face. Then he says, "Well, hell. I guess I've shrunk more, then. Want a martini?"

"Sure!"

"Helen?"

"Okay."

"Eleanor?"

"Maybe a half."

Franklin winks at Helen; they call her mother the Queen of Halves, for her tendency to cut virtually anything she eats in half. Almost invariably she eats both halves.

"Anyone want a Christmas cookie?" Eleanor asks, and they all three answer yes.

They sit around the kitchen table, talking, and Helen finally tells her parents about the house, skipping the monetary worries. At midnight, she is exhausted, but it seems Tessa and her parents could go on all night. "I think I'll go up and just put on my pajamas," Helen says, and Tessa says, "Good niiiiight!"

"I'll be back down," Helen says, and together Tessa and her mother say, "No, you won't."

It's true. Helen has a habit of saying she's "just" putting her pajamas on, then disappearing for the night. Dan used to say, "Why don't you just say you're going to bed?" and Helen would say, "Because I never think I am."

She takes her pajamas out of her suitcase and lays them on the bed, then stores her suitcase back against the wall, abbreviated in height by the eaves of the house. The guest room is in the attic, and Helen always feels she's in danger of bumping her head, though she never does. She takes off her clothing, shivering—the ancient space heater does little to warm the room. But Helen likes sleeping in a cold room; after she's under the covers, she won't mind the temperature. Tessa will be sleeping with her, which neither of them likes, but neither wants the sofa, either. Helen uses the decorative pillows to construct a kind of wall down the middle of the bed. She hopes this will keep her daughter from kicking her. Tessa's kicking is another thing Helen worries about with regard to her daughter's marital future.

She is almost asleep when she hears Tessa coming up the creaky stairs, moving slowly, on tiptoe, across the room lit only by the Christmas tree her mother has put up for them. Eleanor always does this, puts a tabletop tree on a card table in the corner, with little gifts for them beneath it.

"I'm awake," Helen says.

Tessa comes over to sit on the bed, her face a shadowy study of red and green. "Grandpa's lost weight," she whispers. "Did you notice?"

"I don't think he eats that much anymore," Helen whispers back, in an effort to reassure her daughter. She, too, had noticed the way her father's pants hung low on his hips, how his wristwatch was hiked up far on his arm, and she thinks it has more to do with illness than appetite. A little over a year ago, her father was discovered to have a worrisome "spot" on his hip bone. Considering his age, the decision was made to just watch it. She wonders now if that spot has grown, or if some other problem has materialized. When there's an opportunity, she'll ask her mother about it.

Tessa slips off her shoes and gets into bed with her clothes on. She pulls the covers up and closes her eyes. "Good night," she says, yawning.

Helen lies still, thinking, *Don't. She is twenty-seven years old.* She reminds herself of the List of C's, her personal laundry list for self-improvement: Don't control, don't criticize, don't complain. It seems she does all three all day long. But she's aware of it! She acknowledges it! Doesn't that count for something? She closes her eyes to sleep. So what if her daughter wants to sleep in her clothes? It's cold up here! Did she not herself sometimes sleep in her clothes when she was that age? Well, no, actually, at Tessa's age Helen was married and raising her child, and she slept in matching pajama tops and bottoms every night. But her daughter is not her! She is her own person, entitled to have her own individual life!

But did she even wash up and brush her teeth?

Helen raises herself carefully on one elbow and leans across the pillow divide to peer into Tessa's face. Is that mascara under her daughter's eye or a shadow caused by her lashes? She leans closer, squinting, her upper lip hiked high, which always happens when she tries to see better; it's a very unattractive habit—she has been told she looks like a rat when she does it. Tessa's eyes spring open. "Mom! What are you *doing*?"

"*Shhhh!* You need to wash your face and brush your *teeth*!" Helen whispers. "And you need to change into pajamas! What is the matter with you, falling into bed like a—"

"I did wash my face and brush my teeth!"

"Well . . . Put on your pajamas!"

"I *forgot* them!" Tessa's eyes are wide, furious, but then she suddenly starts laughing, and Helen does, too.

"Go and ask Grandma to give you something to sleep in."

"I'm fine," Tessa says. "I don't want to bother them. I think they're asleep. I'll ask tomorrow."

"Want me to go down and get you something?"

"No. I'm all right."

"I could sneak—"

"Mom. Mom."

Helen settles herself on her side of the bed, folds her hands over her stomach, and begins taking idle inventory of the events of the day. She hears a plane passing by overhead and wonders who's on it, wonders what gifts are being carried in the suitcases, what hopes and grudges are being carried in people's hearts.

Tessa yawns, then says, "You know what I was thinking about tonight? I was thinking about the Box. Do you still have it?"

She means the empty box Dan gave her for a Christmas present when she was pregnant with Tessa. It was lavishly wrapped, beautiful to look at, and Helen saved it for last. It was light, and Helen thought there must have been jewelry in there, though there had been no telltale rattle when she shook it. They couldn't really afford for Dan to buy her jewelry at that point, they had agreed he would not, but Helen hoped anyway that a ring or a bracelet was in there, something outrageously expensive that she could wear for one day and then return, if she had to. But when she opened the box, it was empty. She looked up at Dan, her face full of confusion.

"Wait," he said, and came to crouch beside her chair.

"This isn't *funny*," she wailed, and pressed her hand conspicuously against the side of her huge belly: *Look at all I'm doing for you!*

"Wait," he said again, and kissed her temple, the top of her head. Then he sat back on his heels to look up at her. "You know why I gave you an empty box? Because I was thinking, what does she really, really need, what does she not have? And I thought of all these things, these . . . *things,* you know? And then I thought about us, and I thought about the baby on the way, and I decided that we have the most complete, the happiest life I could ever imagine. That if we never got another thing, we would be rich beyond measure. I wanted to give you an empty box to say that." He shrugged. "I guess it didn't come out so well." And Helen kissed him and said that it had come out fine, and he was right.

The Box had become an annual tradition, each year going to a different member of their little family. And although the Box itself became softer and more misshapen with every year, it was always the most beautifully wrapped gift under the tree. The person who received it was supposed to talk about what was "in" the Box—what intangible gifts were presently in his or her life; but that rarely worked. It seemed hard for people to say out loud the things that were most important to them, unless it was in retrospect.

"I still have the Box," Helen says. "It's in the basement with the Christmas decorations." She smiles at Tessa. "I'm sorry I didn't decorate this year."

"I don't mind. I understand."

"I know, you said; but I'm sorry anyway."

"There's only one thing I wanted you to bring out."

"The Box?"

"Yes. I wanted to get it. Because . . . Well, because I wanted to keep up the tradition. And also . . . I don't know, I look at the way some mothers and daughters are with each other, and I just wanted a chance to say . . ." She sighs hugely. "We're basically good, right?"

Helen smiles. "Right.

"Tessa?"

"Yeah?"

"Is this the martini talking?"

"Well, of course. But it's me, too."

Within a couple of minutes, Tessa's breathing changes and she is asleep.

Helen turns onto her side, suddenly wide awake. She is also hungry. Downstairs are the cookies. Maybe she'll have a few and then sit for a while by the Christmas tree in the living room. She likes to sit across the room from it and look at it without her contacts; she likes that soft-focus effect, like Doris Day looking at Rock Hudson in those old movies. Also, despite her years, she still likes to see what presents are marked for her and shake them, guessing at the contents. It took Helen a long time to disavow Santa Claus, and she remembers distinctly the day she finally said she did not believe in him. She was eight years old, and sitting on her back porch steps with her best friend, Cindy McClure, on a hot summer day, and she sighed and said, "Okay, there's no Santa Claus."

"I know," Cindy said mournfully.

And then Helen grabbed her friend, grabbed both of her arms, and said, "But there *is* an Easter bunny." When she saw doubt in Cindy's face, she said, "Why would anyone make up something like *that*?"

"I guess," Cindy said, and for Helen, the day was saved.

She tiptoes downstairs, goes into the kitchen and pours herself a glass of milk, puts some cookies on a plate, and heads into the living room. There she sees her mother, dozing in a chair. She moves beside her, touches her mother's hand, and Eleanor wakes up.

"Hey," Helen says, softly. "Waiting for Santy?"

"I was having trouble sleeping," her mother says.

"Me, too." Helen sits at her mother's feet and offers up her plate. "Want a cookie?"

"No, I've had enough. They were delicious, thank you for making them for us. How are you, darling? Hard time of year for you?"

Helen shrugs. "Every time of year is hard without him."

"It will get better, you'll see."

Helen eats her cookies, staring at the tree. "Where's my ornament?" she asks. She means the reindeer she made in kindergarten, out of clothespins.

"He's on there," her mother says.

"Where?"

"One side or the other. I remember clipping him on."

"I didn't see him."

"Well, he's there."

Helen won't humiliate herself further by going over to look. But she will look tomorrow, when no one's watching. Funny how the littlest things can have such importance. The older some things get, the more precious.

"Mom? How's Dad?" She keeps her voice neutral. She wants to communicate the fact that whatever it is, she can take it.

"Well, we saw Dr. Burns the other day."

Helen turns to face her, hoping for quick reassurance. But what Eleanor does is to put her hand to her daughter's cheek, tenderly, and Helen knows.

"Did they say when?"

"Oh, honey. You know they never tell you that anymore. I know they don't want to get sued, or take away hope, but sometimes I wish they would say. People might want to know. They might need to."

Helen nods. Indeed they might.

fourteen

HENRY BORMAN CLEARS HIS THROAT AND LOOKS CAUTIOUSLY over at Helen. He has just finished reading his page answering the question *Who are you?* He lives about two miles from the library, and his piece described his apartment in the assisted care center, the lamp he always kept lit in the window. It talked about how World War II had made him the man he is, how the fortitude he learned at an early age sustained him today. He said he walked outside every day, and when he finished reading he told the group proudly that he had walked there today. When one of the women shuddered, thinking, no doubt, of the cold wind blowing that day, he told them he was a member of the Polar Bear Club and only three years ago stopped jumping into the icy waters of Lake Michigan on January 1. After the group had commented on his work—all positive comments, Helen was grateful to see, all gentle—he said he'd wondered if he should have put the Polar Bear Club in his piece, and all agreed it would have been an interesting addition. Helen told him he might want to write a whole piece devoted to that experience, and he nodded, saying, "It would make quite a story."

Henry has the largest ears Helen has ever seen. He can't straighten up all the way; he walks as though he's just started to pick something up off the floor, and when he wants to look up, he must turn his head sideways. He warned Helen that his hearing aids act up now and then; but if they ever started to squeal, why, he'd just take them out—he's gotten pretty good at lip-reading. "Go ahead and test me!" he told her. "Just move your lips, and say something. Go ahead!"

Helen looked around at the other class members, all of whom seemed intensely interested in this impromptu experiment. "I'm very impressed," she mouthed, and Henry shouted back, " *'I'm very impressed!'* Right? Am I right?"

She nodded, and Henry beamed.

The other members are as different from Henry—and from each other—as they can be; this is indeed a remarkable mix of personalities. Donetta Johnson, the day-care worker who lives in the West Side ghetto, has yet to take her tan cloth coat off; she sits staring down at the table. When Helen asked the class to go around the table and briefly introduce themselves, Donetta barely looked up. Her voice is low and soft, and there is a richness to it that makes Helen think she could be a great singer. Donetta read about growing up in Alabama, the house crowded with friends and relatives, food always being kept warm on the stove. She came to Chicago for better wages, but *in my head, I'm still home, standing on the front porch, watching my friends come to call. I'm going to finish my work here, and then I'm going home.*

Ella Parsons sits up so close to the table it cuts into her mid-section. She's in her early twenties, a pretty, moderately over-weight girl whose white blouse buttons gap widely, revealing the man's T-shirt she wears beneath. She has on a voluminous blue skirt with a wide black belt, and winter boots with their metal clasps undone. A headband meant to prevent a massive bunch of red curls from falling in her face keeps sliding forward, and each time she moves it back, she slaps the top of her head, hard. Helen believes the strong smell of perfume in the room is coming from her. She herself doesn't mind it; it's a pleasant scent.

Ella read about the old-age home where she worked assisting the occupational therapist. *I'm the happy girl, that's me! I help them so they don't get bored and sad. If you don't help them they will cry for their family and sometimes for their mom even though their mom is dead a long time ago. Mother, Mother, they always say it like that it is never Mom. Mother.* She described the apartment where she lived, her yellow curtains, her pink bedspread. She said she could play poker and her favorite food was pizza with green olives and hamburger. Also, she had a heart murmur. When the group commented positively on her work, Ella sat smiling and squirming and finally shouted out, "Wow!"

Hector Rivera is an inordinately cheerful, short man who appears to be in his forties, and he's wonderfully well dressed. He began taking notes almost as soon as Helen said hello. She can't imagine what he's writing, but then decides it's not her business anyway. His piece focused exclusively on his job delivering television news, and Helen decides that it will be her mission to get him to write about something else.

A twenty-eight-year-old man named Jeff Daley ("No relation to the mayors!" he'd quickly told Helen) had arrived early, and he and Helen had talked a bit about books before the class started. Jeff told her he had floor-to-ceiling shelves in both his bedroom and his living room, and that he was one of those people who couldn't stand book jackets—the first thing he did when he got a book was to throw the jacket away. When Helen had asked why, he said, "It feels like advertising. I only want the story." He said he taught at the Apple store on Michigan Avenue but mainly aspired to be a writer—he wrote longhand, using vintage fountain pens. He showed her one he had in his pocket, a deep yellow color, striped with black. When Helen admired it, he offered it to her, and she gently refused. "I have a million of them," he said. "Pretend we're old friends; go ahead and take it." Still she declined, but when he held it out to her and said, "I got it for a *dollar* at an estate sale," she smiled and put it in her purse. He is magazine handsome: tall, with wavy brown hair and beautiful blue eyes, and Ella Parsons has not taken her eyes off him since she came in.

One of the group members, Billy Armstrong, makes Helen uncomfortable. He's the twenty-year-old mechanic, and to Helen's way of thinking, he looks like a murderer. He has eyes so dark they seem black, very black hair, and extremely white skin marked by acne scars. He wears torn jeans and a hooded sweatshirt, the hood up. Knee bouncing, he read about how he was born a writer and now it was time to go ahead and get published. He claimed the world was full of books not worth the paper they were printed on. Ella's comment on his work was "You use lots of swears."

Cookie Evans is a blond-haired, middle-aged insurance worker dressed in a gray business suit and a pale pink blouse. She is the kind of person . . . Well, Helen hates to say it, it seems unkind, but it's true—She's the kind of person you could have a conversation with for a good fifteen minutes, turn around, and realize you couldn't remember a thing about her. It is Cookie's turn to read now.

Helen straightens herself in her chair and prepares to take notes on what she will hear. Thus far, she has opened the discussion after every person's reading, but she is relieved that her students have no inhibitions about making their opinions known. She's very much interested in these people, even the murderer. Already, she has fantasized her little group onstage doing their graduation reading, their friends and families proud. Also she has fantasized her group doing far better than Saundra Weller's.

Helen looks at her watch: just enough time for Cookie Evans to read, but almost no time for the group to offer comments; it will be a challenge to learn how to budget time here. Cookie pulls her chair closer to the table and begins:

When I was maybe four years old, I told my father I wanted to die. He pulled me onto his lap and turned me hard to face him. He said, "Why would you say a thing like that?"

I was surprised that he was surprised. I told him what I thought he should already know: your sins just got bigger, the bigger you got. It would be better to die early and then you could more easily get into heaven. I have no idea how he answered me. I'm not sure that he did. I only remember that I felt thrilled to be on his lap, to have his face so close to me, to have his coffee cup before me as though I were the one drinking from it. And then I was back on the floor again, left to my own devices. I went to my playroom and got out my kaleidoscope. I lay on my back and looked through it at all the fractured beauty. I turned the wheel slowly. Each thing I saw was so lovely I wanted to keep it, but then I would turn the wheel and there, more beauty, it would never stop. I bent my knees and my dress rode up. It didn't matter. There was no one to see me. I had no friends. I had no visitors. It was a lonely life, but I didn't realize it. It was all I knew: a father who rarely spoke, a mother who disapproved of me, and a dog who lay panting on the floor beside me and occasionally let me stick my finger in his mouth to feel his moving tongue. I didn't think it was sad to want to die. I thought it was practical. I am forty-one years old now, and it seems time to admit that I have been sad all my life. There has not been one occasion of joy in my life that was not overshadowed by sorrow. Also not one day has gone by that I have not turned the wheel of this kaleidoscope or that, and gasped. My name is Claudia.

She stops reading, looks up.

Helen lets out a breath she hadn't realized she'd been holding. "That was . . . My goodness. Thank you. That was very powerful. Very powerful writing. What did the rest of you think?"

Nothing, and then the murderer says, "Well, it was pretty *dra-*

matic." Helen sees Claudia's face color. She reaches to the floor for her purse, pulls it onto her lap, and leaves it there.

"Yes," Helen says. "Wonderfully so, I thought. What else was it?"

"I-I-I," Ella says, her voice tearful, and Helen turns to her. It only goes to show that you should never assume things. She is obviously moved by what she has heard.

"Yes, Ella?"

"I had a dog, too. And he *died*!" And now she puts her hands over her face and weeps. Henry pulls out a gold pocket watch and says brightly, "Well, time to go!"

Helen is glad he said it; it would have been hard for her to.

The students all stand, putting on their coats, and Helen says, "Before you go, I want to give you an assignment. Next time we meet, come with two pages about a room that has great meaning to you."

"What room?" Ella asks, her sorrow forgotten, and Helen says, "That's up to you." Ella stands still, contemplating this, and Helen suspects she will need to talk to her further. But first she wants to speak to Claudia.

"Can you stay a minute?" she asks, as Claudia walks past her.

"No, I have to go." The woman won't look at her.

"You will come next time?" Helen asks.

She nods.

"I thought what you wrote was beautiful," Helen says. Claudia mumbles a thank-you on her way out the door, but it is as though she has been struck rather than complimented. Helen remembers a woman who had been abused much of her life telling her that almost any form of kindness or affection was very hard for her to acccpt. "A hug *burns*," she'd said.

"Teacher?" Ella says.

Helen turns to her. "Yes?"

"You have something on your nose."

Oh, God, how long has it been there? Helen puts her hand up to her nose and quickly wipes under one nostril, then the other.

"You have something on your *nose!*" Ella says again.

"Well, what is it?" Helen asks, wiping harder.

"It's your finger!" Ella laughs heartily. Then her face grows serious and she puts her hand on Helen's arm. "That's my joke."

"Well," Helen says. "It's very funny." She talks to Ella a bit more about the assignment for next week, realizing even as she does that it doesn't matter if Ella does what she's been assigned. So long as Ella brings something to class, Helen will feel like Miss Brooks in the old TV show.

She sits back down in the chair. For the first time in a long time, she feels a lifting inside. Some sense of hope, of purpose, of optimism. There is a knocking at the door and Helen looks up to see Nancy Weldon. "So how was it?" she asks. "Think you're going to like it?"

"Very much. Far more than I expected!"

"See? And how was Ella?"

Helen smiles.

"She'll settle down. She was in the last workshop, and she calmed down after a couple of sessions."

"I *like* her," Helen says.

"Good. So do I. Saundra and I are going across the street for a glass of wine. Want to come?"

"I'd love to," Helen says. "But—"

"Don't tell me you're writing! I know you work in the mornings!"

"No, it's . . . I have other plans. Maybe next time."

"I've got to tell you," Nancy says, as they walk out together. "I am just so thrilled to meet both of you. Don't you love Saundra's books?"

"I do," Helen says. It's true that the books are fine.

fifteen

TESSA IS SITTING IN THE FRONT SEAT OF TOM ELLIS'S CAR AND raving—excessively, in Helen's opinion—about the view from the Golden Gate Bridge. Helen is sitting silently in the backseat, her arms crossed over her chest, wishing she had an emery board in her purse, iPod plugs in her ears. Oh, she knows. She remembers all this outrageous beauty from many years ago, when she and Dan lived here. They used to occasionally drive over the bridge so that they could walk on Mount Tamalpais. After a few hours, they'd descend to the beach and watch the sun set. Then they'd go into the city and eat a cheap but delicious dinner at Sam Wo in Chinatown, and finally they'd return to their tiny apartment, which happened to be across the street from Golden Gate Park. In those days, they would sometimes dream about living in a nice house in California, Helen's homesickness for the Midwest notwithstanding, but it wasn't a possibility then. Now that it is a possibility, Helen finds that her defenses are up. She feels a kind of unwarranted fury and she's not sure why.

She and Dan both had always loved the mix of people in Oak Park: virtually every ethnic background was represented, as were various levels of income. The village had a wonderful mix of restaurants, a beautiful library, three bookstores in one block. Yes, when she told Dan about her dream house, she had said she wanted to live in California, but it was a fantasy! She liked having fantasies, they were part of what made her a writer! But she also amended those fantasies with some regularity—had he forgotten that? When Dan commissioned this house they are headed for, did he really believe it was the best place for them to spend the rest of their lives? She stews and fidgets, fidgets and stews, looks out the window and at her watch.

"A lot of people wanted to tear the house down," Tom tells Tessa, as they turn off the main road. "But the owner wouldn't sell to anyone like that. She was a real feisty old lady, eighty-six years old, who was finally giving in and moving to live with her daughter in the city. But she was determined to hold on to her house until someone recognized the beauty of the place, and your dad did, in spades. She gave him a bargain because she liked him so much. The house is an original California bungalow and we kept the bones, but we really opened it up and let in the light. I think you're going to love it."

"I already do," Tessa says. "It's so *beautiful* here!"

Tom slows down and turns in to a driveway. "This is San Francisco cobblestone," he says. "It used to be on the streets in the city. I had a client who did their driveway in it and there was a lot left over. They just gave it to me, so I used it here."

"This is so cool," Tessa says, looking more closely at the driveway as they step out of the car, but all Helen can look at is the house. It is lovely: small, with shingle siding and a slate roof. There are large mullioned windows, and wild roses growing on trellises on either side of the front door.

Tom holds out the key to her, and she shakes her head. "You go first," she says.

He unlocks the door, pushes it open, and she follows him inside, trying hard to keep a check on her emotions. What she feels, suddenly, is that she has come to see Dan. He is not here, but here he is.

The walls are painted in pale, complementary earth-tone colors; the trim is a pristine white. The living room has a high pitched ceiling supported with closely placed joists. The walls in that space are lined with floor-to-ceiling bookshelves. On one of the shelves are the complete works of E. B. White; on another, there are vintage children's books; and on a third shelf there are copies of her own novels. The rest is gloriously open; ready to be filled.

There is a fieldstone fireplace, and before it are a white sofa and two white upholstered chairs. She remembers a picture in her file with furniture that looked just like this—she had wanted white furniture because her dream house would have a lot of light that would otherwise fade the furniture. Dan must have found that file, for now she sees her ideas everywhere: bamboo floors, laid so that the knuckles show. Open shelving in the kitchen with thick, cream-colored diner-style dishes, a deep double sink with a bridge faucet, an incorporated pie safe with perforated tin doors. She opens the pie safe and sees her design for spice racks, pull-out bins for pots and pans, deep drawers for table linens. There is the six-burner stove she has lusted after for years, and a huge refrigerator—room for drinks *and* food at last. There is a farmhouse kitchen table that has been refitted with a recycled glass top, complete with a silverware drawer.

"Mom! Look at this *bathroom*!" Tessa calls, and Helen goes into the small room that nonetheless holds everything she wanted: a shower made by water falling off a rock ledge, no curtain, no door. There is a free-standing, oval-shaped tub, built-in cabinets with many long and narrow drawers, and divided shelving above that for bath linens. She touches the cream-colored towels: exactly right. "This is all artisan tile from Sausalito," Tom says, behind her. She nods. She can't speak. She is full of such a mix of conflicting emotions: excitement, wonder, pain, appreciation, regret.

There is a bedroom-size closet with a place for everything, including purses. There is a three-way mirror and an upholstered stool to sit on. There are hatboxes, wire baskets for accessories, slanted shelving for shoes, even tie hangers. Behind a paneled door are a linen-lined laundry basket, a washer and dryer, and an ironing board.

The bedroom has hand-printed, Japanese paper weave on the walls, and the room-size bed is covered by a dove-gray linen duvet. There are bookshelves and swing-out lamps built into the wall, a flat-screen television. In the ceiling are tiny lights that form the constellations of Sagittarius and Libra, her and Dan's birth signs. There are French doors that lead from the bedroom into the garden, and she pushes those doors open now and steps outside into the soft air and sunshine.

"Tessa?" she calls. "Come out and see this *garden* with me!"

"In a minute," Tessa says. "I'm watching a hummingbird—he's right outside the window!"

Helen follows stone steppers into the garden and then on to a small wooden shed, furnished with only a simple desk and chair, a perfect writing space modeled after E. B. White's. She stands there, taking in the view from the little window on one wall, and then sees Tom approaching. She comes back outside and closes the door behind her, already protective of this little space, not wanting anyone else to come inside.

"Do you know the names of all the flowers growing here?" she asks him.

"I made it my business to find out," he says, smiling. "Let's see. You've got night-blooming orchids, freesia, dahlias, oriental lilies, lantana, penstemon, princess flowers, mock orange, jasmine—"

"Where's the jasmine?" Helen asks; she loves jasmine.

His face grows serious. "Are you ready?" he asks.

"What do you mean?"

"Follow me." He heads for a live oak tree in the far corner of the yard.

As they get closer, she sees a tree house, high up in the branches. And then, as they get closer still, she sees that it has been designed to look like a sailboat: Dan got a part of his wish after all. There is a wooden spiral staircase leading up to the boat, and Tom points to the center post, on which vines with small white flowers are growing. "There's your jasmine," he says. "You can smell it from here.

"Want to go up?" he asks.

"Yes."

"Want to be alone when you do?"

She nods. "Thank you."

"I'll go and talk to Tessa. Take all the time you need."

Helen climbs the steps into what is made to look like a state-room: there is a small bed, a table and two chairs, porthole windows. She takes the ladder staircase up three steps to the upper deck. Here is a bow with two teak deck chairs. There is a mast, on which is anchored a sail made from handkerchief linen; it flutters in the wind, and the sound is lovely. She stands still, listening, and feeling the tears she has kept at bay until now start down her cheeks. She walks to the other end of the boat, to the stern, where she finds a ship's wheel. She puts her hands to the polished wood and steers this way and that, wondering about the kinds of things she and Dan might have talked about up here. A friend of hers who had little boys once told her about how her father was building a tree house for them. "Oh, fun, what all are you putting in it?" Helen asked. "Nothing," her friend said. "It's not the things you *have* in a tree house, it's the things you *think* about there."

Helen goes back down below and sits at the little table.

Champagne, they would have had, their first night here. Joy. She looks out the window at the house; she can see Tessa and Tom through the window; she can hear the sound of their laughter.

She cannot live here. Every day here without Dan would tear her heart in two.

"If you don't want to live there, let me!" Tessa says. They are sitting in a small Indian restaurant near their hotel recommended by the concierge, and the meal was indeed quite good. Now they are lingering over mango ice cream, and Helen tries once more to explain to Tessa why she wants not to live in the house, but to sell it.

"I know it's beautiful; I know it's utterly unique, but it would be so hard for me to live there without Dad. And think about what we'd be giving up if we left Chicago."

"I don't think of it that way," Tessa says. "I think of how living here would open up my life!"

"You can't afford to live here alone," Helen says. "Do you know what the taxes are on that place? You'd be paying more than double what you are now, just for taxes! And then you'd have bills, besides."

"I know that, but I would be able to afford it. I could get a second job."

"Jobs are very hard to come by in this area—everyone says that."

"And what's that rah-rah speech you've given me a thousand times? *Forget about statistics; when it comes to the individual, it's zero or one hundred percent.* And anyway, I could get a roommate."

"No, you couldn't." Helen answers so swiftly she astounds herself; she doesn't even know where that answer came from.

"Why not?" Tessa asks, and twin spots of pink appear on her face; she is angry.

"This house is not a dormitory."

"What are you talking about?"

"I mean that it's very special; it needs to be treated in a certain way."

"Right. Good thing you're going to *sell* it, since it's so very *special*." Tessa's voice is loud, now.

Helen looks around the little dining room. No one seems to be paying attention to her and Tessa, but the couple at the table next to them are acting a little too nonchalant.

"Keep your voice down," Helen says, quietly.

Tessa leans forward over the table to say, "Did it ever occur to you that the decision is mine, too? He was my father. I would like to live in a house that my father built."

Helen stares at her daughter. What she wants to say is "Built for him and me, Tessa, not for you." But her daughter has a point. She says, wearily, "Let's talk about this tomorrow. I'm exhausted. At home, it's midnight." She signals for the bill, and they wait for it in silence.

That night, while Tessa sleeps, Helen lies awake. In her mind, she walks through the rooms of the house again and again.

Being in the place was almost more than she could take in. She felt as though she were looking directly at things yet not quite seeing them. People talked about dream houses, but this really *was* a dream of a house, made real for her by Dan. But Dan is no longer here, and her life is in Chicago. In addition to that, she needs to live somewhere where she can walk to stores and restaurants and parks and public transportation and movies and the library; she never wanted to live somewhere where she would be dependent on a car for such things. She thinks, too, that she probably really does need the seasons, their lessons of birth and rebirth, the rich variety they offer, even when the offering is a freezing day full of howling winds and driving snow. For every nasty day, there are many more that can break your heart with their shy beauty; nothing so ostentatious as California's beauty, no. In the Midwest, the beauty is quieter, but realer, somehow—it grounds her. And her house there is the one that Dan did live in rather than the one he was going to live in; this means more to her than she can say.

She peers over at Tessa, wild in sleep as always, her covers tangled around her. She knows her daughter as an intelligent and responsible person, but she doesn't really believe Tessa is ready to take on the responsibility of a house, and Helen doesn't want the responsibility of two. She stares up at the ceiling and quietly sighs. Maybe the next writing assignment she gives her group should be for them to write a piece on this theme: *a great gift you are given backfires.*

In her mind, she goes around the table they sit at, seeing all her students' faces. When she gets to Jeff Daley, she nearly gasps. She knows he's single and "between relationships"; she heard him tell Claudia that he'd been broken up with his girlfriend for a while. She'll invite him to dinner with Tessa and her. Naturally she is thinking that the rest of the story is that they become an item and Tessa decides the hell with California. Naturally she knows the odds are against this. Naturally she decides she will try anyway. In the morning, she will tell Tessa that they both need more time to think. That she will not sell the house right away, she will hold on to it for a few more months and then they can decide.

She thinks now that she can sleep. She can sleep and tomorrow they'll have sourdough toast with their breakfast before they head home. The little house will wait there: magical, glorious, unclaimed. She doesn't want to live there. But she's really not ready to sell it yet, either, how can she?

Oh, Dan, she thinks. In a way, it's the Monkey again. Years ago when she and Dan were in an art gallery, Helen had admired the whimsy shown in an artist's conception of a monkey turned butler. It was a four-foot-high statue and the monkey was dressed in a little suit, holding a tray, and he was remarkably lifelike: his curled-back lips, his hairy feet. For her birthday, Dan bought the monkey for her. She hadn't wanted it; she had simply admired it. She didn't know how to tell Dan that, so for some time she kept the thing up in their bedroom, off in a corner. She and Midge started calling any gift they found inappropriate a monkey. One day Dan overheard her talking to Midge on the phone, saying, "Well at least she didn't give you a *monkey*," and the jig was up. She was afraid he'd be hurt, but he was fine; he told her to return it and get something else. But he was alive then. When someone has died, it's a lot harder to get rid of something they gave you—everything has terrible value. Helen thinks that's why her mother used to say she was going to have a garage sale to end all sales—she said it and said it but never got around to doing it. She doesn't say it anymore. It would be impossible to stack her father's alpaca sweaters on some card table for strangers to rifle through now, when everything is so uncertain. And if—when—he dies, how to do it then? Helen thinks if anyone picked up anything belonging to her father at a yard sale, she'd snatch it from their hands. And then do what with it?

In her mind, she wanders the rooms of the little house, seeing all the wonders there. How many people would think she was absolutely crazy for not relocating immediately? But she is not those people; she is her odd self. The kiln has been fired; she is a person persnickety about keeping her house clean but not above spitting on her desk to rub out a coffee stain; she will never be an athlete or a mathematician or a skinny person or someone whose heart isn't snagged by the sight of fireflies on a summer night and the lilting cadence of a few good lines of poetry.

Once, when Helen was ten years old, she was sitting on the front porch with her grandmother; she had been staying at her grandparents' farm in Wisconsin while her parents went for a weekend out of town. She had been telling her grandmother all the things she intended to do, once she was finally grown. Her grandmother encouraged her imagination; she saved all the stories and poems Helen wrote. She died before Helen's first book was published, and Helen dedicated it to her memory. But on that summer night, the sky dramatic with the smoky pastels of sunset, she told her grandmother she would live in Paris. Fly an airplane, lead a safari. Act in a movie. Sleep in a bed like an eagle's nest, amid the branches of a great tree. Rescue orphans and zoo animals.

Her grandmother had rocked and listened. Then she'd said, "I was thinking you could help Grandpa milk the cows tomorrow, and then we could pick blueberries and make a pie." Helen stood and stretched. All the fantasies she'd been considering seemed to fall from her lap, and at first she felt sorry about that. But then she was relieved that she could stay with the familiar, internal boundaries she had never really chafed against. Even then, she was a girl who would take the chair closest to the door, and then sit there every time.

sixteen

THE ROOM THAT HAS GREAT MEANING TO ME IS MY KITCHEN, DONETTA
Johnson reads. *It has great meaning because it brings me memories. Like of my mother and my grandmother and my husband
James who liked to make coleslaw. Just about every night he
would eat coleslaw if you let him and everyone said it was so
good but his recipe died with him. The only thing is I know it did
have barbecue sauce in it. This room also has great meaning to me
because it's where my children used to like to sit after school and
have some snacks and do their homework. And now they are
grown and flown away. But when I am in the kitchen, seems like
they are too. I can be washing dishes and it is almost like I can feel
them behind me. Hear them, even. Sometimes when I eat dinner,
I set an extra place for one of them. And so you see all these people I love are still with me when I am in my kitchen and that is
why it has great meaning to me.*

Donetta turns her paper over. "I don't know if that's what you meant, 'bout writing 'bout a room," she says. "I don't know if I did it quite right."

"You did it very well," Helen says. "I really liked it when you talked about all those other people being with you even when you were alone." She looks around the room. "What about the rest of you? What did you like?"

Jeff Daley says, "I liked the clear style, that you just told it like it is, but you really made us see more than was on the page. And feel it, too."

The other students, emboldened as usual by hearing the first comments, begin to offer their opinions. Ella Parsons says she wants to taste that coleslaw; Henry Borman wonders if it wouldn't be a good idea to describe the room: the table and chairs, what's on the walls; Hector Rivera says she might say what her husband did for a living.

Helen listens, but not well enough: she's distracted by thoughts of the trip she and Tessa took to San Francisco. She can't stop thinking about the house. Last night, she dreamed she was there, standing out in the front yard, the sunlight bright around her. She was waving at two people in a red car who were pulling into the driveway. She was shouting "Welcome home!" but one of the people in the car was her.

"You should make this a short story," Billy Armstrong tells Donetta. He is sitting with his chair tipped back on two legs, his arms crossed in a way that can only be read as defiant. His delivery is as scary as his countenance; what he says sounds less like suggestion than like diktat. But just as Helen is about to defend Donetta against his brashness, Donetta smiles and says, "Oh, I like that idea! I'm going to do that! Can I do that?"

"Of course," Helen says, and begrudgingly smiles at Billy. "Okay, only two of you left. Who wants to go next?" When no one answers, Helen says, "How about you, Hector?"

Hector's face brightens and he straightens in his chair. She finds it dear that her students won't volunteer to read, but then are so pleased when they're asked to. There are ways in which people never grow up, and Helen feels grateful for that.

Hector reads loudly, overmodulating a bit, like a Latino Ted Baxter reading the news. His piece is uninspiring, a rather monotonous page about how his study is his favorite room, and it mostly focuses on a shelf holding his awards.

"Aw, man, what's the *dark* side of you?" Billy asks, and Helen rushes to say, "What did you like about the piece, Billy?"

"Nothing."

"Well, have you any specific *suggestions*?"

"All's it is, is a love poem to himself. I don't *see* the place. We're supposed to *see* the place."

"So what you would like, perhaps, is a description of the furniture, the desk, maybe the pictures on the desk?"

Billy shrugs. "*Something.* Christ."

"I liked the way your piece told us a lot about you," Jeff says. "I feel like you're a confident and happy man."

"I am!" Hector says, and laughs.

"I guess I would like to know more about how you got that way," Jeff says.

Hector's forehead wrinkles. "From telling about my favorite room?"

A silence falls, and Helen asks, "Well, what do we think? How might he do that?"

"He could wheel in his chair!" Ella says.

"Wheel in his chair," Helen says. She has no idea what Ella means.

"Yes, wheel around and around like Mr. McManus, he wheels around and around because he is always happy and excited and he tells everyone hi all the time even if he just saw them. But he drools."

"Okay," Helen says. "Anyone else have any ideas?"

Claudia Evans says, "You might say something about how you felt when you got the award; it might have suggested some memory from your past."

"It did!" Hector says, and starts taking notes. "I used to pretend a pop bottle was an Academy Award. I sprayed it gold, and I kept it in my room under my bed and every night I would take it out and sleep with it."

"Make it a short story," Billy says, and pushes his chair back from the table. "I gotta go early today."

Helen looks at her watch; only ten minutes left. "Before you go, Billy, let me give the assignment for next week. I'd like you to write a page about a big surprise you once got that made you happy, but something else, too: sad, shocked, maybe even angry." They all stare at her blankly. "What I mean is, tell me about a time that you got a surprise that was . . . complicated." Again, they only stare. Why doesn't she just say, "What if you got news that your dead husband had built you a house in California?" Or "I can't afford to go to a therapist, so why don't you all help me out?"

"Another option," she says, "is for you to tell me about your first kiss." Now their faces light up, and Helen has a pretty good idea what they'll write about.

Oh, it's terrible the way she's asking the group to help her rather than the other way around. She recalls, guiltily, a time when Tessa was three and was badly misbehaving. Helen lost patience and yelled at her, then grabbed her by the arm and spanked her, saying, *You! Don't!* Do! *That!* Tessa wailed at the top of her lungs, her pride hurt as much as her bottom. Helen stood there wide-eyed, her heart pounding, wanting to weep herself, wanting to fall to her knees and beg her daughter's forgiveness. Instead, she fled to her bedroom, closed the door, and sat at the edge of her bed, terrified at the way such strong emotion had suddenly overcome her. Where had it *come* from? It was too hard having children, she remembers thinking. It was too hard and too important and she would never do it right. Tessa deserved more than Helen could ever be.

And then she did start crying; she sat rocking at the edge of the bed, using the time-honored rhythm in a vain effort to comfort herself. She heard a little knock at the door. When she told Tessa to come in, her daughter walked over to her, put one hand on her knee, looked up into her face, and said, "Why are you crying?" Helen said she was crying because she felt bad about hitting Tessa. "I'm a bad mommy," she said. Her daughter gravely assessed her, then said, "No, you're not. You're a *good* mommy." And Helen, full to the bursting point, embraced her, and silently vowed never to behave in such a way again. Though surely she had, at one time or another. Had and, oh, does.

"My turn!" Ella says, after Billy has taken his leave. She smoothes wrinkles out of the page before her, a lined page from a yellow legal tablet, covered with loopy script, and in a loud voice begins to read:

My meaning is in the shower room at the home where sometimes I help wash the ladies in D ward. They can't do it because they are too far gone so we have to do it. They have purple spots and brown spots and their bosoms are all long and saggy like those balloons they make dogs out of. Their stomachs have big folds. They have it is like little piles of blue spaghetti on their legs. That is their veins. Sometimes they laugh in the shower but this one, Mrs. Lundgren, every time she has a shower she yells and tries to scratch and pinch you. She doesn't understand and so we have to tell her it is a shower it is a shower we are cleaning you up. But she yells and even sometimes she screams which you think you're going to get in trouble even though you are not doing anything wrong. Their hair gets flat like a drowned rat and then you have to comb it for them which they also can't do that and if you put a ribbon in oh boy they love it. We don't have enough ribbons for all of them but some of them do. It is only yarn anyway. Why the shower room is meaning to me is because it is always interest-

ing to see someone naked and I like it more than the activities room which I have been there too long. And also I like the shower room because I like when they do things I do too. The supervisor always tells us, they are not so different from you and me, you know. If you learn that, you can learn compaction, and that will make you a better health care worker. Which I am.

Ella looks up expectantly and Helen wonders how to temper what she wants to say, which is that she actually loves this piece, for its bright energy.

Henry Borman is the first to comment: "Now there's some honest writing!"

"You know, talk about *see*," Donetta says. "I can see those ladies as clear as can be. And when they be pinching you—whooee! You are one patient person!"

"Yeah!" Ella says.

Helen looks at her watch. "I'm awfully sorry, but we're out of time. Perhaps we can talk more about this next time."

"Wait!" Ella says. "I have to tell you one single thing: I learned to speak French!" She rattles off a bunch of gibberish that might be some language somewhere, but is most certainly not French. The room is silent, and then Donetta says, "You said that very well! You know, I always wanted to learn French." She and Ella walk out together, chatting like longtime girlfriends, and Helen sits still at the table, thinking. A friend of hers—Anne Jensen, as it happens—once described such acts of kindness as hold knots on life's climbing rope, and Helen thinks it's true.

Not long ago, she was waiting in line at the post office, irritated at how long it was taking. Finally, there was just one old man ahead of her, a gentleman with a walker. He made his laborious way to the clerk and held up a window envelope, a bill being paid. He said, "I've got a little problem here. As you can see, the paper inside the envelope has moved up and now you can't read the address where it's going." The clerk took the envelope from the man and examined it carefully, front and back. Then he said, "Hmm. You know what might help?"

The old man stood watching intently.

The clerk tapped the envelope sharply on the desk and the paper fell into place.

"Oh," the old man said. "I see. Well, thank you."

"Good to see you, Charlie," the clerk said. And then, after he'd given the old man plenty of time to get out of the way of the next customer, he called, "Next?" Helen came forward, mailed her package, and then headed home. A simple thing. But the world she stepped out into was so different from what it had been before.

seventeen

"Wow," Midge says. "That house sounds literally incredible. I know it was important for you to go alone, but now I'm kind of sorry I didn't go with you."

"Tessa took pictures. I'll ask her to email them to you."

"You have a lot to think about, huh?" Midge asks. There is the sound of the phone dropping and then she hears Midge saying, "Ow! *Ow!* Damnit!" She comes back to the phone, saying, "I dropped the iron. On my *foot*. I'll call you back."

Helen gets back to surveying her pantry. She thinks she has enough ingredients to make a cake from scratch. Tessa's coming over for dinner, and, unbeknownst to her, Helen has invited Jeff Daley to come, too. Jeff doesn't know Tessa is coming, either. No need to push things. She looks at her watch. Three more hours. Maybe she'll get her hair done. She calls to make an appointment with her stylist, who is Tessa's age. And married. With a child.

Helen has heard plenty of stories from people who fell in love at first sight. This would not be the case for her daughter and Jeff Daley. They sit stiff-backed, forcing inane chatter over a mostly uneaten dessert (triple chocolate cake!), while Tessa's eyeballs seem to grow ever closer to leaping out of her head. It is all Helen can do not to push herself away from the table and say, "Fine! It didn't work! Let's all just *stop,* now!" But of course one does not do such a thing under circumstances such as these. One finishes one's meal and, after what can be seen as a polite interval, takes one's leave. That, at least, is what Jeff does. He compliments Helen on the dinner, and tells Tessa it was nice to meet her. Tessa grunts. Then he wraps his scarf around his neck, puts on his jacket, and goes out into the night. Helen stands at the door, watching him walk away, thinking, *But look at all they have in common! He doesn't zip his coat either!*

Tessa's response to what Helen thought was a clever plan is to stomp into the living room, fling herself onto the sofa, cross her arms tightly over her chest, and say, "Mom. Mom. Mom. What were you *thinking?*"

Helen comes to sit beside her daughter. When Tessa gets like this, she looks like she did as a toddler. Helen starts to share this; then, in an uncharacteristic fit of discretion, does not. She speaks carefully, slowly. "I was thinking I would invite a lonely person to dinner, who happens to be your age. I thought I'd invite you, too. End of story."

"Bullshit."

"Pardon me?"

"Bullshit, Mom!"

"Well, Tessa, since you seem to be so acutely aware of what's really in my head, why don't you share my real motivation with me?"

Tessa sighs. "You are trying to find me a boyfriend here so I won't go to California."

Damnit. Helen makes her face go neutral. "No." She says the

word in a long, drawn out way that makes it sound almost like a question: *Noooooooo?*

"I'm going home," Tessa says, and heads to the closet for her coat.

"Where are you going?" Helen asks anyway, and her daughter only looks over her shoulder at her, sparing her the eye roll she deserves.

"Do you want to watch a movie?" Helen had walked over to the library to check out *Midnight Cowboy,* one of the classic movies that Tessa has not yet seen, but wants to. Helen figured after dinner, they'd talk about how wonderful Jeff was (though Helen was going to be very careful not to be too enthusiastic) and then watch the movie.

"Yeah, I really feel like watching a movie now."

Well, two for two. Helen gets up off the sofa and goes over to the coat closet. "What," she says. "What did I do that was so awful?"

"You set me up for such humiliation!"

"What's *humiliating* about meeting a nice person? Suppose one of your friends had introduced him to you!"

"Then it would have been one of my *friends* who introduced him to me."

"Meaning what?"

"We need to not talk about this anymore," Tessa says. "I'm not going to talk about this. You won't listen, anyway." She goes out the door, closing it quietly behind her. Helen is left with the dirty dishes, the foiled plans, the unwatched movie, the knowledge that she really must stop this. She knows it. She really must stop.

She sits at the kitchen table, feeling a thin stream of cold air coming in from under the back door. It's freezing outside. She goes out onto the front porch and calls to Tessa, who is halfway down the block.

Tessa turns around. *What,* her body is saying, though she says nothing.

"Do you want a ride to the el?"

"No, thanks," Tessa says. "I want to walk."

"Leftovers?" Helen asks, though thank God this is too quiet for Tessa to hear. She waves; Tessa waves back, and there, that will have to do.

Helen goes again to sit at the kitchen table. She wishes she smoked; she'd like to shove a cigarette in the middle of the un-eaten cake on her plate.

It comes to her that a good long-term relationship can have its downside. If the great ideal of being accepted completely for oneself is achieved, where is the room for growth? Rather than protecting her so much, Dan should have complained about her most glaring faults. Then she might have had the opportunity to change, while working with a safety net. Now he is gone, her in-adequacies are revealed—not only revealed but amplified—and she will need to do her psychic homework by herself. She starts to get angry at Dan, to blame him for her overdependence, her foggy way of moving through the world, and then realizes the inanity of it. At least she's not as bad as the woman she once met who con-fessed she had no idea where the thermostat was until after her husband died. Such women still exist. Literature and popular cul-ture want to make women cowgirls whirling lassos over their heads, but such women still exist.

She tidies the kitchen, then goes up to her study and turns on the light. She regards her desk, the books on the shelves, the clock with the second hand going round and round. She stands staring at her computer, her arms crossed. Then she switches the light off and heads up to her bedroom. She keeps volumes of poetry beside her bed. She'll go there. Flannel pajamas, lamplight, the spare and exquisite execution of language. Maybe later, another piece of cake.

eighteen

"DID YOU READ THE REVIEW OF JILL COSSEN'S BOOK IN *THE NEW York Times*?" Saundra Weller asks. They are in Panera, across from the library, waiting for Nancy Weldon. Helen has agreed to meet the two women for a snack.

"I did," Helen says. "I thought it was wrongheaded and unfair. Practically sadistic."

"I thought many of her points were well taken, actually. But can you *imagine* reading that about your *own* book?"

"I can, in fact." Helen has long preached that one must separate the creative part of writing from the business of it; over and over, she has said that the writing part is all about heart and risk and honoring your truest intentions, and the business part is all about, well, business. But it's hard to stay true to yourself when you can be so demoralized by a few lines in print from a critic more interested in school-yard bullying than in thoughtful analysis. She wonders, sometimes, what those critics feel after they've written such indictments. She wonders if they lean back in their chairs and—

"*Hello?*" Saundra says.

Helen starts. "Sorry. What did you say?"

"I was asking if there was *anyone* in your class who has shown the tiniest bit of promise." She looks about to see if Nancy is coming yet, then leans closer to Helen to say, "Because I have to tell you, most of mine are utterly hopeless, as predicted. But I have one who's actually quite brilliant. A woman named Margot Langley. And she reminds me of . . . Well, dare I *say*. But it's true; she reminds me of a young Alice Munro or Penelope Lively. That kind of observational power, that kind of depth."

"What's her name again?"

"Margot Langley."

Helen sits back in her chair. "That sounds familiar. Has she been published already?"

"Oh, no. No. But believe me, I'm going to make sure all that changes."

"Margot Langley . . ." Helen says, and then suddenly remembers. The letter she got deriding her books. It could be a coincidence. But no, because Saundra says, "She knows you, actually. She said she'd read a few of your books. Or . . . Well, she read one, and looked at a few others. She read *Telling Songs*." Saundra takes a drink of her cocoa, stares over the top of her cup at Helen. Waits, spider to the fly.

"Huh," Helen says, nodding, willing her face to stay absent of any expression. Then, seeing Nancy headed for them, she offers the woman a bright smile. After Nancy sits down, Helen says, "Saundra was just asking if anyone in my class showed promise. I think they all do."

Then, turning to Saundra, she says again, "I think they all do."

· · ·

"May I stand to read?" Henry asks.

"Of course," Helen says.

"I think it lends a little something to your piece if you stand up and read it. We always used to stand to read when I was in school. Elocution, you know."

"That hurts," Ella says.

"Elocution?" Henry says, standing, adjusting his shoulders.

"Yes! And you have to wear a diaper and get strapped down and you can't even move."

"Do you mean electrocution?" Helen asks.

"That's what he said!"

"No, he said *elocution.*" She is about to launch into an explanation when Billy the murderer says, "They sound the same, fuck it, just read."

Probably a better idea, Helen thinks, and nods at Henry to go ahead.

"Okay, so I just call this 'First Kiss.' " He pulls down his cardigan, adjusts his squealing hearing aid, and begins reading about being a soldier, fresh off the farm, eighteen years old and yet to be kissed. The girl in the backseat of the Studebaker. Her perfume, his cologne, those colliding scents. Helen sits back and listens, and begins to see those young people on that dark night, parked in an empty lot behind a liquor store. She sees the girl's pin curl waves, the shine of his army insignia in the dark.

It's getting easier in the group. They know each other; they trust each other; each week, they try harder, and each week, they get better. Next time they meet, they'll need to talk about the graduation reading; for now, she turns her attention to Henry's revulsion as the girl crams her tongue into his mouth, his observation that her tongue conjured up images of fat rolls of bologna hanging over the butcher's counter, his admission that he feared Hitler less than the moment he would have to pull away and face this girl and *say* something. Henry's piece elicits a round of applause, and the tops of his ears pinken with pleasure.

The rest of the students read their work joyfully absent of the fear and hesitancy that were so often present at the beginning. Donetta was in fourth grade, on the school playground, when she was suddenly smooched by a sixth grader, and then lived in fear that she was pregnant until she was set straight by her older sister. Hector, twelve years old and seeking shelter in a drugstore doorway from a rainstorm, leaned over and kissed the woman he would later marry. Billy kissed his pretty cousin in the basement of their grandparents' house and she promptly gave him a bloody nose; Jeff was first kissed—on the mouth, lingeringly—by one of his mother's friends, when his mother had gone out of the room for something. He was twelve; the woman was in her thirties. Afterward, she had put her finger to her lips and winked—*Don't tell*—and he had not, until now. Helen had ached for him, hearing this story, for all it suggested about how his life had been since. It occurred to her for the first time that an overly good-looking man must suffer many of the odd hardships of an overly attractive woman. She listened to him read in his quiet, gentle voice, noticed for the first time a cowlick at the back of his head, and liked him even better.

For Claudia, it was a popular jock in high school who kissed her on a bet, and at first, when he cornered her at her locker, she thought she was being robbed. Ella, at ten, had kissed a seven-year-old girl whom her mother had recruited to play with her. The little girl began to cry and asked to go home, and Ella got the strap. *My daddy counted when he hit me and whoa! I counted, too.*

"When was your first kiss?" Ella asks Helen, after she has finished reading.

"Oh, no," Helen says. "I'm the *teacher*." She remembers it, though, a hot summer night when she was nine, a group of neighborhood kids playing hide-and-seek, a boy who hid with her in the bushes suddenly turning her head and kissing her and her sitting frozen, wanting to run away from him, but not wanting to be tagged out of the game.

She gives her class their next assignment: Eavesdrop on a conversation; then use it to inspire a conversation between two characters you make up. Through dialogue only, give the reader an idea of how each person looks. She watches them eagerly scribble their assignment down, and becomes aware of some kind of spreading warmth inside her. At first she is alarmed, wondering what that is. But then she recognizes it. Happiness.

nineteen

HELEN SPENDS ALL MORNING ON THE PHONE. SHE STRAIGHTENS out a problem on her Visa bill; she makes a doctor's appointment for her annual physical; she buys tickets for Midge and her for an upcoming play at the 16th Street Theater; she has a brief conversation with her father, carefully avoiding asking him how he feels, since lately, the question seems to annoy him. Just as she's ready to take a shower, Midge calls and they have a conversation full of things that make them laugh, and then the sound of them laughing makes them laugh, and then they get into quotes from *Blazing Saddles,* and Helen looks at her watch and realizes they've been talking for forty-five minutes. No wonder her ear hurts. She remembers how anxious she used to be to get off the phone in the mornings, if in fact she ever answered a call at that time. She remembers the frustration of trying to explain to people that when she was writing she was *working.* Even if you made your living writing, it seemed hard for people to think of writing as really working. A colleague once told Helen he had begun saying,

"Think of me as a surgeon, performing operations at home. There are times when I just can't be interrupted." Now, though, she is gifted by the pleasure of a leisurely conversation with a friend, by sitting at the kitchen table in morning sun, laughing.

Just after Helen hangs up from Midge, the phone rings again, and she picks it up, saying, *"Raisinets!"*

Silence.

"Uh-oh," Helen says. "Midge?"

"Nope. Tom Ellis."

"Oh, sorry. Sorry. I was just talking to my girlfriend and we were revisiting scenes in an old movie."

"Blazing Saddles?"

"Yes!"

"I'm just calling to see how you're doing. What you've been thinking about the house."

"Well, as I told you, I want to give it a few weeks." It stuns her to realize how little she's thought about the place, lately. "We're okay for a bit longer, right?"

"Sure. I'm keeping an eye on it, as I promised. I also just . . . Okay, the truth is, I wanted to see if *you* were okay. It can't have been easy for you to—"

"I'm fine." She doesn't want to think about that house or Tom or even Dan. Her heart is light in a way it hasn't been for a long time: she feels like she's been walking with an egg balanced on a tablespoon and she wants nothing to break her concentration. She wants to go and meet Tessa for lunch at a restaurant and she has to get the directions from MapQuest. Not that that always helps. Her sense of direction is roughly equal to her skill with numbers. If she's out for a walk in her neighborhood and a car pulls over with someone seeking directions, Helen says she doesn't live there. "Just visiting," she always says gaily. And oftentimes if she drives somewhere she's been many times with someone else in the car, she will suddenly forget how to get there. "What are you *frowning* about?" Midge asked, last time this happened. She was taking Midge to a boutique she particularly liked and had visited often.

"I'm not frowning," Helen said.

"Are you lost?" Midge asked, and Helen said no. But she was.

She tells Tom, "You know, I was just on my way to meet Tessa for lunch and I've got to run," she says. "May I call you later?"

"Sure. You can call me anytime."

"I . . . Well. Thank you. I appreciate that."

"You're welcome."

"Okay."

"Okay."

She laughs. "Good-*bye*!"

He laughs, too, then says, "So long."

Still she stays on the line.

"Hang up!" he says.

She does. And then she smiles the whole way upstairs, thinking, *Who* does *that anymore, lets the woman hang up first? Who does that kind of thing?*

She finds the little French restaurant Tessa wants to go to, and prints out directions. Then prints them out again, in larger print.

Helen gets to the restaurant twenty minutes late and apologizes to her daughter. "I got lost," she says.

Tessa says nothing, shakes her head.

"What? I did! You know I'm not good with directions!"

"How could you get lost? This restaurant is three blocks from my apartment!"

"Okay. I'm going to explain this to you again."

Tessa holds up a hand. "No need."

"Well, apparently there is. When I try to get somewhere that's unfamiliar to me—"

"Mom. Mom. I know what you're going to say. You're going to say that it gets all messed up in your mind, north, south, right, left. The grid rotates in your mind. You're going to tell me about how all people are good at some things and bad at others. You're going to say that you can't help it. Forget I said anything. I'm sorry. I won't say anything else ever again about your sense of direction. Or lack thereof."

"Fine." Helen picks up the menu.

"Though how you can get lost when you're three blocks from—"

"Okay, you're paying," Helen says.

"I know. I intended to. To celebrate my new job at *SanFrancisco* magazine."

Helen puts her menu down. "What do you mean."

"I don't have the final, final word," Tessa says. "But all signs point toward my being hired."

"Oh! Well, that's . . . It's amazing that you found a job so fast. Good for you. That says a lot about your talent."

"Thank you."

"But can I just . . . Are you sure you want to do this?"

Tessa looks straight into her mother's eyes. "Yes."

"Oh. Okay." She opens her menu, cannot read a word. She stares at the page and asks, "When would you start? If you're hired?"

"I'll start in a month."

"Oh." Is this the only word she can *say*? "Well, congratulations."

"Not yet. One more person has to agree to the hire; but it seems like there'll be no problem at all. He's just out of town right now. But after he comes back and gives the final word, *then* you can congratulate me."

"Yes. I will. And . . . where will you live?"

Tessa opens her mouth, then closes it. "Okay, Mom. Not in the house. I get it. Okay?"

"I've been thinking a lot about it." *Lie.* "I just . . . I don't see how I can keep it, Tessa." *Lie.* "I'm sure if you think about it, you'll understand." *Lie.*

Tessa opens her menu. "I've got to get something quick. I have a lot of work to do."

"Me, too." *Lie.*

Two days later, Helen goes to the mailbox and pulls out the usual assortment of garbage. But here is a letter, familiar handwriting on the envelope. Tessa. Helen opens it on the spot, the door still open, the cold air blowing in. Inside is a blown-up portion of a map, a few streets in downtown Chicago. There is a large *X* at the center, beside which Tessa has written, *I live here.* She has included a note on a yellow, floral-shaped Post-it that Helen bought her, thank you very much. The brief message reads, *Mom, Your mission, if you choose to accept it, is to memorize this map. A quiz will be given at my place after your class next Wednesday night. Dinner will be provided. By me. Regrets only. T.*

Helen studies the map. Hah. Easy. She throws the map away, starts to go to the cookbook shelf to find a recipe for dessert Wednesday, then doesn't. Instead, she sits at the table and reminds herself that State goes *north and south;* Madison goes *east and west.* That or the other way around. Then goes up into her study to decide upon the next exercise for her class. For her other, *grateful* children.

twenty

"What do you think I should do, Midge?" Helen asks. "Be honest."

It is 10:00 A.M. on a Monday morning, and Helen is lying on her bed with the phone, letting her toenails dry. They look awful. She gave herself a pedicure after she paid the bills this morning and decided she must start cutting out extravagances, but now she sees getting a pedicure is a necessity. For one thing, manicurists actually get the polish on the nails.

"I don't know," Midge says now. "If our daughter moved to San Francisco, I might move there so my goddamn arthritis would calm down."

"It's damp in San Francisco, you know, it can be very damp." Helen does not add what she is thinking: *Wouldn't you miss* me?

"If you don't move there, I think you should let your daughter live in the house and pay you rent. I never really understood how you could sell it, despite all the reasons you told me. It sounds like Tessa will have enough money to do that if she gets the job. Why not let her live there? Not that I'd let Amanda do that, if it were me—I wouldn't let her live there; she'd wreck the place in half an hour. But Tessa's not like that, and if she were my daughter, I'd let her live there. And then I'd visit a lot, especially in the winter."

"I'm not letting Tessa live there."

"Didn't you tell me one of the reasons for holding on to the place was to see if Tessa could get a job and afford to live there?"

Helen says nothing.

"Helen. Isn't that what you told her? Isn't that what you said?"

Helen studies the swirls of paint on her ceiling. "Do you ever do your own pedicures?"

"Why don't you take a trip out there again yourself?" Midge says. "Just go and spend some time in that house, by yourself, and then see what you think. Even if you decide to sell it, at least you'll have been able to say good-bye to it."

Helen's throat tightens.

"Helen?"

"Um-hum."

"Are you crying?"

"Nope."

Midge speaks gently. "Seems like you should go out there, though, huh?"

"Uh-huh. Yup."

"So . . ."

"I will."

"When?"

"I'll *go,* I said!"

Helen awakens at four in the morning and cannot go back to sleep. Might as well get up and make some coffee. She goes downstairs and sees what looks like water pooled on her kitchen counter. She moves closer, puts her hand to it, looks up. There is a bulge in the ceiling, and drops are falling from it. *Burst pipe!* she thinks, recalling last winter when temperatures plummeted and homeowners were advised to crack their faucets. But it hasn't been that cold, has it? She stares at the bulge, positions an aluminum bowl under the drip, and listens to the steady *plunk, plunk, plunk.*

She will not call Tessa. One, she's a little mad at her, and two, she needs to learn to handle things herself. Three, this would be beyond Tessa, anyway, and actually, the truth is that's reason number one, two, three, four, et cetera. She will not call Midge, either, because she's a little mad at her as well.

Whom to call, then? An emergency plumber, she supposes, but what plumber? She looks in the yellow pages, finds a long list. She'll pick one with a big ad; if they have a big ad, it must mean they have a lot of money. If they have a lot of money, it must mean a lot of people use them.

There are a few plumbers with big ads, and one of them says, "Honest." What does that mean? Are there rip-off artists who are plumbers? Well, of course; there are rip-off artists everywhere. She remembers her friend Alice telling her about two men who came over to fix her toilet and charged her a fortune for what turned out to be a really minor problem—Alice's husband came home from work, heard about what his wife had done in an effort to handle the problem herself, and told her that all the toilet had needed was a gasket, which he had intended to replace himself that weekend. Alice said, "And the worst part is, I knew it! I could hear them talking to each other in these low tones and all but giggling, and I *knew* they were going to rip me off, but I was too afraid to say anything. And they were just slobs—they had mud all over their boots; when they came in they just threw their smelly jackets on the floor and the dog tried to *roll* in them!" So much for using the yellow pages.

She could ask her neighbors for a recommendation, but it's

the middle of the night and anyway, since Dan died, she asks them for help too often. She gives them baked goods for recompense, but she can tell she has worn her welcome thin, and she understands completely. Last time she brought chocolate chip cookies to the Adamses, the wife said, "Oh, hon, we still have some from you."

No. She will handle this herself. She stares up at the ceiling, imagining it suddenly opening up with a terrible gush of water, of plaster. She sees huge chunks of ceiling hitting her head, water rising up to her ankles and beyond. She wonders if she can get electrocuted from standing in water that rises to the level of the baseboard outlets. She picks up the phone and dials the police.

"Thank you so much," Helen says. "I hope you'll understand if I say I hope I never see you again."

The plumber smiles in a kind of halfhearted way, and it occurs to Helen that he's heard that one before. "Seriously, though," she says, "I appreciate your coming, and if I ever have another plumbing problem, I'll be sure you call you." *Whoever you are.* The policeman who answered her call—after explaining in a not entirely unsympathetic way that the police were not handymen—redirected Helen to the yellow pages. She closed her eyes and put her finger down on an emergency plumber, who arrived two and a half hours after she called him.

As the man is putting on his coat, Helen says, "Would you like a cookie?"

He shrugs. "Sure!"

She offers the bowl to him, and he bites into one. "Good!" he says. "Thanks! Okay, then, so I'll just be—"

"Hold on," Helen says. She dumps the rest of the cookies into a bag, hands them to the man.

"You don't have to do this," he says. "You paid me."

Helen's eyes fill, embarrassing her. Why is she *crying*? Maybe it's because she's tired. Maybe it's because in her own clumsy, distinctly roundabout way, she has handled a plumbing problem, and this, perhaps more than anything, has confirmed Dan's death. Maybe it's because she has felt for so long that she is walking a tightrope and now she has looked down to see that the ground is closer than she thought—all she has to do is step off. "Please take them," she says, offering the cookies to the plumber again, and he does.

After he leaves, Helen goes to look at the hole in the kitchen ceiling. Now she'll need to get that fixed. As well as the other hole he put in the upstairs wall, before he discovered that the problem was not a pipe at all but a gap in the grouting of her shower that was letting water trickle down. "Oh," Helen said, standing by him. "Are you supposed to check that periodically? The grouting?"

"Yup." He pointed to a gap at the bottom of the shower stall. "See that?"

She leaned in and looked. "Uh-huh."

"That's *huge*."

She nodded sagely. "Okay, so then obviously the thing to do is . . . I guess I just call . . ."

"A tile guy?" the plumber said. He didn't seem at all surprised that he had to tell her that. When she had first called him, he'd told her to turn off the water to the house. When she hadn't responded, he'd said, "Do you know where the main water shut-off is?"

"No."

"Okay," the plumber had said. "It should be right by the meter."

"And the meter . . . ?" Helen had said.

"It's . . . round? With a bunch of numbers on it?"

Helen had been exuberant; she knew that one! But where, she had asked him. Where was it? Not in the kitchen, right?

Helen goes to the closet and gets her coat. She'll walk to the bookstore, she will find a book on home maintenance. Damnit. And then she will take herself out to dinner and order macaroni and cheese. And then she will come home and go to bed early. Tomorrow night, she is going to have dinner with Claudia. She called early, while the plumber was there, and Helen accepted her invitation. Claudia said she wants to talk to Helen about something; she wondered if they could do it over dinner, at her place. "I'd be delighted," she told Claudia, then told the plumber. "That was one of my students. I teach writing." He said nothing, and she added, "I'm a writer. I've published quite a few books."

"Yeah, my wife reads, sometimes," the plumber said. "Helps her fall asleep. Me, I'd rather take a pill."

twenty-one

CLAUDIA LIVES IN A MODEST HIGH-RISE DOWNTOWN, NOT FAR from the lake. Helen takes the elevator to the fourteenth floor, thinking of how, if she lived here, she wouldn't be able to fit her weekly haul of groceries into this tiny elevator. Never mind that she now shops for one: she has a hard time passing up any bargain. Or anything that isn't a bargain that looks good. Or anything in a food store period; those people are geniuses at making you *want*. The right arrangement of papayas makes Helen desperate to have some. The yellow color on a box of cereal conjures up an image of her at the breakfast table full of cheer, and she'll buy it as though it were a prescription that will make her exactly that. And when they put out samples? Oh, then Helen is a dead duck.

She exits the elevator and walks down the hallway, looking for Claudia's apartment. There is the smell of something in the air . . . curry? She checks the numbers, realizes she's walking the wrong way, and starts back in the opposite direction. A door opens, and Claudia sticks her head out. "Hi," she says. "I heard the elevator. I thought it might be you."

She's nervous; her voice trembles. She's wearing a blue skirt and a white blouse beneath a yellow ruffled apron. Low heels, nylon stockings. There's something touchingly anachronistic about the scene; it borders on the ironic, but Helen feels sure that Claudia doesn't mean it that way. Helen wishes she herself had dressed up a bit; she's wearing old brown slacks and a pilling beige turtleneck. She holds up the bottle of wine she's brought, a few flowers wrapped around the neck with blue velvet ribbon. When Claudia sees it, she smiles so sweetly Helen wishes she'd brought better wine, more flowers.

The apartment is small, sparsely furnished, but with a great deal of art on the walls. While Claudia goes into the kitchen to stir the pot—they're having chicken and dumplings, she said—Helen moves from image to image. There is a grouping of botanical prints, a watercolor of nasturtiums in a jelly jar, a primitive piece featuring a farm in the middle of rolling green fields. Most imposing is an oil that Helen finds fascinating. It is a panorama of New York City; she recognizes the Chrysler Building, a subway stop, Radio City, and, sadly, the Twin Towers. But nothing is where it should be—the buildings are all mixed up. There is traffic on a freeway in the middle of the painting, but the cars are all stopped and people have gotten out of their vehicles, leaving their doors open, to mingle with each other. They are dressed in jeans and sweatshirts, jeans and T-shirts, a few faded and ill-fitting dresses. Many touch each other: embrace, shake hands; a child and an old woman press foreheads together. Three little black girls play jump rope. A large patchwork quilt lies open on the road, and there is food spread out on it like a picnic: platters of chicken, bowls of salads and beans, bags of opened potato chips, cakes and cookies. All around the quilt, like a living border, are gigantic ants wearing telephone headsets.

The painting also shows many men in black pants and white

shirts, but they are very small, perhaps one eighth the size of the other people; and whereas the full-size people are smiling, laughing, the little men are all grim-faced and isolated, seemingly wandering around without purpose. Each man leaves red footprints behind him—blood? It is an obvious political or social statement, but there is something else about the painting that is angrier than that, darker.

"That big painting is really interesting," Helen says, coming into the kitchen, where Claudia is tossing a salad. "Who did it?"

"A guy I used to know." Claudia speaks quickly, then bows her head to her task, her mouth tight.

Okay, Helen thinks. *We'll leave that one alone.*

It is after dinner that Claudia brings up the reason she invited Helen over. "I have something I'd like to give you," she says. "But before I do, I need to ask you a few things."

"Of course," Helen says, and thinks, *A manuscript.*

"I've written a book," Claudia says, and Helen smiles.

"You don't have to read it," she says quickly. "I'm sorry, I just—"

"I would be glad to read it," Helen says. "I'm smiling because I was hoping that's what you would tell me. I would love to read it."

"I want you to know that much of it is . . . Much of it might be hard to read."

"Is this nonfiction?"

"Yes, it's a memoir. A kind of fractured memoir. And I'm a little worried that if it ever got published . . ."

"Your family?" Helen asks.

"No, they're all gone. Long gone. It's just me. I have no living relatives that I know of. Isn't that funny? I'm the end of the line. But I'm worried about . . .

"Well, I'll just say it. If you publish something like this, if you say some things that . . . If you write a deeply personal book and it gets published . . ." She looks up, frustrated.

"Why don't you let me read it first," Helen says, gently. "And then we'll take it from there."

Claudia covers her face with her hands—they are large hands, the knuckles reddened—and makes sounds that are either laughing or crying, Helen can't tell, and she doesn't know what to do. Should she gently touch Claudia's shoulder? Look away until she collects herself? But then Claudia pulls her hands down and Helen sees that she was laughing. "I guess I'm more nervous about this than I thought! I feel so confused. I'm scared that it might be publishable, and scared that it won't be, that someone will read it and not care.

"Oh, I hope this isn't an imposition, asking you to take a look at it. I just feel you're . . . I trust you. I hope it isn't an imposition. I had to tell you in private, I couldn't bring the thing to class. I can hardly talk about it, as you can see. I'll go and get it."

She returns from her bedroom with a brown paper bag. The manuscript isn't very thick; Helen doubts that it's much over one hundred pages. She regrets the smallness of heart that makes her grateful for that. The truth is, she suspects this could be a very fine work. But she has been fooled before: the first few chapters of a bound galley or a book about which she raved to everyone, but then ultimately was disappointed by.

They talk more over a dessert of apple crisp, but it is idle conversation, anemic and superficial. Helen would like to know more about Claudia, but the woman is clearly unused to sharing intimacies, to letting people in. And why must she? Are people not entitled to keep their own counsel, to live lives of relative isolation, if that is their choice?

And yet. Looking at Claudia, almost anyone would sense a longing on her part, a wish for someone to reach a deep place in her. It is in her eyes. But the someone to reach Claudia is not Helen: she can see that, now that Claudia has turned her manuscript over, she would like her teacher to go.

And so she thanks Claudia for the meal, and says she'll see her in class. Claudia closes the door quietly, seemingly with great care, and Helen imagines her next clearing the table, rinsing the dishes with a kind of single-mindedness almost monastic in nature. She sees again the sparseness of the apartment, the single chair by the curtainless window, turned to look out on a world far below.

As Helen waits for the elevator, she reads the first page. It is the same thing Claudia read in class the first day. A good start, Helen thinks. She flips to another page, and reads, *I drew mustaches on the male clothespin dolls, thin black lines of authority, of destiny.* She flips again and reads, *He is a senior, and he occasionally backs me up to my locker to tell me about his weekend conquests, the girls he nailed in the backseat, their garters and underpants. I don't know why he does this; I don't know why I don't walk away.* Near the end, Helen reads, *She wears the blue nightgown, still. A little box in the corner has been added to the room, stationed beneath the dying plants. A humidifier? I ask the nurse. Deodorizer, she whispers. It is not working, though. The room carries the smell of death, which has been described as sweet. It is not sweet.* The elevator comes and Helen closes the manuscript. It feels suddenly like a live thing.

twenty-two

"OKAY, EVERYBODY," HELEN TELLS HER CLASS. "LET'S SEE IF WHAT you've done will let us not only hear your characters, but see them. Who wants to go first?"

No hands.

"Oh, come on. Must I choose one of you?"

Now two hands shoot up, Billy and Donetta. Helen is about to call on Donetta when she smiles shyly and says, "He can go first."

Billy runs his hand over the top of his severe crew cut, pulls his pages from his back pocket, and unfolds them. "A'ight, this is between a grandmother and her grandson Anthony, okay? I heard a guy on the el telling this story about his grandmother. A lot of this is direct quotes. The rest I made up." He clears his throat. "Okay, so two characters, Anthony and Grandmother."

Anthony says, "Oh, man, you got to knock so loud? You gotta stop coming around here all the time! My neighbors are complaining."

Grandmother says, "Let me by, I smack you face. I got lasagna. Heat it up a little, we eat, then I want you to pluck my chin hairs."

Anthony says, "Shit, man."

Grandmother says, "I got salad too."

Anthony says, "You got to start calling, yo. I could be sleeping, you knock on the door like that. I could have somebody over. I could be fucking somebody, I got a girlfriend now says I look like James Dean."

Grandmother says, "You look like Dean Martin, Anthony. I tell you that since you five years old. You look like Dean Martin."

Anthony says, "You look like Dean Martin! You really do, man, that long face. And don't call me Anthony. I'm James now."

Grandmother starts blabbing away real fast in Italian.

Anthony says, "English, English!"

Grandmother says, "Madonna! It's Anthony, Anthony, Anthony! First Anthony, my husband, second, my son, third, my grandson, you don't take from me what don't belong you! You not so big I can't still hit. I can reach you face, and smack, Big Mr. Six Feet Tall."

Anthony says, "Fine, you can call me Anthony. You never listen to nothing."

Grandmother says, "Good boy. Now listen, Anthony, I need you to steal me some night creams. My skin is so dry. Look here, I touch and it fall like snow."

Anthony says, "Use Vaseline, why don't you? I'm tired of stealing shit for you."

Grandmother says, "Maybe you like to change shirts."

Anthony says, "Why?"

Grandmother says, "Maybe I kill you and I no mess up you nice shirt. We bury you in that one."

Anthony says, "What the fuck kind you want?"

Grandmother says, "Estée Lauder. Get the big size, save money."

Anthony says, "I'm stealing it."

Grandmother says, "We eat and then you pluck my hairs. You got Kleenex to put them in?"

Anthony says, "Why you gotta wrap them up? Why you gotta carry chin hairs home in your purse?"

Grandmother says, "Look at me, nice blue suit, nice leather shoes. Always my hair in a bun, my face washed, I got nice bones in my face. Sophia Loren. You think I look like chin hairs? Anyway, I don't leave them here, you give to a gypsy to put a maledizione on me. Or you show your friends, make fun."

Anthony says, "Who the fuck would want to see your chin hairs? If anybody wants to see chin hairs, they look at me. I got me a fine soul patch."

Grandmother says, "After dinner, you shave it off. Disgustoso."

Anthony says, "Over my dead body."

Grandmother says, "Okay. Set the table; we eat, then I kill you and then I shave you."

Billy folds his papers and leans back in his chair. "That's all I got so far. I'm going to make it into a short story and submit it maybe to *The New Yorker*, I might give it to them."

Helen crosses her arms and leans back in her chair. She doesn't have to say a word. The class has eagerly jumped in to critique, and they are so complimentary and excited that Billy smiles. A few teeth missing near the back on one side, but a nice smile, she finally sees it. Nancy told her recently that she had once been in Billy's apartment, and it was neat as a pin. "And you know what was on his kitchen wall?" she said. "A *puppy* calendar!"

When it's Donetta's turn, she says she has always remembered overhearing a conversation between her parents when she was a little girl lying on the sofa, where she'd fallen asleep. When she awakened to the sound of her parents' voices, she kept her eyes shut and listened.

She reads in her soft voice, imitates the pleasure and flirtation in her mother's voice: *I thought* you's *the handsomest man in the room, but I for sure didn't need to* say so; *you already taking care of that. Flexing your muscles to that crowd of women. Shining your smile so hard in their faces, flashing your dimples. I thought, That man needs to be taken down a notch. And I'm the woman to do it. I may have a crooked smile and a no-count booty, but I got personality. I knew if I could only get you to look in my eyes, you'd be a goner. And didn't I get you to look, you know I did.*

Helen looks around the room at her students' faces. They are listening so intently, with such obvious enjoyment. In this little room, at least, a love for the written word is alive and well. An appreciation for the effort and the artistry. Helen finds it funny that she is paid for such pleasure, for such validation; she should pay them.

Claudia has not come today, and Helen wishes she could hear this. She wishes, too, that she and the others could have heard what Claudia might have written. Maybe she'll call her later, and tell her that they all missed her today. And she'll tell her that she's very much enjoying her manuscript, and has in fact slowed down her reading dramatically in order to savor everything there— some of the pages she's read multiple times. It's hard to know, with someone like Claudia, how much to offer. Helen worries that too much attention might scare her away.

Henry reads next. His efforts are less successful, but talk about an A for effort; the man should be onstage.

"*You* made this?" Helen says.

Tessa does not dignify Helen's response with an answer; instead, she simply serves her more of the chicken.

"What's in the sauce?" Helen asks.

Tessa sits at the table. "I'll give you the recipe. A friend gave it to me. It's his mother's signature dish."

His. Helen does not ask who the "he" is. Does not ask.

When they have eaten the pie Tessa serves for dessert (bakery, but still), she clears the table and puts before her mother a map like the one she sent her in the mail, but this time the names of streets are absent. She hands her mother a pencil and says, "You have five minutes."

Helen looks at the map, then up at her daughter.

"Go," Tessa says.

Helen starts to laugh, and Tessa says, "Mom. Remember when I fixed your garbage disposal? Et cetera, et cetera, et cetera? This is a favor I want you to do for me. Fill in the streets. Start with mine."

Helen, smirking, writes in Tessa's street, then the street at either end of her block. Then, though there are only six other streets to name, she is stuck and she begins to feel the kind of stomach-clenching anxiety she used to feel when she was given a math test. Ridiculous. She looks over at Tessa, rinsing off plates and then putting them in her little dishwasher, and it comes to her why Tessa is giving her this quiz: her daughter is moving away. And this "favor" is not for her, but for her mother. "Tessa?" she says. "I need help."

Tessa doesn't even turn around. "You can do it," she says.

"You got the job, huh?"

"Yup." She stays focused on her task, the running water, the dishes.

Helen gets up from the table and puts her arms around her daughter and Tessa begins to cry. "I have to go, Mom."

Helen strokes her daughter's hair and in a voice whose calm does not surprise her after all, she says, "I know you do. I know you do. It's fine. It's good! I'm very proud of you." Tessa gently pushes her mother away and says, "Finish your quiz. Your time is almost up. Before I leave, you're going to know every street in this city."

Helen finishes the quiz, getting only two streets wrong, then talks animatedly with Tessa about what her new job will entail. It's a good job; Tessa will be doing more of the kind of writing she has always wanted to do. Helen talks about how exciting it will be for Tessa to meet new people, to learn a new city. After she leaves Tessa's apartment, she goes to her car, slams the door, puts the key in the igntion, checks the rearview to back up, and sees the sorrow in her eyes. She's pretty sure Tessa saw nothing like that.

When Tessa was fourteen, she came home from ice-skating with a huge gash in her chin. "I think it might need stitches," she said, and pulled away the washcloth the rink had given her. She needed stitches all right. Dan grew pale and fumbled in his pocket for car keys to take them to the ER. Helen sat in the back of the car and talked to Tessa about who was at the rink that night, about whether or not Tessa had mastered the jump she had wanted to. While Tessa lay on the table to get stitched up, Dan sat in a chair all but wringing his hands (actually, he kept cracking his knuckles until the doctor asked him to stop). Helen stood beside Tessa, her fear of blood gone, her fear of anything gone. She kept Tessa occupied by talking to her, once nearly making her laugh, for which *she* was admonished by the doctor, and though she was staring into her daughter's eyes, her hand on Tessa's hairline, she was also watching every single move that doctor made. It wasn't until hours after the event, when she and Dan were in bed, that Helen heaved a sigh of relief so great it prompted Dan to ask, "*What?* What'd I do now?"

She tightens her hands on the wheel, switches lanes, and accelerates so that she has to pay attention to the road before her.

"Why do people have to turn into grown-ups?" she'd once asked her mother. She'd been seven years old, sitting on the kitchen floor playing jacks, and she was miffed that Eleanor wouldn't stop peeling potatoes and play with her. Eleanor had smiled down at her and said, "Sometimes they want to. But mostly, they need to."

twenty-three

Saturday morning, Helen answers the phone thick-voiced, and hears a man say, "Oh. Sorry. Were you sleeping?" Tom Ellis.

She looks at the clock: ten-fifteen. She'd been up until after two, and had almost finished Claudia's manuscript. It was longer than she'd thought—the pages were double-sided, and for some reason the latter half of the manuscript was single-spaced. Twice, before it had gotten late, she had tried calling to tell Claudia how much she was appreciating—and admiring—her work; twice there had been no answer and no voice mail for her to leave a message. It compounded the sadness she felt about Claudia; there was something so defeated about someone not having voice mail, as though the person might have thought, *Ah well. Who would call?* But then she reasoned that Claudia might simply be smarter than most people, eliminating the need to check one more thing. Email had almost replaced telephones, anyway. But she didn't want to send Claudia an email, it couldn't convey the kind of enthusiasm she felt, and besides, she wanted the immediacy of the response from her student, who had been so nervous about handing her work over. She decided to wait to talk to her personally, after class.

"I'm awake," she says. "Hi, Tom."

"Hi, Helen." A beat, and Helen feels it as a moment of telephone flirtation, the silence more provocative than anything he might have said, and then, "Listen, I have an interesting proposition for you. A couple out on a walk passed your house and . . . Well, they shouldn't have, but they looked in the windows. They looked in the windows and went in the backyard, and were out looking at the tree house when your neighbor spotted them. She came over to see what was going on. She told them you hadn't moved in and she didn't know if you were going to. If there's any way these people can live there, they want to."

"You mean . . . they want to buy it?"

"Yes."

"But . . . at what price?"

"Almost any within reason."

"How do you know?"

"Well, they just called me—your neighbor gave them my number; I met her when I first started work on the place and I gave her my card. But these people are just over the moon about the house."

Over the moon, Helen thinks. *Who says that anymore, besides me?*

Call waiting. Helen asks Tom to hold on and switches over. It's her mother. "I'll call you right back," she says. "I'm in the middle of a major real estate negotiation. I might change my name to Trump."

"Helen, I need to talk to you now."

"Okay, just let me . . . I'm on the other line. Hold on, I'll be right back."

She switches to Tom. "I'm sorry; I have to go; it's my mother. But for the meantime, the answer's no."

And yet she had been going to tell him to show the people the house, to solicit an offer. Why has she suddenly changed her mind? "I'll call you tonight," she tells Tom, and switches back to her mother.

"Okay, I'm here."

Silence.

"Mom?" Some knowing cold moves into her stomach. "What. Is it Dad?"

Eleanor begins to cry. "You know, he was fine last night. And this morning I got up and made coffee, and read the paper a little. And he didn't get up so I went in to check on him, and . . . It was in his sleep. It was in his sleep, honey. He didn't feel anything. The doctor said."

"But . . . what *was* it?" Helen needs a face for this enemy. She needs to insulate herself with facts so she doesn't have to confront the feelings.

"A stroke. Isn't that funny, when we were all so scared of cancer."

Helen swallows, and turns to look out the window. It has begun to snow; she may not be able to get a flight.

"I might have to drive up, Mom, it's snowing pretty hard here."

"Here, too. Don't come right now. There's nothing to do."

"But—"

"I'm fine, Helen. Really. I can call someone if I need to. But I think I just want to be by myself for a while. The weather is supposed to clear here tomorrow; come then. We'll have the funeral on Monday."

Helen might have expected that her mother would want time alone. She was always deeply private about things that hurt her. She mended alone and in her own way, usually not even seeking consolation from a husband who would always have been more than happy to provide it. Her father once told her about a time he came upon his wife leaving the bathroom, her face splotchy from crying. When he asked her what was wrong, she said, "What do you mean? Nothing." When he said he could tell she'd been crying, she said, "Well, I'm not crying now. What do you want for lunch?" Helen isn't sure where her mother got that kind of fortitude. The gene had certainly missed her.

Helen takes in a great gulp of air, and begins to rock back and forth.

"Helen?"

She makes her voice light. "Yes?"

"Sweetheart, I'm so sorry we can't be together right now. But listen to me, listen to me; it's all right. I mean it. We had quite a life together. It's all right."

"I know," Helen says, though she feels at this moment that she doesn't know one single thing.

She sits holding the phone tightly until they have finished talking. When she hangs up, she starts to call Tessa, then does not. Instead, she stops rocking and simply sits there, her hands on her knees. She remembers her father saying earnestly to her when he was first diagnosed with cancer, "I'm not afraid." He said, "Hell, I never expected to live this long. Don't think I don't know how lucky I am." She remembers him teaching her to whistle, bending over her palm to remove a splinter, standing on the porch, his hands in his pockets, watching her drive off with David Peters on her first date. She remembers him eating the first thing she ever made out of the *Junior Cook Book* he bought her—French toast—and saying, "Holy smokes. This might be the best thing I ever ate." She remembers his pants hanging low on his waist, and the way he leaned onto the kitchen counter this last Christmas Eve, unaware that she was watching him from the living room. His arms were trembling a bit, but he steadied himself; he pushed off and rejoined the party, smiling.

Helen gets off the bed and kneels beside it. She holds back a sob long enough to say, "Thank you for my father." And then she lays her head down and lets go.

Out loud, she condemns her circumstances. She knows that there are far worse things happening in the world—if not on her block—than have lately happened to her, but at this particular moment, that makes no difference at all. Not at all. She pounds on her mattress, grinds her teeth, and for one satisfying and painful moment, pulls on her hair so hard it hurts her neck, too.

At eleven o'clock, she calls Tessa. When her daughter answers the phone, she says "Hi, Mom," in a clear, unweighted, friendly way.

"We have to fly to Minnesota," Helen says. "Tomorrow. Bring a nice dress. Okay?" So much for the speech she had planned: Grandpa was old, he had a good life, he was prepared; for everything there is a season; now we must turn our thoughts to Grandma. She cannot do it. She cannot say the words. She can barely speak.

There is a long silence, and then Tessa, understanding, says, very calmly, very gently, "Okay. Want me to come over?" What is Helen's love for her daughter right then? She wouldn't even try to say.

"That's okay," she says. "I'll pick you up tomorrow around noon."

Later that night, Helen calls Tom and tells him what has happened. They have a kind of abbreviated memorial service for her father: Helen shares a few choice anecdotes about him, and Tom makes the usual sounds-like-a-swell-guy comments. Then Helen sighs, and says, "Oh, Dan." She realizes her mistake immediately. "*Tom,* I mean. Sorry."

"Don't be. It's fine."

"I guess I . . ."

"I'm flattered."

"So, I'm coming out there next weekend," she says, and another part of herself says, *Oh?* "I know I have to decide what to do with the house."

"You have some time," Tom says.

"I want to see it again," she says. "I can do it now."

"Send me the itinerary," Tom says. "I'll pick you up."

"Again?"

"Of course," he says, in a way that makes her laugh.

"It's a date," she says, and it occurs to her that in a way, it is.

She hangs up the phone and then sits still at the kitchen table for a long while, looking at everything around her as though it belongs to someone else. Then she goes into the living room to turn out the lights. First this one, then that, and then they are all out and the room is lit only with the milky light of the moon. Enough to see by. But barely.

twenty-four

HELEN AND TESSA DO NOT SPEAK MUCH ABOUT FRANKLIN ON THE plane; there seems to be a tacit agreement that to do so will make for emotions that do not fit into seats 11A and 11B. Instead, Tessa leafs through a magazine, offering commentary on this dress, that lipstick. Helen points to a blond man astride a motorcycle in an ad for jeans, and says, "Do you think he's handsome?"

"Don't start," Tessa says. "Or I'll sign *you* up for Internet dating."

"I only asked if you thought he was good-looking."

"You want to know what I think?" Tessa says. "I think he's gay. I think every man in here is gay." She closes the magazine and excuses herself to go to the bathroom. Helen picks up the magazine and flips through it. Tessa is probably right. But not all men are gay. Where do men who are not gay *go*? How does one meet them? Oh, how does one meet anyone these days? It seems to Helen that people have given their real lives over to virtual ones, that they spend most of their time asleep or interacting with screens. What exactly does Tessa do about the need for . . . touch? "Oh, God," Midge said when Helen once talked about this. "You didn't ask her about *sex,* did you?" And Helen said no, as though she were outraged at the notion of having done so, even though the truth was, she had thought it.

"I think you need to take up needlepoint," Midge said.

Tessa comes back to the seat and puts the magazine in the seat pocket. "Remind me to check around my seat for my personal belongings before I exit the aircraft," she says, and Helen smiles. Then Tessa sighs and asks, "Did Grandma and Grandpa really meet in the back of a dime store?" and Helen tells the story they both know so well: how Franklin bumped into Eleanor and made her purse fall down, how they knocked heads when they both bent to pick it up and then went out for ice cream sodas, then to a movie, then for dinner, for a walk that lasted until dawn, and then separated to go get ready for work, but met for dinner again that night.

When the plane lands, they both fall silent, and Helen imagines that they are both thinking about the same thing: going into a house where Franklin no longer is or will ever be again. She remembers Tessa saying about Franklin, when she was six years old, "He's my favorite grandfather." Never mind that he was her only grandfather; Dan's father had died before Tessa was born. Helen knew what she meant: he was her favorite grandfather of all possible grandfathers. As he was Helen's favorite father.

With Tessa sound asleep beside her, Helen looks at the clock: a little after two. She herself has not yet been able to sleep at all, and now, downstairs, she hears her mother running water in the kitchen. She'll be making herself a cup of tea, no doubt.

Helen quietly gets out of bed and makes her way down. From the darkened dining room, she sees Eleanor standing before the sink, staring out the window, the teakettle in her hand, the water running and running.

"Mom?"

Her mother jumps and then turns to her, and for a moment Helen has the terrified thought that her mother does not recognize her, that something has happened to Eleanor, too. But it is only that she was so deeply caught up in her reverie; she laughs, now, and says, "Want a cup of tea?"

"Sure." Helen comes into the kitchen, squinting against the light; not long ago, Franklin had installed a bright overhead to help with his failing vision. "Your mother can't see like she used to," he said, and Eleanor only rolled her eyes.

"Can't sleep?" Eleanor says, when they sit at the table together, and Helen shrugs. "Me neither."

Helen takes her mother's hand.

"I'm all right," Eleanor says. "Truly."

"I just want you to know, Mom, that if you want to, you can come and live with me."

Eleanor smiles.

"Really. I have plenty of room. The guest room—"

"Helen. Please don't be insulted. But the last thing I would want to do is move in with you."

"What do you mean? Why not? I'm not saying you're not competent to live alone. You know I'm not saying that, right?"

"Well, I hope not! But no. Thank you. I don't want to live with you. I love you very much, but you'd drive me crazy."

Helen's mouth falls open.

"Believe me, it just wouldn't work out."

"Why not?"

"Well, to be honest, you're a little too . . ."

"What? I'm a little too what?"

Eleanor looks at her, considering. Then she says, "I like to have things the way I like them."

"You could!"

"And I need my privacy."

Helen says nothing.

"You know," Eleanor says, her tone softening, "we're alike in some ways, but very different in others."

"How?" Helen asks. "How do you think we're different?"

"Some of it is generational," Eleanor says. "Our generation didn't . . . Well, we kept our own counsel far more than you do." Helen thinks, *It's not just generational. Tessa is like you, she keeps her own counsel, too.* In many respects, in fact, Tessa is more like Eleanor than Helen is, and sometimes Helen is jealous of that.

Eleanor goes on. "We didn't need to air all our dirty laundry and run to therapists every five minutes. Life comes with problems, you just have to *accept* that. And you have to try to lead the simple life; to not constantly ask questions about the whys and the wherefores of everything. To do that is to invite trouble."

"Well, I think a life absent of inquiry is not a life I want to live."

"That's your choice," Eleanor says. "But one thing I would say to you, Helen, is that you must respect the choices that others make."

"I do! Don't I? You think I don't?"

"I think you need to let Tessa grow up. You need to let up on her. I've been meaning to say that for a long time. And as long as I'm being honest, I think you need to stand on your own feet a little better than you do. You're capable of more than you know. Ever since you were a little girl, you've had a habit of hanging back and letting others do for you what you should do for yourself."

"Why didn't you say something about it, then? You were my mother!"

"I tried. But you were such a *dramatic* child. So quick to have your feelings hurt."

"Well, I'm sorry I was such a disappointment to you."

"Oh, Helen, stop it. This is what I mean! This is what happens—what has always happened—when someone tries to offer you constructive criticism."

"This is not constructive criticism! This is an assault on my character. I can't believe that you—"

"Helen."

"*What?*"

"Do you want more tea?"

And now she laughs and says yes, for what else is there to do? Her mother is right; she is terrible at taking criticism. At listening.

When Eleanor sits back down, Helen says, "Did Tessa ever complain to you about me?"

"I'm not going to talk about that. I think we've had enough of baring souls, don't you?"

"But just tell me. Did she?"

"Yes. And I defended you."

"Why? You just told me how awful I am."

"Oh, for heaven's sake. I suppose one of *my* faults as a parent is that I am not generous with praise; it's not the way I was raised, to carry on about every little thing a child does. But of course there are so many wonderful things about you, Helen, surely you know that I know that. And I will always defend you against anyone who says anything negative about you."

Helen looks out the window into the darkness and sees her own face reflected back. "I sure am going to miss Dad," she says.

"Yes."

"And I can't help it; I'm worried about you being here alone, Mom."

"Oh, Helen. I hurt, of course I do, as I know I will for a while. I look for him in the morning when I wake up, before I remember. But I am at peace. We knew it was coming. The only good thing about knowing death is imminent is that you have the opportunity to say some things you might not otherwise say. We talked about everything. My goodness. *Everything.*"

She offers no specifics, and Helen realizes she does not want her to. The glory in a good marriage is the things that belong only to the couple.

"Have you decided what to do about the house in California?" Eleanor asks.

Helen shakes her head no.

"Well, it will come to you, what to do." When Helen looks over at her, her face full of doubt, she says, "It will! In time, you'll know exactly what to do. And you know what? Whatever you decide will be the right decision. I have a feeling that Dan's real gift to you in building that house will turn out to be your having a kind of faith in yourself that you've never had before. And once you have that, everything's going to be a whole lot better."

Helen sighs.

"Really and truly," her mother says.

In the chapel the next morning, Helen sits between her mother and her daughter, staring straight ahead at the many bouquets around the casket. She is thinking of all the people who ask that donations be made to this place or that in lieu of flowers, and she is glad her mother made no such request.

There is a great comfort, a pride, even, in seeing so many flowers. Everything that is done now is not for her father, of course, who is unequivocally not here, yet people have their stubborn ways of thinking. *Here you go, Franklin, this is for you, you always loved daisies.* One can't let go of everything all at once. A few days after Dan died, she lay in bed, fully believing that she could feel his presence, that he had come to see her on his way to wherever souls went. She had lain so still, her eyes closed, feeling him so intensely nearby that she was a little afraid of opening her eyes and seeing him, though if he *were* there, she would have wept with gratitude. Who doesn't long for one more time of seeing someone they've loved and lost? And yet what would you say, what would you do, if it were possible?

Her mother has said that she'll take home one smaller bouquet; the rest will be donated to a nursing home after the service—it's all been arranged: the home where the flowers will go, the person who will bring them there, and the time at which they will do so. Everything has been all arranged—the service, the luncheon afterward, the holy cards, the sign-in book. Helen did nothing but come to her mother's house and then come with her to this chapel, for this service. In the same way, Tessa did nothing for her father's service but attend it, weeping quietly from start to finish. It was exactly what Helen wanted, to spare her daughter from having to do things that would break her heart, but that in some respects eased Helen's pain. It gave her something to concentrate on. It was something she actually did well, planning Dan's funeral. It was the last time she felt truly competent, in fact. And now a thought comes to her, a thunking kind of realization: that she is the kind of person who must do things for or on behalf of another. For her, the taste of the ice cream, the red of the sunset, the humor in the movie must be shared to *be*.

The service begins and Helen hears Tessa sigh. She thinks about taking her daughter's hand, decides against it, then takes it anyway. She feels her mother take her other hand. The three of them make a little force against this big one.

twenty-five

AGAIN, CLAUDIA IS NOT PRESENT IN CLASS, AND HELEN HAS STILL not heard from her or been able to reach her. None of the other class members know where she is, either. *Well, no point in short-changing those who are here by dwelling on those who are not,* Helen thinks. She's hurt though, the kind of hurt that harbors a fair amount of anger. She feels Claudia is poised for something so positive to be added to her life, if only she'll step up and take it.

The assignment was to write a piece on loss. Jeff reads first, an affecting piece about his cocker spaniel dying when he was five, and how this was the first time he understood that all things die, himself included. He spent a lot of time sitting with his mother on the sofa that day, she trying to explain the hard ways of nature, he clutching his elbows and staring straight ahead, arguing against the need for anything to die: couldn't it just happen that every-thing here on earth now would just *stay*? Nothing his mother said made any difference until she asked her seemingly inconsolable little boy if he'd like to help her make cupcakes, and then he instantly laid down his sorrows for a chance to lick the mixing bowl.

Billy wrote about a car he had as a sixteen-year-old, a '65 Mustang convertible he'd gotten into prime shape and then lost when his father took off with it. It was clear from his piece that the car was the bigger loss.

Henry wrote a kind of overdue eulogy for a soldier with whom he'd sat as the young man lay dying. It was during World War II, in Germany, and Henry reads, *He kept looking at the sky above him, a beautiful blue that day, and he held my hand and talked to me about how he could go home now, and see all the people he loved. And I didn't know what to say back to him, because I didn't know which home he meant, his farm in Iowa or heaven. I held his hand, I saw the color leave his face and I offered him sips of water, he was so thirsty. Just before he died, he looked at me and said, "It's not so bad, Henry," and that was all. I closed his eyelids and felt a shaking start inside me but outside I stayed calm because I couldn't think about how I had just lost my friend, I couldn't think about his folks and his girl, I had work to do. But all these years later, I guess I just want to say something about the generosity of a man who, while losing his life, offered a kind of solace against the time when I would lose my own.*

There is a long moment of silence when Henry finishes, and then Billy leans back in his chair and says, "That was fucking good, man!"

Ella gasps. "You said a swear again! Now that's *enough*!" Billy looks over at her, laughing, but she looks right back at him and finally he apologizes in a manner more sincere than sardonic. "Try to use other words to express yourself," Ella tells him. Then, turning to Henry, she says, "You made me cry. That's how much I liked what you wrote. When I cry is when I like things the most."

Donetta reads a funny piece about the time she was at a mall and lost her purse—which, as it happened, was on her arm, hidden beneath a shopping bag. This was pointed out to her as she was frantically reporting the theft to the beefy man from security.

The last person to read is Hector, who has finally moved away from writing about himself and his job as a newscaster, and reads a piece about the loss of manners. He describes the way his parents brought him up to say please and thank you, to hold open doors for those behind him, to dress carefully. He describes an airplane trip his family took when he was a little boy, all of them outfitted with new clothes and his mother wearing her hat and white gloves, then contrasts this with the last plane trip he took, where several people were dressed in what looked like pajamas, and where one teenage girl not only was dressed in nightwear but carried a teddy bear. He ends his piece with a memory of his father sitting out on his porch last summer in his straw hat, his striped blue shirt open at the neck, his linen pants still holding a crease. *He offers a cordial "Good evening!" to everyone passing by. I watch the people who smile and speak back to him, and I wonder about all we have lost by our current lack of civility, and what might be gained by a return to it.*

Helen listens to her students read with a growing sense of pride and wonder: these people are launched into something all their own, and she helped create it. When class is over, she walks out with Hector, telling him that he should consider presenting this piece at the reading. "Really?" he says And then, "Wow, it's coming up soon, isn't it? Only two weeks away. Did I tell you my wife is sending out engraved invitations?" He laughs, and then his face grows serious. "I'm sorry there's only one more class. I've really enjoyed this."

"You should take another one," Helen says.

"Are you teaching again?"

"Oh, no. No, this was just . . . I won't be teaching again."

She minds admitting this; the class has offered her much more than she ever would have thought possible.

twenty-six

Saturday morning, Helen sits at the computer using the last of her frequent-flier miles for a trip today to San Francisco. An early evening flight, returning on Monday night. She waits for the confirming email and prints out the itinerary. Then she calls her daughter.

"Hi, Mom." Tessa's voice is clipped, a bit impatient.

"I know you're working," Helen says. "I just wanted to let you know I'm taking a trip today, and I'll be back Monday night. I'll have my cell."

"Where to?"

Helen doesn't want to tell her. But how can she not?

"It's . . . private." She waits for some sort of explosion, but all she hears is "Oh. Okay. Have a good time."

Helen sits for some time staring at the phone after she's hung up. That's *it*? Then the phone rings, and Tessa says, "Wait."

"Fine, San Francisco, but I'm not moving there. I'm just going there. I'm not moving there."

"Why are you going?"

"I have to take care of some things about the house."

"Are you selling it?"

"I need to go and see it again."

Silence. And then Tessa says, "Stop by here if you want, when you get home."

"Okay."

"Mom? I just want to say . . . It's your house and you have to be the one to decide. I understand that. Whatever you decide is all right with me. Really."

Helen pulls the phone away from her ear and looks at it. Then she says, "Listen, it's been great talking to you, but could you put my daughter on?"

"Very funny," Tessa says. "I have to go back to work. I'll see you Monday night."

Helen hangs up the phone and sits with her arms crossed, thinking. Something is going on with Tessa. She is too soft, lately. Too accommodating. Too generous. This is different from the overly solicitous behavior people can show each other after a funeral, a death. And then Helen sits straight up in her chair. Tessa's in love! Oh, she can't wait to hear all about it. Tessa might not tell, but Walter the doorman will. Helen will bring him some toffee chip cookies so he'll tell her everything about who has come in the lobby door to visit Tessa, and maybe even at what time he has gone out of it.

The softness of the air outside is nearly an assault. Helen stands at the curb outside the airport, waiting for Tom Ellis, and takes off her coat. She'd gotten sleepy on the plane, but now she's wide awake. She looks at her watch, still set for Chicago, where it is 10:00 P.M. Here, it is only 8:00—she's younger! A blue Prius pulls up slowly in front of her, and she bends to see if the driver is Tom. It is not; rather it is a man about her age meeting a woman who appears to be his wife: the woman moves to the trunk of the car for the man to put her suitcase in, and they kiss hello with an old and easy affection that brings tears to Helen's eyes.

She hears her name being called and sees Tom a few car lengths away, waving at her. She has a sudden thought that maybe she'll make her apologies and then go right back inside and take the next flight home. When she'd told him she'd be fine coming out here, she thought she would be. In the last couple of days, whenever she imagined seeing him, being alone with him, it was with a kind of schoolgirlish eagerness and excitement. But here he is now in the flesh, a man she hardly knows, walking toward her and smiling, and she feels no sense of eagerness but instead a kind of panic. Her odd impulse is to smack him. But she smiles back; he takes her suitcase from her, and by the time she sits in his car, she has relaxed somewhat. Enough to breathe, anyway.

"Nervous?" he asks.

"No!" She laughs in a tittering, Aunt Pittypat kind of way and then, embarrassed, turns to look out her window.

"Yes, you are. I am, too."

She looks over at him. He's wearing khaki pants and a black sweater, the sleeves pushed up. Loafers, which Helen happens to love, but who wears loafers anymore? "What are you nervous about?" she asks.

"Well, truth be told, now that I've said I'm nervous, I'm a little more relaxed. You?"

She smiles. "Yes."

"Are you hungry?"

"Yes."

"Want to get something to eat?"

"Yes."

"Are you always this agreeable?"

"Yes."

"You're lying, right?"

"Of course."

As they drive toward the Golden Gate Bridge, she looks out the shadowy outline of the hills. It is awfully pretty here. Credit where credit's due. She looks down and sees that her blouse is rumpled up around her midsection, and when she's sure Tom's not looking, she straightens it.

If the measure of the man is the restaurant he takes you to, Tom Ellis is her kind of guy. This place, Sonny's, is just the right size: about ten tables, and a counter with eight stools. There are home-made pies in a glass case, and there's a chalkboard menu featuring comfort foods. "I want everything on there," Helen tells Tom, and he says, "Let's get it, then."

She laughs, and he says, "I mean it. We'll have some now and then we'll both have meals for the next couple days. You're staying until Monday, right?"

"Well, yes, but . . ."

"And we'll stop for breakfast things for you at the grocery store before I take you home."

"Why are you being so . . . *nice*?"

His face changes and he looks down at the table, then up at her. "I liked your husband very much."

She nods, her throat tight.

"And . . ." He shrugs. "I like you. I feel like I got to know you from building that house—I like the way your mind works. Anyone who saw that place would want to know who *thought* of all those things. And here you are."

"I didn't think of everything."

"You thought of most of it."

Helen cannot think of what to say next. "Thank you," she manages, and then, "I guess you sort of have an unfair advantage."

"In knowing more about you than you do about me?"

She nods.

"I'm an open book."

"Nobody's an open book," Helen says.

"You're right. But I'll tell you the truth about anything you ask me."

A young, red-haired waitress comes over, a pleasant girl seemingly unaware or uncaring about her great beauty, and Tom places their order. "Really?" she says. "Everything on the menu? A lot of people say that, but they never *mean* it." She tilts her head, pointedly appraising this older and quite attractive man, then says "Cool" in a way that sounds like *Call me.*

After she leaves, Tom says, "We need a new word for *cool.* You're a writer. Can you think of one?"

"*Awesome,*" Helen says and he smiles, and there are his laugh lines. His hands cupping his coffee mug. If Helen could pick one part of a man's anatomy that she loves most, this is it: hands. Unbidden, the image comes to her of waking up beside Tom, a wide ray of sunshine lying across them as they turn to each other and blink good morning. She looks away, at the older man seated hunched over coffee and pie and the newspaper at the end of the counter. *What's his story?* she thinks in a way that is automatic, and an answer starts to come to her: his long-dead wife, his crush on the waitress, his dishwasher mended with duct tape, the magic tricks he performs for the boy next door. She is content; she is hungry and food is on the way. Also, she has not been with a man for a long time, and Tom Ellis is so very pleasant to look at, to talk to.

By the time they have finished eating, though, Helen's mood has changed; she feels tired, unsure of herself, a little foolish. Lost. She looks at her watch, and Tom says, "It's late, I know. Why don't I take you to the house." Then, before she can even start to worry about what that might mean, he says, "I'll just drop you off, and then you're on your own. But you can call me if you need anything."

They drive in silence, the delicious smells of their food the only things talking. Then they are there, in deep darkness, the front of the little house illuminated only by the car's headlights. "I won't come in," Tom says. "But why don't you make sure everything's okay before I take off?" She takes her suitcase and packages of food, refusing Tom's offer to carry some of them for her, and uses the headlights to find the lock and turn the key. Once inside, she turns on the lights and checks quickly for—what? Killers? Raccoons? Ghosts? In any case, there is nothing there but the inviting rooms of the place. She goes outside to signal to Tom that everything's all right. He leans out the window to say, "I'm ten minutes away if you need *anything*."

"Thank you!" she calls, waving, and goes back inside. She stands still for a long moment, her hands clasped, just feeling the place. Then she walks slowly around the house, taking in the rooms in a way she was unable to before. She puts away the food into the fancy new refrigerator, touches the rocks that surround the fireplace, looks through the mullioned windows at the backyard, dimly lit by a shrouded moon.

In the bathroom, she turns on the shower briefly, and she then goes to the bedroom. She flicks one of the switches and the constellations light up. She crosses her arms and leans against the doorjamb, shaking her head. What he missed, by not being able to show her all this! What *she* missed, by not getting to see his face as he saw hers.

She moves slowly through the house, all but holding hands with Dan's spirit, thanking him for this and every other beautiful thing he ever did for her. When she gets back to the bedroom, she lies in the middle of the wide, wide mattress with her coat for a blanket, meaning to rest for a minute, then get up and change into her pajamas. She stares out the French doors at the night sky, at the stars, much clearer here than at home. She closes her eyes to listen for night sounds, insects, the wind, and feels herself drifting down toward sleep.

. . .

Morning in the house is like something Helen has never seen. She goes to the kitchen and makes coffee, the small sounds amplified in the silence, and then drinks it from one of the diner-type mugs; the weight and the feel of the mug is as perfect as she imagined it would be. She moves to one of the living room windows and takes in the Easter egg colors of dawn, purer here, somehow.

She puts on her coat against the early morning chill and goes out to the tree house, carefully climbs the dew-wet stairs, and sits in a deck chair at the bow of the boat. She can smell the pencil scent of the tree she sits in, along with the sharper smell of eucalyptus beads that lie scattered under a tree nearby. In the distance are gently rounded, high, green hills, and above them a plane moves slowly across the sky.

Despite the bit of chill in the early morning air, the sun feels warm against her face. For the first time in a long time, she is outside without gloves, and the pleasure in this is immense. Only two days ago she was walking to the mailbox with her head down in a fierce wind, her eyes watering from cold. Here, people come out of their houses in February wearing no coats and stretch their hamstrings before jogging past trees and flowers. Putting aside the issue of how Tessa might feel about her mother moving to the same area she's moving to, Helen closes her eyes and tries to think objectively what it would be like to live here. Would she be able to work again? If she got what she thought she could for her house in Oak Park, she wouldn't have to earn much money. She could take a part-time job in a bookstore and be all right. She sees herself in some small but well-stocked store, comfortable armchairs set out for browsing, a tabby cat moving from one customer to another, his back arching in pleasure with each person's affections. She would look different, she would look like she lived in California. She would wear a wide silver bracelet, many rings. Her gray hair would be permed in a hip sort of way, her clothes a kind of yoga cool. She sees herself assisting a customer with finding something good to read. How pleasant it would be to only be a reader again! She could work in the store a couple days a week and spend the rest of her time puttering—that was part of the fantasy she had described for Dan when they talked about retiring. It *is* possible to do it. It is.

She thinks about the unnecessary clutter she has in her house, how she would have to get rid of so much of it, and the notion aggravates and discourages her. Then she remembers a woman on her block who moved out and gave almost everything away. She'd told someone that she'd thought about trying to sell things, but it just seemed like—and in fact was—so much *work*. But to give things away—that was fun! There was a secondhand furniture store she'd always liked and she made a deal with the owner: take everything she didn't need for her new, vastly smaller house, but take it all—then it's free. She had a lot of pantry staples, and a woman three doors down said hell yes, she'd take her vanilla beans, her garlic chili sauce, her fusilli and cumin and adobo peppers in sauce. And the woman moving loaded up her son's red wagon with those things and took a walk down the block, her heart light. Every day, Helen thought, so many people tap the bull on the shoulder and say, "Excuse me. I'm just going to grab your horns." Why doesn't she? Why *doesn't* she? As for Tessa being displeased about her mother following her, well, Tessa will be in the city, not living with her. And Helen is allowed to make a decision that is for and about herself, is she not?

She settles back against the chair, sips her coffee, and fills her mind with only the sight of the hills and the sky and the trees. There is a bird making its call over and over, and to Helen it sounds like *Here! Here! Here!* Now comes the whistle of a cardinal, and Helen leans forward and whistles back. She is alone, and not lonely. If you leave one home, you can find another. Here? Here? Here?

twenty-seven

Sitting at her airport gate, finishing a turkey and avocado sandwich she is eating out of boredom, Helen stares into space, seeing the little house she locked up this morning, then kissed the front door of, before she made her way to the end of the driveway to wait for Tom. It's cloudy today, rain is expected, and Helen is glad for it. It would be even more heartbreaking to leave on a beautiful day.

Tom had a meeting with new clients and could not take her all the way in to the airport, but he did take her to Manzanita, the stop where she could catch the Marin AirPorter. The big bus had a rainbow painted on the side, and Helen loved that. The seats were high and comfortable, the view from the oversize windows was fine, and the driver was a happy man who greeted each passenger as though he or she were a close friend. It felt less like public transportation to the airport than a safe carnival ride.

Before she boarded the bus, she kissed Tom good-bye, a chaste kiss, and their first; but she believes they both felt the promise and the intention in it. They hadn't had much time being together—Helen had wanted to be alone in the house, and Tom was busy with his work. But the time they had was deeply satisfying: they talked without awkward pauses, laughed easily, and discovered that they had a great deal in common. Birthdays in May. An aversion to science fiction. Dog mania, although Tom was between dogs, having recently lost his fourteen-year-old golden retriever. They both also love chickens. Dan could never understand her affinity for chickens, but Tom thought they were beautiful and funny. "*Funny*, yes, that's it!" Helen said. They were on the Tennessee Valley Road, walking toward the ocean when he said that. Turkey vultures circled overhead and the fields were full of wildflowers. They brought a picnic of meat loaf sandwiches (still happily eating the diner's leftovers) down to the water's edge and for a long time simply watched the foamy waves race onto the sand, then get pulled slowly back out to sea. They talked about the art of Mary Cassatt, they talked about how their mothers still hung clothes on the line, even in winter; and they talked briefly about why Tom had never married. He told her about finally meeting the woman he fell madly in love with at age thirty-five, and how they had lived together for many years, eschewing marriage. Then, one Sunday afternoon when they lay together on the sofa reading the "Vows" column, they decided to take the big step themselves. On the Tuesday before the wedding planned for Saturday, September 15, 2001, she was in New York for a business meeting and went to have breakfast at Windows on the World at the Twin Towers before she took her flight home. It was still hard for him to talk about it. Since then, he'd not had any kind of relationship. He put his head down, shrugged; then, turning toward her, he said, "I *guess* there's still time," and she noticed how his eyes matched the sky at that particular moment, how his voice was rich in timbre and kind in tone. Looking down at the sand in which she was idly drawing lines with a stick, she remarked on the quality of his voice and asked if he would read aloud to her sometime. "Of course!" he said, as though he'd been just about to suggest it himself.

Tom Ellis, she thinks, and sighs, looking down at her boots.

Not long after Dan died, she and Midge were talking about the prospect of Helen dating again, and Helen was saying that apart from thinking she might never overcome this sorrow, she wasn't sure she was at all interested in dating. So much work. So much awkwardness. And the idea of sex! Helen and Dan had enjoyed an active sex life, but to be with a new man that way? Helen couldn't imagine it. Didn't want to imagine it. Now, though, she can imagine it. She begins with a very dark room. Preceded by a bottle of wine.

Twelve more minutes until boarding time. Helen leans back in her seat and closes her eyes, recalling last night when she was in the house, sitting before a fire she'd built herself, which was probably the reason it kept going out. She fed it with paper from the Sunday *Examiner* she'd bought at a coffee shop she'd walked to that morning. She'd sat there for a while, watching the people she guessed lived nearby ordering their drinks, trying to gauge her compatibility with them. No one spoke to her, but then she didn't initiate any conversation, either. She left feeling awkward and disappointed: age six or sixty, it was hard to be the new girl.

Last night, sitting on the sofa in the living room, she stared into the flames thinking about everything her marriage had been—and had not been. In the time since Dan died, she had recalled often enough the wonderful times they had together, the appeal of his easygoing nature. But last night she considered the other side: the colossal argument they'd had one Thanksgiving Day when he decided she was getting bitchy from trying to make too many dishes, and he dumped the pumpkin pie filling she'd just made down the garbage disposal, saying, "Stop it! You do this every year and it is not *worth* it!" She stood there for a moment, her eyes wide, and then she ran up to the bedroom and slammed the door. She sat on the bed, fuming, realizing that he must have been thinking this for years and yet never said a word. She thought about how she had scraped her knuckles badly while grating nutmeg for a pie filling that was now making its way to the sewer. Then, as long as she was at it, she thought about every other thing that was wrong between them. And at that time, there was plenty wrong. Television had begun to dominate their evenings. Dan was spending too much money gambling on sports games. They argued regularly about what to do when they went out. "I never saw the point in listening to live music, so stop asking me to do it!" Dan said one night, nearly shouted, after she'd suggested they go to a blues bar. "If I like a musician, I want to listen to their CDs, not live music, with everyone *talking*. And I don't like these girlie movies and plays you drag me to, either." "*Les* Misérables?" she shouted back, about the play they'd most recently gone to. "*Les Misérables* is a *girlie* play?"

Things were so bad around that time that she had suggested counseling, and Dan had said—oh, she'll never forget this—Dan had said, "For all the good *counseling* would do, you might as well write our problems on a piece of paper, put on a costume, have a ceremony, and burn them." So she did that. One morning after he left for work, she wrote out all the gripes she had with her husband, put on a change of clothes in lieu of a costume, said a Hail Mary in lieu of having a ceremony, and then burned the list in the kitchen sink. On that list, in addition to the other complaints, was the way he volunteered to clean the kitchen and then only half cleaned it: left the grease on the stove, the crumbs on the counter. The way he picked at his teeth in public. And especially the way he dressed so carefully for work at a time when, at an office picnic, one of Dan's women co-workers warned Helen that another woman co-worker was spending an awful lot of time in his office, the door closed. When Helen had confronted Dan with this, he'd said, "I am not doing anything, I swear to you. She flirts with me, okay? Is that so bad? Don't you like it when men flirt with you?" She had stood before him in her breast-milk-stained nightgown that morning, her hair uncombed, her glasses filthy with specks of who knew what, and quietly said, "Just who do you think flirts with me these days, Dan? Even you don't." And he had checked his watch and said, "Look, Helen, I have to go to work."

Sitting there in the house Dan had built for her, she fed the fire and continued thinking of things that were not so perfect in their marriage. Why? To clear the way for a new love in her life? She admitted to herself that such was probably the case, then wept loudly—wailed—for what she hoped was the last time over a man who was just a man, no more perfect than any other man, a man she had married for love, yes, but also because of timing and circumstance. Another man might have done as well or better in a marriage with her, who knew? Still, something stubborn stirred in Helen's stomach, resisting that most practical thought. Dan may have been just a man who happened along, but he was also her love. Her own. She let the fire go out, and went to bed.

When she boards the plane, Helen sits next to a woman who is the image of Helen's fantasy of herself as a California woman: she has loosely permed hair, wears an artful, asymmetrically cut suit, and many interesting rings. "Going home?" the woman asks, and Helen rankles against being so easily pegged as a midwesterner.

"Yes, but I might move here," she says.

The woman nods. "Might want to consider that pretty carefully."

"Oh?"

The woman laughs. "I'm sorry. I didn't mean that the way it sounded. Well, actually I did, I guess, but it's certainly not my place to tell you where to live!"

"It's okay," Helen says. "I appreciate your honesty. But . . . why did you say that?"

The woman looks past Helen's shoulder, out the window, where rain has begun to dot the glass. "I miss Chicago in a way I never knew I would. The city itself, which I happen to think is beautiful, and also has just about anything anyone could want; but mostly I miss the people. There's a kindness in the Midwest that you don't get out here. Oh, not that the people in California aren't nice, but . . ." She shrugs. "I don't know. I guess I wish I'd thought things through a little more, maybe lived out here on a trial basis before I sold my house."

"Did you ever think of trying to buy your house back?" Helen says. "I've heard stories about that happening." Her own house appears in her head, her airy bedroom, the window above her kitchen sink, the bird's nest built at the curve of the gutter.

"Yeah, I've heard about that, too. I tried it. I went right up to the door and asked if there was any way the new owners would sell it back to me. I asked them to name their price."

"What did they say?"

"They said no, they didn't want to sell it. Not at any price. Then they invited me in for dinner."

Helen laughs. "Did you eat with them?"

"Almost. But it would have made me too sad to see things so changed. And to know I couldn't have back what I wanted so badly."

"What about another house?"

The woman smiles, shakes her head. "It was all a pipe dream, really. What I wanted back was a whole life I had purposefully lost. It's . . . Well. Never mind. It's more than you want to hear, believe me. But I do suggest that you think hard about moving. Once it's done, it's hard to undo."

The pilot interrupts them, saying they're going to be delayed taking off. The woman rolls her eyes and takes a neck pillow from her oversize purse. Within a minute, she's snoring, a dainty ruffled sound that makes Helen smile as she stares out the window at the rain, coming down harder, now, so that the drops hit and then bounce back up.

When she arrives in Chicago, it will be cold and dark. The

wind will whip around her and rush up under her coat as she waits for the cab. But she will be home. She thinks about all she would miss, if she were to leave. The way that spring feels like a miracle every year, how she spends the first warm days sitting out on the front porch steps, willfully paralyzed, watching robins hop heavily across the lawn. The conversations on the el, the miniatures in the Thorne Rooms at the Art Institute, the bar at the top of the John Hancock, the changing colors of the lake, the high quality of the many small theaters. Midge, of course.

She looks over at the woman sleeping next to her, someone who regrets a rash decision. Then she imagines herself in the little house, bringing in the mail and sitting at the lovely new table to read it. Then she thinks about having her cab stop at Superdawg in Chicago on the way home, where she might get two Whoopskidawgs, she loves them and she loves the *fact* of them. She's pretty sure there are no Whoopskidawgs in Mill Valley.

Oh, it's impossible to make the decision! On the one hand, the house is a miracle offering that she simply can't refuse. On the other hand, it was meant for Dan and her, the two of them. And in addition to Chicago being home, it seems her life there is beginning to change in ways she is only now starting to understand. Shouldn't she see it through?

Tom. Well, he has said that his favorite city next to San Francisco is Chicago. Maybe he'll move there. She thinks of them walking down Oak Park Avenue together, hand in hand, and something inside her seems to revolt at the notion. She thinks of him sitting at the breakfast table with her in the little house in California, and that doesn't feel any more comfortable.

There is nothing to do but not decide right now. A solution will come of its own accord. She has to learn patience and trust. At some point.

She stares out the window, wondering if she is too old to learn certain things. Is it true that one can become so fixed in one's ways that it really is impossible to change? Or are there preordained stages in life—altered somewhat by each person's eccentricities, of course—but preordained stages through which people must pass, meaning that one is changing all the time whether one wants to or not? She remembers the day Tessa turned seven and at breakfast said to her and Dan, "This is the first old age, right?" She and Dan had found that so amusing, but now she wonders if there wasn't some preternatural wisdom in Tessa's remark, if there *isn't* some rule of definitive change that accompanies each interval of seven years, no matter who you are, or where you live.

When the plane finally begins to taxi down the runway, gathering speed, she turns away from the view. If she does sell the house, she will personally interview anyone who wants to buy it. It has to be the right person, it has to be such an exceptional person.

She's not selling it. She's going to live in it.

Somehow.

She'd better sell it.

Enough! She closes her eyes and tries to disconnect from herself, to switch from this ping-pong turmoil in her brain to sleep.

twenty-eight

"I'm not telling you anything," Walter, Tessa's doorman, says.

"Come on, Walter," Helen says. "I just want to know if she has a boyfriend. You don't have to give me details, just say yes or no." She knew she shouldn't have asked him this without cookies in hand.

Helen has taken a cab to Tessa's apartment on the way home from the airport, and she and the doorman are sitting on lawn chairs in the storage room behind Walter's desk. He has propped open the door so he can see if anyone comes into the lobby, and now he goes to peer through the crack, ostensibly to have a better look, though Helen thinks it's really to break away from her pleading gaze. As soon as he sits back down, she starts in again. "Seriously though, does she? I'm pretty sure she does." Walter raises an eyebrow and the tenor of his voice rises right along with it. "What's the matter, y'all don't talk?"

"She doesn't tell me everything."

"She *shouldn't* tell you everything!"

"She shouldn't tell me if she has a *boyfriend*?"

Walter purses his lips, says nothing.

Helen looks at her watch. "Walter."

Someone comes into the lobby and Walter rises quickly. "Duty calls," he says and then looks at her. "You staying in here?"

She nods.

"I'm not coming back," he says, but she knows he will.

And he does. He stands before her, his arms crossed. "I'm sorry, but I'm not going to tell you anything, Helen. I don't feel it's my place. And I don't want to. Tessa's my friend." He smiles at her. "You're my friend, too—although you feel more like my daughter."

"Stop stalling, Walter. I've got to go."

"All right, Helen, I will stop stalling. I'm going to tell you something I've been wanting to tell you for a long time. But it's not what you want to hear. Helen, I say this because I care about you both: you've got to let her go. You're way too tight up against her."

"I am her *mother*!"

"I know you are," Walter says. "And you show her a whole lot of love and concern. And leftovers. Now you've got to give her some respect and let that girl stand *up*."

Helen stares into her lap, fiddles with the clasp on her purse. The purse that Tessa helped her pick out after Helen had held up an alternative selection and heard the usual rejoinder. "You know she's moving out to California, right?"

"She told me. I'll miss her, but I'm very happy for her. She found herself a good job."

"Did she find anyone to take the lease? Can you at least tell me that?"

"Not yet."

"Not yet you can't tell me or not yet she hasn't found any-one?"

"She hasn't found anyone."

Helen nods. "I'm worried she'll be stuck with two rents."

"Let her figure it out."

Now she is angry. "Do you have children, Walter?"

"Do you remember *being* a child, Helen? Do you remember when you wanted to move away from your parents, how hard it was to do, but how important?"

In fact, she does remember. Oh, that yellow brick road, that wild need she had to get *out*. The very notion of buying her own bag of bread was exotic. The summer she was nineteen, just fin-ished with her first year of college, where she had lived in a dorm, she told her parents she wanted to move into an apartment with a young woman she'd met at the office where she was working for the summer. They didn't want to let her go. For one thing, they had met the young woman and had reservations about her char-acter and they were right—the girl was in the habit of bringing home men almost every night, and it was a one-room, studio apartment. Still, Helen moved into the place in August, and her parents gave her four bags of groceries to get started. A couple of weeks later she met Dan. Immediately, she began spending more time at his place than at her own, finding it infinitely more private.

Helen stands, brushes crumbs off her lap. "Do you want an-other cookie?"

"Give them to my girl."

"She's not your girl."

"Is too."

"Is not."

"Ask her. She'll tell you."

Helen sighs. "Thank you, Walter. For everything you've done for her."

She starts to leave the storeroom, then turns back to face him. "And . . . I just want you to know I heard you, okay?"

"Okay."

Helen walks over to the elevator and presses the button. Just as it arrives and she's stepping in, Walter says, "Helen? He's real good-looking. And *nice.*"

Helen doesn't bother holding the door open to hear more. She knows that's all she's going to get.

Tessa's apartment is fragrant with the scent of exotic spices. "Did you make Indian food?" Helen asks, trying not to sound incredulous—and failing.

"I ordered out," Tessa says, "but I could have made it."

Helen takes off her coat and sits down on the sofa. Tessa moves a stack of papers and Helen sees penmanship on the top page that is not Tessa's—some writing, some numbers. "Is that . . . ?"

Tessa turns around. "What?"

Is that your boyfriend's writing? "Is that biryani I smell?"

"Yes. Do you want some?"

"No thanks. But it smells good." *What's that writing about? What are those figures for?*

"Well, I have tons left. You can take some home if you want."

Am I ever going to meet him? Why can't I meet him? "Okay. Maybe I will."

Helen tells Tessa how lovely it was to see the house again, how she appreciated it even more the second time around. "It's just so hard to let go of it," she says.

"What was it like waking up there?" Tessa asks.

Helen smiles, shakes her head.

"I thought so," Tessa says. "Did you sit in the tree house?"

"Yes, I did. I sat in the tree house and I looked out and the view was so beautiful. And I saw two deer. I know people hate them for the way they eat their gardens, but I love them."

"Me, too," Tessa says. "I'd feed them."

"So," Helen says. "How are your plans progressing for your move?"

"I just talked to someone who I'm almost positive is going to sublet the place. She's coming for one final look tomorrow and if she takes it, she'll buy my furniture, too. Whatever her decision, though, I'm going out there in two weeks."

"Uh-huh," Helen says. She feels the sting of tears starting and stands up. "Be right back. I've got to go to the bathroom."

In the tiny room, she looks at her daughter's toiletries: her toothpaste and perfume, her piles of makeup, all of it sent to her on what is nearly a daily basis. Helen picks up one of the cases with eye shadow, and rubs a violet color over her lid. It looks awful, and she turns on the water to take it off. Tessa's sink is dirty, and so she gets the cleanser out from under the sink and begins scrubbing. There. Next, she puts cleanser into the toilet and starts scrubbing that, too.

Tessa knocks on the door, then opens it and sees her mother standing there holding up a toilet brush like the Statue of Liberty. "Mom. Mom. Mom."

"You want your bathroom to be clean if that person comes back to look!"

Tessa closes her eyes, rubs her forehead.

"Fine." Helen puts the toilet brush back in the holder, and joins her daughter in the living room.

"So. I guess you're excited to go, huh?" she asks cheerfully, to make up for cleaning the bathroom.

"I am. This is going to be a great job, and I already have a place to stay in the city, in Pacific Heights."

"Really!"

"Yeah, a friend of a friend is over in France, and I can stay in her apartment for a month. That should give me plenty of time to find my own place."

Helen leans back against the sofa, looks around the apartment. It seems so odd to think of someone else living here. After Tessa leaves, it will be difficult to drive by this street.

Tessa has asked her something she hasn't heard.

"What?"

"I said, 'How was Tom?' "

"Oh. Fine. We had a couple of meals together."

"He's a really nice guy," Tessa says. "Seems like he could be fun to be with, too. Is he?"

Helen looks at her watch. "I'd better get going." She puts her coat on, picks up her purse, kisses her daughter good-bye. When she walks down the hall, she can feel Tessa's eyes on her back. *How do you like it?*

twenty-nine

"BUT WHY DIDN'T YOU SLEEP WITH HIM?" MIDGE ASKS, THE NEXT afternoon.

Helen only looks at her.

"*What?*" Midge says, puffing a little; they're walking at a pretty rapid pace. "Time's awasting."

"First of all, this isn't the sixties. I hardly know him."

Midge waves her mittened hand. "Ah, you know him well enough. It sounds to me like you covered a lot of ground in just a few days. Didn't you even *kiss*?"

"Not that it's any of your business, but yes, I kissed him. I kissed him good-bye."

"Tongues?"

Helen says nothing.

Midge laughs. "Okay, no tongues. Well, next time."

"How do you know there'll be a next time?"

"Because you didn't want to go to George's for breakfast, that's how I know."

Helen starts to protest, but her friend is right. If you go to George's you have to get hash browns. And she's not eating hash browns for a while. Just in case. She had half a bagel for breakfast, and a little bowl of strawberries. And now is starving to death, but never mind.

Passing Austin Gardens, Midge points to the park. "Let's go sit down."

They make their way to a bench near the entrance and Midge dusts off a good three inches of new-fallen snow. It's the powdery kind that lifts lightly in the air and glitters as it falls. They sit quietly for a while, enjoying the warm sun, the lack of wind. It's the best kind of winter day, where breathing in the cold air does not hurt, but refreshes. Midge described it once as taking your lungs to the dry cleaners.

"I just think it might be too soon," Helen says, finally.

"For sex?"

"Yes."

"Well, then just make out! You know, heavy petting, like in the old days. It's fun. It would be *good* for you. Don't you want that old pelvic ache back again?"

Helen turns to face her friend. "You know, sometimes you just don't get it. I know you think I've had enough time to grieve. But I'm not like you, Midge. I feel things more deeply. I—"

"Okay," Midge says. "Let me tell you something, Miss *I-Feel-the-Pea*. I feel the pea, too! All of us feel the pea! The difference is what each of us chooses to do about it! Or *has* to do about it!"

Helen feels a kind of lurch inside that is complete acknowledgment of what Midge has just said. Helen has always thought of herself as being different, as feeling more than others. Sometimes she views it as a gift, more often as a curse. But it had not fully occurred to her, until now, that if someone doesn't react as she does, it doesn't mean they feel any differently.

"You're right," she tells Midge, her mouth suddenly dry, a weary embarrassment upon her. She turns away, focuses on a squirrel who has climbed down a tree and now holds statue still, as though eavesdropping.

"You know that story about the person who's thirsty?" Midge says.

Helen shakes her head no.

"Well, the person is complaining and complaining and complaining that she's *so thirsty*. 'Oh, my God, I'm *thirsty,* I am *so thirsty.* She's given a drink of water. And you know what happens then? She says, 'Oh, my God, I was *thirsty*! I was *so thirsty*!' "

Helen looks at her hands. "That's me?"

Midge doesn't answer. Then, more gently, she says, "Helen, you're my best friend. I love you for lots of reasons. But the truth is, you've never stepped up in some kind of essential way and part of the reason is that Dan never made you. He protected you, and in fact he encouraged your helplessness. I think he thought it was charming. Maybe it made him feel like a man."

Helen starts to defend her husband and Midge interrupts, saying, "I know. I loved Dan, too, believe me. And I think he did most if not all of this subconsciously. But without him, here you are, still asking someone to fix everything for you."

"You mean Tessa," Helen says.

"Well, yes." Midge leans closer. "Look, I don't mean to—"

"It's okay," Helen says. "I'm getting it from all sides. I know it's time for . . . I know it's time. But I just want to say one thing. If I ever write a novel again, it's going to be in defense of weak women. Inept and codependent women! I'm going to talk about all the great movies and songs and poetry that focus on such women! I'm going to toast Blanche DuBois! I'm going to *celebrate* women who aren't afraid to show their need and their vulnerabilities, to be *honest* about how hard it can be to plow your way through a life that offers no guarantees about *anything*! I'm going to get on my metaphorical knees and *thank* women who fall apart, who cry and carry on and wail and wring their hands because you know what, Midge? *We all need to cry!* Thank *God* for women who can articulate their vulnerabilities and express what a lot of other people probably want to say and feel they can't! Those people's stronghold against falling apart themselves is the disdain they feel for women who do it for them! *Strong.* I'm starting to think that's as much a party line as anything else ever handed to women for their assigned roles! When do we get respect for our differences from men? Our *strength* is our weakness, our ability to feel is our *humanity*!

"You know what? I'll bet if you talked to a hundred strong women, ninety-nine of them would say, 'I'm *sick* of being strong! I would like to be cared for! I would like someone else to make the goddamn decisions; I'm sick of making decisions!' I know this one woman who is a *beacon* of strength, a single mother who can do *everything,* even more than you, Midge. I ran into her not long ago and we went and got a coffee and you know what she told me? She told me that when she goes out to dinner with her guy, she asks him to order everything for her. Every single thing, drink to dessert, because she *just wants to unhitch.* All of us dependent, weak women have the courage to do all the time what she can only do in a restaurant!"

Midge looks at her. "Hmm. I'm very sorry to tell you this. That all sounded pretty strong."

Helen laughs, and then they sit quietly until Midge announces that her butt is frozen and Helen says how convenient, now it won't hurt when they saw off all that excess flesh she keeps bitching about.

"Yeah, we can superglue it to your pancake boobs," Midge says and Helen says that would be fine.

When Helen gets home, there is a message from Tom, saying he's just making sure she got home all right, and to call back when she's got time. She picks up the phone, then decides to call him tonight, just before she goes to sleep. She'll save it up for herself that way. Also, she'll decide what it is she really wants to say to him, and how.

thirty

HELEN READS THE LAST CHAPTERS OF CLAUDIA'S MANUSCRIPT and leans back against the pillows. She feels such admiration for this shy writer's powerful prose; such determination to help get her everything she deserves as an artist. It is ten-thirty, too late to call, but Helen gets Claudia's number and tries her again anyway.

When she hears her student say hello, Helen feels a sudden tightening in her throat. "Claudia?" she says, in a pinched voice not quite her own.

"... *Mom?*" Claudia says, and at this Helen begins to laugh.

"Oh! Ms. Ames! I'm sorry!"

"Call me Helen, please. And I'm the one who should apologize for calling this late. But I have to tell you, Claudia, I am absolutely overwhelmed by your manuscript. In the very very very good way!"

"You are?"

"I would love to help you try to get this published. It's beautiful, and I don't think it will be hard to find it a home. You know, the reading for the class is coming up, and there'll be an agent there, Maureen Thomas, who's very good, and I think she will absolutely love this. She comes from an all-woman agency; and I really admire the clients they have. There'll be an editor at the reading, too. For her to do anything other than listen is more of a long shot, but still, she'll be there, and she's a great editor." Helen was in fact amazed to learn that Kate Demian was coming to the reading, and so were Saundra and Nancy—in the end, they decided that Kate must have just wanted a free trip to Chicago for some reason or another—editors of her stature didn't usually show up at things like this.

"I didn't think I could come to the reading," Claudia says. "I missed so much class. After I gave the manuscript to you and then didn't hear anything right away, I was too embarrassed to see you. I thought you hated it. I was afraid to even answer the phone."

"I took as long as I did because I kept rereading passages! But oh, please do come back to class! There's one left—why don't you come? Everyone will be so glad to see you—we've missed you. The last assignment is to write a piece on risk. That seems appropriate, doesn't it?"

Claudia laughs. "It does. Okay, I'll come. I'll do the assignment and I'll do the reading, too, from my book. I wonder if . . . Do you have any suggestions about what I should read?"

"You can close your eyes and point to a page. It's all wonderful. Truly. Pick anything you like, about five pages' worth—each person gets only ten minutes."

"Well, I just . . . Thank you so much. I can't tell you how happy I am to hear you say all this. I'll see you in class tomorrow. Thank you."

Helen hangs up the phone and lies still for a long while, imagining Claudia at the podium, reading in the darkened auditorium. Helen wants to sit somewhere where she can see Maureen Thomas's face. If she were the agent, she'd rush the stage the moment Claudia finished, an agency rep form and pen in hand.

She flips through the pages of the manuscript. What raw pain is here, but how beautifully and universally expressed. She understands now what Claudia might have been trying to ask when she first gave Helen the manuscript: *If this is published, where will I hide? What will protect me? I'm writing to try to get myself out from under this pain, but will a public sharing of it only bind me more tightly to it?* Helen wishes she could tell her student that moving her experience out of herself and into the open will only help. But the truth is, she's not sure. It's a risk that Claudia will have to decide to take, or not.

Helen picks up the phone again and dials Tom's number, realizing after the fact that she has it memorized. She means to exchange pleasantries, to tell him about Claudia, to make a delicate inquiry as to the next time they might expect to see each other. But when he answers and finds that it's she, he says, "God, Helen. I miss you!" And she immediately blurts back, "Midge says we should have had sex!" And then she actually blushes, covers her mouth like a schoolgirl and blushes, sitting there alone in her mismatched flannel pajamas, surrounded by books and papers, wads of Kleenex, orange peels, and the candy wrapper from one—*one*—piece of chocolate.

"I was thinking we should have, too," Tom says. "I was thinking that just now, in fact."

"You were?" She laughs. She pushes aside a stack of papers as though making room for him beside her.

"Yes. That's the truth. I was just now lying here, thinking about . . . what we missed."

"Oh, but, Tom. You know, it's . . . I was in a marriage for a long time. And when you're with somebody that long, you see them in a certain way. I mean, I would look at Dan and I would see him as he used to be even as I saw him as he was. And I knew he saw me the same way. It was a kind of safety net, that long history. After he died, I felt like sex was just . . . over for me. And I didn't mind, really, until I met you and you kind of woke me up.

But I feel a terrible shyness about being with someone now. I mean, I'm *old*."

"You're not old. You're fifty-nine. You're a kid!"

She doesn't even start.

She hears sounds that suggest he's changing positions and she does, too; she turns on her side, hunkers down more with the phone, hears him say, "Listen. You think women are the only ones who worry about what their bodies look like? I keep a picture of me in my twenties on my bedside. It's pathetic. It's like Woody Allen's track medal—remember that movie where he swings the track medal in front of some young woman's face? I have a brief memorial service every time I take a good look into a full-length mirror. And . . . Okay, have you noticed the prevalence of Viagra ads? They're not for the girls, you know. They're not for the girls to *take*, anyway."

"Have you . . . ?"

"No. Not yet. Haven't had the occasion to. But it's not out of the realm of possibility that I'd need to take it, if the occasion arose. So to speak."

She says nothing.

"I'm making you uncomfortable, aren't I? I'm making *myself* uncomfortable. I'm sorry; I sound like some sleazy guy with hair transplants, sitting in a bar and hoping to score. Let's start over. How are you, Helen?"

"We wouldn't have to have sex right away," Helen says. "We could just . . . lie there and hold hands. I used to love watching movies and holding hands." She sighs, a quiet thing. Dan, passing her the popcorn and kissing her temple.

"I did, too," he says. "I loved all that. I'll tell you what, Helen, next time you come out here, we'll go to the movies and hold hands. And then if you'd let me . . . Here's the fantasy I was just enjoying, okay? I want you to lie on my bed with me and I want to hold you right up next to me. That's all. Except . . . I don't know, I'll bring you raspberries with the dew still on them; I've got a huge bank of black raspberries growing in my yard, and I'll bring you some. We'll go to Chinatown and then to hear some music—I know a bar that books great jazz acts. We'll walk through the tea garden in Golden Gate Park. I'll take you to look at puppies."

"Only if we can get one," Helen says, and he says, *"One?"*

Helen hesitates, then says, "You know, we have a Chinatown here and we have Millennium Park and we have great music to listen to, live. Blues. Would you like to come here and visit?"

"I thought you'd never ask," he says, and Helen bites her lip so hard it hurts. And then she feels a sudden, terrible disloyalty to Dan for exulting in the fact that here is a man who can have dogs and *wants* to hear live music.

"I just have to tell you," she says. "If there's a heaven, I'm going to have to be with Dan."

"As I'm going to have to be with Laura."

"Was that her name?" Helen asks, softly.

"That was her name," he says. "But she is gone, and Dan is gone, and here we are on earth, Helen, with an unknown number of days left to us, and I really can't wait to come and see you."

"How's the house?" she asks, because she cannot go further down this road. And he tells her she has time, but she should decide soon; the couple who wanted to buy it are beginning to look at other properties. She talks about real estate, and buyers, and time lines, and in her head she lies down beside him, and she can feel his arms pulling her close, and she can smell his skin, and she can feel the regular rhythm of his breathing, which coincides with her own.

thirty-one

ONE HOUR BEFORE THE LAST CLASS IS SCHEDULED TO BEGIN, Helen is sitting in the café across from the library, waiting for Saundra Weller to arrive. They will be discussing the particulars of the reading, which student will read when, what they might realistically expect from the agent and editor, what they will serve at the reception. Helen is early by a good twenty minutes, and has already had two cups of coffee as well as a cherry cheese turnover, which is the counterwoman's fault, because after she gave Helen her coffee she looked right at her and said, "What else?"

All around the café are people in conversation, or sitting hunched before their computers, or eating solemnly, staring into space. There is one man reading a newspaper; otherwise, no one is reading anything.

Such a discouraging time for people who love reading. Independent bookstores are struggling, all those magical places built by people who loved books from the moment they could hold one, and wanted to share that love with others. Helen recalls one such store where she did a reading a couple of years ago, how inviting the place was, with its broken-in armchairs and lamps glowing a deep yellow, with the cat named Melville, who slept on his back in the front window. It was a browser's paradise, books so thoughtfully and attractively displayed you wanted everything you saw, whether it was a nonfiction book about cod, or a volume of poetry, or a fat novel with ragged-edged pages, or a cookbook featuring winter soups. It was a time—the only time, as it happened—that Helen had arrived far too early for her reading, and she spent forty minutes wandering around the store. In the children's section, she eavesdropped as a mother read *Scaredy Squirrel* to her son; both mother and child laughed aloud at the inclusion of sardines in Scaredy's emergency kit, and at his first step in what to do in case of emergency: "panic." Helen laughed, too, and stopped just short of asking if she could sit down and listen to the rest of the story.

In the classics section, she had picked up a copy of *The Magic Mountain* and recalled the summer between her junior and senior years of high school, when she read it, how she lay in bed hours after she should have gotten up, the sheet growing warmer against her skin as the sun rose higher in the sky, her mother poking her head in now and then to see if she'd gotten up yet, but never suggesting that she should: Eleanor didn't have many rules about child rearing, but one of them was this: Never interrupt reading.

About ten minutes before Helen was scheduled to start her reading, the owner, Suzie, had offered her a cup of ginger tea, and they'd sat together in Suzie's cramped office at the back of the store. Suzie had told her how she'd left a high-paying job in advertising to open her store. "Now I'm on the side of the angels," she'd said, grinning. "And every day is Christmas." Books were everywhere: stacked up on her desk, overflowing from bookshelves, piled high in corners of the room, in boxes that needed to be unpacked.

When Suzie introduced Helen, she told the audience that one of the best things about books is that they are an interactive art form: that while the author may describe in some detail how a character looks, it is the reader's imagination that completes the image, making it his or her own. "That's why we so often don't like movies made from books, right?" Suzie said. "We don't like someone else's interpretation of what we see so clearly." She talked, too, about how books educate and inspire, and how they soothe souls—"like comfort food without the calories," she said. She talked about the tactile joys of reading, the feel of a page beneath one's fingers; the elegance of typeface on a page. She talked about how people complain that they don't have time to read, and reminded them that if they gave up half an hour of television a day in favor of reading, they could finish twenty-five books a year. "Books don't take time away from us," she said. "They give it back. In this age of abstraction, of multitasking, of speed for speed's sake, they reintroduce us to the elegance—and the relief!—of real, tick-tock time."

It was an inspiring speech, but she was preaching to the converted. The crowd gathered to listen to Helen read were people who were already convinced of the worth not only of books but of authors. But the decline of reading was continuing. It seems impossible that not so many years ago, people read newspapers twice a day, morning and evening editions. They read newspapers and came to their own conclusions about what they had read— what a notion! Helen remembers Dan once throwing up his hands in exasperation after a politician gave a stirring speech that was followed immediately by mind-numbingly repetitive analysis.

Maybe it's not such a bad time to come to the end of her career as a writer. She doesn't see how the growing trend of screens taking precedence over pages can be overcome. Books aren't loud enough; they're not showy enough; they don't move quickly enough; indeed, they don't move at all. They require stillness, reflection, imagination, and these things are out of step with the times. Thank heaven for the popularity of book clubs; sometimes Helen thinks they're the main reason publishers—and authors—are still in business.

She looks at her watch. Ten more minutes. She pulls out a pen and idly begins making a list of possible jobs for herself on a napkin. Her leave of absence, if one might call it that, is up, she's going to need to start bringing in some money.

Waitress, she writes, and stares at the word. Why not? She likes the easy camaraderie in being a waitress; as a young woman she had worked in a steak house and it was one of the best jobs she ever had. When the women customers would pass on the potatoes that came as a side, the waitresses would order potatoes au gratin and then put the oval dish of bubbling cheese, potatoes, and butter on the little table in the back of the kitchen that was reserved for them, and they'd all share. At the end of the night, the staff would gather at the bar for a couple of drinks, and Helen always liked the jokes and the casual intimacies, the raspy voice of the senior waitress, Della was her name, a onetime hot blonde who, in her words, knew her way around the block and back, and liked nothing better than to offer Helen advice about men. "Pay attention to what kinds of socks they wear," she said. "You can tell a lot about a man from what kind of socks he wears. Hole in the back, okay; hole in the front, forget about him."

Helen liked wearing the black uniform and the white waitress shoes; she liked coming home with leftovers every night—she rarely bought groceries in those days. But then she remembers the gigantic trays of food she hauled around and the very notion makes her back ache.

Nanny? she writes. She looks up and sees Saundra Weller coming toward her, and she crumples the napkin.

Saundra sits down at the table, slides her heavy winter coat from her shoulders. "How are you?" she says, and, without waiting for an answer, pulls from her enormous black bag a thick bound manuscript. "Guess what this is."

"No idea."

"Margot Langley's novel."

Helen sits back in her chair. "Really."

"Yes, and I have to tell you, it is simply magical. I told her I'd get her a few blurbs before we even submitted it. Patricia Honeywood just called and gave it a *wonderful* quote. And her last book was on the list for twenty-three weeks!"

"*You're* going to submit it?"

"Well, I spoke to my agent, who's agreed to represent Margot, but we've all agreed that I should personally hand it to Kate Demian. Who is *wonderful,* so discerning. I am absolutely sure she'll want it and I'm thinking she'll offer high six figures, easily. A million isn't out of the question. I made a few editing suggestions, of course, and Margot was just so good in recognizing the need for those changes and . . . Well, here we are!" She holds out the manuscript. *"Pour vous!"*

"You know, I'm actually buried with galleys that publishers have sent." Not true. Number of galleys Helen has at present? Zero.

"Oh, come on, Helen. Really. A favor for a colleague? I just had this copy made for you—why don't you have a look, read twenty pages or so. I promise you, you'll love it. And then if you would just quickly get the blurb to me before the reading, something beyond the usual plot summary, of course, something that talks about the lyricism of the prose, and the great intelligence and imagination shown here. Four sentences should be just right."

"Let me ask you something. Does Margot know you're asking me to do this?"

"Yes. She does. I had to talk to her a little about . . . She was unaware of the importance of gathering blurbs from a number of sources. She had a wish list, but your readers represent a segment of the population she can't afford to ignore."

"I'm sorry. I really haven't time right now." Helen looks at her watch. "We need to talk about the reading. Funny thing, I have a student who has completed a manuscript, as well. And it's really good."

"Oh. *Ooookay.*" Saundra offers Helen a weary smile. "I'll read your student's book, all right?" She looks at her watch.

"Oh! No. No, thanks."

Saundra mutes her astonishment at this refusal and finally puts Margot's manuscript back in her bag. On her face Helen can read a kind of anger. But she will not read one page of Margot's manuscript. Absolutely will not. Not a single word. Still, she's curious about something. "What's the title?" she asks, and Saundra says the book doesn't have one yet. It has to be a *great* one. Saundra says she will think of one.

Helen sits in the empty classroom, her coat on, though open: she is not willing to leave quite yet. Her students, after having presented her with parting gifts of a silver pen and *The Book of Positive Quotations*, have all gone. Their pages today on risk were the best yet: some funny, some poignant, all full of the telling kind of detail she has been urging them to display. Claudia read first at the request of her classmates, who were delighted to see her back. She wrote about sneaking into her parents' room when she was twelve, examining the contents of every one of their dresser drawers. In her father's drawer, she found a stash of cigars beneath his underwear along with a roll of fifty-dollar bills bound by a deteriorating rubber band, and she found a box of condoms whose pale yellow color sickened her. She described the filmy negligees wrapped in tissue paper that she found in her mother's drawers, garments she had never seen or imagined before—she held the blue one up before her, and saw her own blouse clearly through it. She found a stack of letters written to her mother by a former suitor, and she found her mother's unlocked diary. She read to the point where her mother wrote about her disappointment in her daughter—her plainness, her debilitating shyness; then she stopped reading and very carefully repositioned the diary back under her mother's slips.

The piece then described Claudia's near miss at being caught, how, when she heard the crunch of the gravel that meant her parents were pulling into the driveway, she fled to her room and felt her heart knock in her chest, and she described how, when her mother opened the door to announce that she was home, Claudia saw her differently, though not angrily. *I felt no malice toward her. I felt no need to forgive. She had put into words a truth she needed to move outside of herself, in what she believed was a secretive way. Of course it was not secretive, even before I found the diary. Of course it was not. See a four-year-old standing before a mother who is tying a bow at the back of a dress full of ruffles and ribbons. See the disappointment in the mother's face when she turns her daughter around. The child sees it. But she was my only mother. I stayed in my room, and when she called me for dinner, I came. When she asked if it was good, I said yes, because it was. We ate, each of us stabbing and stabbing and stabbing at our plates.*

Hector, in a return to form, wrote about his first audition for television; and Billy talked about the one and only time he jumped out of an airplane. Donetta wrote about donating a kidney, a piece that both moved and astonished everyone. "You *really* gave away one of your *kidneys* to a *stranger*?" Billy asked.

Donetta shrugged. "You want to see my scar?"

"Yeah," Billy said, and then Donetta, smiling widely, said that would be hard, since what she wrote was fiction. She looked at Helen shyly then, and asked if it was all right that she'd brought fiction.

Ella, misunderstanding or choosing to ignore the assignment, wrote about the first time she understood that hamburgers were from cows. She wrote, *I looked at what was in my hand. It was a hamburger like before and all the catsup and mustard and pickles. But underneath was the animal in the field with brown eyes that never did a thing wrong and they did not get to choose anything about their life. And they never got mad but if they wanted to they could smash a big man right up against the side of a barn and that's it, Charlie, lights out. But they only stood in green grass in spring with little babies that loved them and they loved their babies too, you could tell from how gentle they looked down and even if they gave them a little poke it was gentle. And the babies how they nursed with their little tails flicking, which is their happiness. And in winter just standing there with no complaints even on the coldest days with steam and snot coming out their noses. Well all of a sudden I threw the hamburger away in the trash but it was too late for that cow. The moral of this story is every day is a surprise.*

Well. Truer words were never spoken. Jeff wrote a three-page essay about meeting the woman he feels destined to be with. It was a setup, a blind date of sorts; he met her at her mother's house, where he had been invited for dinner, and although he was instantly attracted to her, she seemed to despise him. It was a short evening, he said wryly, but later that night, as he sat waiting for the el, he saw the woman come onto the platform and risked speaking to her one more time. Helen sat frozen in place, understanding right away who that woman was.

After class, Jeff stood fussing with papers and his backpack until the others left; then he came up to Helen and said, "So."

"So!" she said.

"I'm kind of scared to tell you this. Actually, I'm really scared to tell you this. But I'm going with her to California."

"You are?"

"She's going to talk to you about it; she's just not ready yet. But I told her I wanted to let you know today, and she said that was my prerogative."

Helen had no idea what to say. She had no idea what she even felt. Too much of too much, that's what she felt.

"I love your daughter, Ms. Ames. I am so in love with her."

Then she smiled, and Jeff did, too.

"I know very few people believe in love at first sight," he said. "But I swear, for me it was love at first sight."

"I believe in love at first sight," she said.

"You and your husband?"

She nodded.

"Yeah, Tessa has told me a lot about you guys."

Helen studied him, wondering what all Tessa had chosen to share. Then she said, "Don't take this the wrong way, okay? But I'm really glad this class is over!"

He laughed. "I'll see you at the reading."

"Is Tessa coming?" she asked, just as he was going out the door.

He turned around. "She is."

"Well, good, that's good." A moment, and then Helen said, "Take care of her, okay?" It came to her, saying this, that part of her overdependence on Tessa after Dan died was bound up with her anxiety about being the only parent of an only child. She saw that she had been more worried about Tessa's inability to form a serious relationship than she had admitted, even to herself. She was miffed that Tessa hadn't said anything, but mostly she was vastly relieved.

"We'll take good care of each other," Jeff said. "We already are. It's kind of great."

Helen gathers her things, and turns the light out. In the darkness, she stands thinking. She told Midge once that she became a writer because she wanted to make a family of the world. She hadn't quite envisioned it happening this way, but here it is.

She thinks of Tessa in her apartment the other night, the clear-eyed earnestness with which she spoke. Then she thinks of her holding on to her mother's hand one cold afternoon when Tessa was three years old, and they were taking a walk to the library. They were pushing Tessa's yellow umbrella stroller, loaded up with books, past snow piles at the side of the road that had been dirtied with sand by the plows. Tessa said, "Doesn't it look like crumb cake?" and that was exactly what it looked like, and suddenly the sight of that snow did not make Helen winter-weary but instead delighted her.

She thinks of the time Tessa was six and so ill with a violent flu she would not eat for days, and the pediatrician who called to check on her said that if she didn't eat today, he was going to have to hospitalize her. Helen sat at the bed beside her feverish daughter and held up a spoonful of red Jell-O and told Tessa that her bear, Snugs, had come in the middle of the night to speak to Helen, and he had said he felt really bad that Tessa wouldn't eat and in fact had had bad dreams on account of it, and he really hoped Tessa would eat some Jell-O so he wouldn't have bad dreams like that again tonight, they were dreams of those flying monkeys that Tessa also once feared. Tessa looked closely into the face of the bear lying next to her and then picked him up and put him in her lap. And then she ate some Jell-O, one shuddering bite and then another and one more, and Helen thought, *I will never know such gladness and relief again.* But of course she did, because that's what children are capable of: creating freight train feelings in their parents with a bite of Jell-O, with a single glance, with a sigh that they make in sleep. Helen stands in the darkened classroom and sees Tessa stirring mud puddles with a branch of blooming forsythia, pointing to a setting sun and saying, "The sky's coming down." She sees her posing in her first high school dance dress, her braces glinting, her corsage wildly off-kilter.

Helen has a strong sense that Tessa and Jeff are so right for each other that they will end up marrying; and however prematurely, she regrets for Dan that he will miss the wedding. She knows that a father's transferring his daughter to her husband is meant to be symbolic, but for Helen, to whom the task will fall, it now seems quite literal. *I give her to your care.*

On a few occasions in her life, Helen has felt deep happiness as a kind of pain. The day she married Dan. The day Tessa was born. Now comes another such time. She sits down and puts her hand to her chest and rocks. Thinks of all she has lost and will lose. All she has had and will have. It seems to her that life is like gathering berries into an apron with a hole. Why do we keep on? Because the berries are beautiful, and we must eat to survive. We catch what we can. We walk past what we lose for the promise of more, just ahead.

thirty-two

Yawning, Helen lies in bed reading the last page of Margot Langley's manuscript. When she got home from class, she'd found it on her porch with a note from Saundra saying, *Please?* Helen started to throw the thing out, but then, right after dinner, decided she'd just read a page or two—she *was* curious. After that, she'd convert the manuscript into scrap paper; she's low on scrap paper. But the book is really good. It's more than that. It's that rarest of things: a literary novel that is entirely accessible. Its style is elegant and subtle, its impact profound. She became tearful reading certain parts; she laughed aloud at others.

The story concerns a woman who immigrated to the United States in her twenties, and follows her life, her daughter's, and then her granddaughter's. The details—of nineteenth-century New York City cobblestone streets, washed and glistening in the morning sun, contrasted with the hectic energy of those streets today; the clothing, all those swishing skirts and Gibson girl blouses giving way to blue jeans and stilettos; the Sunday dinners moving from heavy, five-course meals served on crocheted table-cloths to take-out sushi eaten directly from the carton; the ache of homesickness combined with the heady hope for a new life in a new country, the clashing of values and beliefs over the years, the way that an understanding of ancestors can make for a simultane-ous peace and charged expansion within oneself. This book de-serves every bit of help she can give it. The question is whether she *should* give it help. She is still in possession of the letter Margot wrote to her, and she thinks for a moment about going to get it. But what would be the point? She remembers what it said about her own novels: *insipid*. Besides, what needs to be decided here should be outside of what was in that letter. Hadn't she just re-cently, on the occasion of her disastrous speaking engagement, told a roomful of people that it was necessary to separate the au-thor's work from the person? Should she not look at Margot's book in that way, as a work of art separate from the creator? And as someone who mourns so acutely the decline of reading, shouldn't she do everything she can to support good literature as a way to draw people back into this most worthy of pastimes?

She tosses a couple of pillows aside, turns out the light, and lies down. Gradually, the objects in the room come into focus: the bureau with her many bottles of perfume, the chair in the corner, a stack of books beside it, the closet door, cracked open. She'll have to get up and shut it; she is fifty-nine years old and still afraid of an open closet door at night. Just as she still leaps into bed from a fair distance away, lest the monster who lives under the bed reach out and grab her ankles. She did this sometimes even when Dan was alive; it was almost a reflex. He laughed at it, and she told him at least her fantasy wasn't as bad as Midge's. Midge used to fear that a man with a knife lived under her bed, and he might at any moment decide to push his long blade slowly up-ward. Of course, Midge no longer lay rigid, listening for any sound of movement. She had banished her fear at about age nine. Helen's has persisted a bit beyond that point.

Ah, well. Add it to the list. Assume financial responsibility. Learn home mechanics. Overcome night fears. Acquire sense of direction. Recognize daughter as a grown-up. Grow up herself.

Yesterday afternoon, in what Helen had described to Midge as The Miracle in the Deli Department of Jewel, Tessa had finally called her mother's cell phone to tell her about Jeff, and there was nothing girlish about her declaration of her feelings for him. The childish one had been Helen, who had burst into tears and then emphatically denied that she was crying.

Helen turns on the light, picks up the last page of Margot's manuscript. Reading those last few paragraphs again, she is even more convinced of its worth. Damnit. Maybe the title will be terrible, and she can rejoice in that.

She'll give it an endorsement, an enthusiastic one. So the woman doesn't like her writing. Can't Helen rise above her own hurt feelings to help promote a book worth reading? Maybe if more books of this quality are published, the tide will turn: book sales will rise, bookstores will not founder and close; the important role of books in people's lives will be recognized and embraced.

She knows that some people, Midge, for example, would tell her not to offer any help at all. They would suggest that she was crossing some boundary she shouldn't cross and was compromising her personal integrity. They would say that if Margot Langley held her in such contempt—and took the trouble to write her a letter saying so!—she was undeserving of Helen's attention, much less praise. And a case can certainly be made for that point of view; one should defend oneself, care for oneself. That's true. One should not kiss the hand that slaps one's face. Should one. Maybe she won't help after all. The woman will get other blurbs. Anyone who reads this and has the slightest appreciation for literature will help. Surely that is so. And yet she wonders even as she thinks this if it is true. The literary world is full of jealousy, full of people afraid that if someone gets a piece of the literary pie, they will have to give up their own.

She turns out the light again, lies on her side, and closes her eyes. She thinks about a report she heard on the radio about a family whose home in Africa was destroyed by their neighbors. The interviewer asked one of the family members if he thought he could ever move back there. He said, "I don't know," with enormous sadness. And Helen thought, *But he will go back. Because it is his home.*

What she decides now is not so far from that. She will craft the best blurb she can for Margot's book. She will try to help an author who detests her, because of the home she wants to build inside herself, because of how she wants to live. In the end, to forgive, to tell the truth, to honor what is worthy of admiration, hurts less than the alternative. And there is this: if she offers words of praise to Margot, it will free her from the stinging criticism Margot offered her. Odd to think it works that way, but for Helen, it does. She does not regret it now, nor has she ever.

thirty-three

WHERE IS KATE DEMIAN? HELEN WONDERS. SHE LOOKS CARE-
fully around the auditorium again. Maureen Thomas and her as-
sistant are in the front row, seated with Nancy and the students
who will be reading. Helen and Tessa are seated in the back. At
the reception that took place earlier, Maureen told her that she'd
heard there was a lot of talent in the two groups this year, and
she'd been looking at Margot Langley when she said this. Helen
regarded her, too, the lanky, redheaded woman who, earlier, had
perfunctorily thanked Helen for her endorsement. There was
nothing in her manner to suggest she remembered sending Helen
the letter. "Did Nancy mention a student named Claudia Evans to
you?" Helen asked the agent, and Maureen widened her eyes as
she bit into a cookie. "Awfully *dark,* huh?" she said, delicately re-
moving a crumb from the corner of her mouth. Kate Demian was
not at the reception due to a late flight, but had reportedly landed
and was on her way to the Harold Washington Library, where it
was believed she would be in plenty of time for the reading.

But now Helen does not see her, and her disappointment is acute. From all she knows about Kate, she would be Claudia's ideal editor. Among the books she has edited are—

"Mom!" Tessa says.

Helen looks at her. *"What?"*

"Wake *up*!"

A board member has come to the stage and begun a rather lengthy introduction to the friends and family and newspaper reporters who have come to hear these readers. There are easily one hundred and fifty in the audience; maybe more. With the exception of those Helen suspects are Billy's friends, the people are dressed up in Sunday finery and their faces are full of pride. The ages range from what appear to be grandparents to a sleeping baby, resting like a potato sack on a man's wide shoulder.

Nancy is introduced, and she steps to the podium and makes opening remarks, then names Helen and Saundra Weller as the teachers this year; they are asked to stand and be applauded.

Then Nancy introduces the first reader: Ella Parsons. Helen and Nancy had agreed that Ella should go first so that she wouldn't have to wait to read; in past years, she had gotten loud backstage in her impatience. Ella marches purposefully toward the microphone, leans in close to it, and says, "This is about one time in my work," so loudly it appears that every person in the audience jumps. "Whoa!" she says. "Wait a minute." She squints out into the audience. "Where's the remote?"

Someone comes from behind the curtain and adjusts the microphone—and Ella, too, moving her away from the microphone—and she starts again to read from her piece about Halloween in the nursing home, how the residents handed out candy to nursery school students, except for Mabel Gruder, who ate hers. *Those little kids and the residents, they are on the different ends of the line, but they still have some same things. Like they both like candy and both have to get taken to the bathroom. When you see the lit-*

tle hand reach for candy in the big hand, sometimes it makes me feel like crying.

Helen looks around at the audience. They seem as engaged as she has been every time Ella has read something, and it gives her a rush of pleasure.

When Tessa was seven, she gave her first piano recital. Helen was seated in the front row, and when Tessa came out from backstage in her little pink dress and seated herself on the piano bench and began playing, Helen started laughing uncontrollably. It was nerves, but she couldn't account for the form they took. She shook with laughter, her hand pressed against her mouth, for the entire duration of the piece. Later, she asked Dan if he thought Tessa had noticed and he said no, but that Tessa was the only one who *didn't* notice. "Whatever made you do that?" he asked, and Helen said she didn't know.

But it's happening again. As Ella reads, Helen begins to laugh and cannot stop. She can feel Tessa staring at her, and now she is squeezing her arm, whispering, "Mom. Mom. *Mom!*"

"I can't *help* it," Helen whispers back.

Tessa pulls a Kleenex from her purse and Helen shoves it into her face. Finally, she does stop laughing.

When the audience applauds for Ella, Tessa says, "I can't believe you laughed at her!"

"It wasn't at her; it was nerves!"

"Well, calm down," Tessa says, looking at the stage, where Jeff has just come out.

He lays his papers on the podium, adjusts his tie, and begins. He describes a road trip he once took with his parents, his place in the backseat, and despite the brevity of the piece, it is full and rich. At the end, Helen sees Maureen lean over to say something to the person who came with her, sees her nodding and smiling.

"That's the prologue to the novel he's writing," Tessa says, with a kind of proprietary pride.

Now it is Claudia's turn; and Helen checks the audience once more for Kate Demian: she is nowhere to be seen. Helen fixes her gaze on Maureen Thomas, who listens attentively to Claudia, but there is something in the set of her shoulders, in her crossed arms, that makes Helen think she will not be asking to see any more work. Claudia reads from the beginning of her book, and when she has finished there is a brief moment of silence before the applause begins. Maureen turns to her companion, her chin lowered, one eyebrow raised, and now Helen knows that she will not be asking to represent Claudia. Helen supposes she shouldn't be surprised, but she is. She stares into her lap and applauds, then looks up at Claudia and applauds harder.

thirty-four

HELEN SITS IN HER OFFICE, CLEANING OUT FILES. SHE HAS DE-cided to turn this room into a guest/reading/television room. Sprawled all around her are pages with ideas for stories that no longer make any sense to her. It occasionally was a problem before, coming across fragments she'd written in the car, in the middle of the night, or standing in line at the grocery store; it was a problem finding those fragments and then trying to remember what she meant by *a cage full of flowers* or *ironing underwear* or *phone call and the Mustang convertible.* But it never mattered before; her head was so full of ideas that she didn't need those prompts anyway—she saved them in case she ever ran out of ideas. But now that she is out of them, these scraps of paper don't help. She understands that it was never the specific ideas anyway; rather it is the ability to write at all that has left her.

She sits back in her chair, inspecting a paper clip as though it is a rare artifact. She recalls visiting E. B. White's writing shed, and the comment she made to Dan afterward about how White's inability to access words must have been the greatest loss he endured. How idiotic that notion turns out to be.

Odd to feel embarrassed sitting by oneself in one's own home, but that is what she feels now. She used to harbor the illusion that without Dan, she would write so much better, so much more. Of course she would be lonely and in many respects unfulfilled, but wasn't it loneliness and discontent that fueled the better artists? Without her anguish, what would Frida Kahlo have been? Even Dorothy Parker—didn't she *need* whatever kept her glued to the sofa, drink in hand, staring at the phone? Helen used to think, oftentimes with bitterness, that once you were married, you were permanently on call. If you had children, the problem was compounded. Never mind the supposed advances the women's movement brought; it was women who felt most keenly the obligations to children; they were hardwired to put others first.

How many Sunday mornings, full of a kind of self-importance, did she tell Dan, "I'm going up to my study to work—I just got an idea. You're on your own."

"Okay," he would say, quite agreeably, yet she would read into it a kind of petulance or regret. Inevitably, she would be unable to work after all, and she would come down from her study to be with him, images of martyrs burning in her brain. So yes, how embarrassing, how scorchingly embarrassing to remember this! For what she sees now is that her love of Dan and Tessa, her obligations and ties to them, is what provided her with her life's work—and Dan knew it. It is true that she wrote before she even met Dan, she wrote from that first day in the basement as a way to understand the world and to find comfort, but it was Dan who encouraged her to turn from writing fragments to writing stories and then novels; it was Dan who got her to publish, Dan who got her to turn what she loved into what she did. Her family, Dan first, but then Tessa and Dan, were not only the place she came down to when she was through working; they were the place she took off from.

She tosses the paper clip into a drawer, and begins to throw away more pages, and more, then suddenly stops. She picks up the phone, and dials. Then she starts pulling pages out of the trash.

About six months before Dan died, Helen and Midge went to see a psychic Midge had told her about. Midge went first; then Helen. The woman used a beat-up pack of tarot cards, and the last card she pulled from it showed a woman standing on a beach weeping into her hands, many empty goblets turned on their sides before her. "This is your future," the woman had said, and Helen had said, "Hmm. That doesn't look too good." She was embarrassed, she remembers, disbelieving; and she wanted nothing more than to hurry up and get this over with, then flee past the crummy black curtain and into the crummy waiting room, where Midge sat—right after this, they were going out for a nice lunch to celebrate Midge's fifty-ninth birthday.

"That's right," the woman said. "It is not good in the direction she is facing. But look here." She tapped the card with one of her dirty fingernails, showing Helen the upright, full cups behind the figure of the woman. She leaned closer and spoke quietly. "All she has to do is turn around. Love always presents itself for your consideration, if not in one way then in another. You have to learn to see it. Then you have to learn to take it, which is harder."

"Okay!" Helen said. "Well, thank you."

"If you want," the woman said, "I can offer an additional prayer for you, and burn sage. Ten dollars."

"No thanks," Helen said, laughing, and when she got into the car with Midge, she said, "Don't ever take me to one of these places again!"

Midge backed out of the parking place and then looked over at Helen. "You'll see," she said. "What she says always comes true. Sometimes it takes a while, but it always comes true."

Now, as Nancy Weldon answers the phone, Helen sits up straight in her chair. "Nancy? It's Helen Ames. I know I said I wasn't interested in teaching next year, but it turns out that I am. Is it too late?"

"Of course not!" Nancy says. "Oh, I'm so glad. So was it the news about Claudia that changed your mind?"

"What news?"

"You don't know?"

"No, what news?"

"Well, I . . . I don't know if I should tell you. I thought surely you knew. I'm so sorry."

Helen leans forward, closes her eyes. "Did something happen to her?"

"Well, *yes*. But I don't want to spoil the surprise!"

"Oh, it's *good* news!"

"It's *very* good news."

"Did Maureen take her on? Is she going to represent her?"

"Oh, dear," Nancy says, laughing. "I think you need to call your student."

Outside, Helen sees a truck pull up. A man gets out with a huge bouquet and starts up her sidewalk. She tells Nancy she'll call her back, and goes to answer the door. She signs for the flowers, then reads the card:

Dear Helen,

I am in New York City interviewing agents, as Kate Demian wants to publish my book next fall. I can think of one other person who will be as excited as I am. This comes with such gratitude, and love.

Claudia

Helen tries Claudia's number: no answer. She calls Nancy back to share with her this happiest of coincidences, then asks, "When did Claudia meet Kate Demian?"

"At the reading, apparently. I just found out today."

"Kate wasn't at the reading!"

"She was," Nancy says. "She arrived late and sat way in the

back, in the sound booth, in fact. You left before she came out. She went straight over to Claudia, introduced herself, and asked for the rest of the manuscript, which she read that night in the hotel. She called Claudia the next day."

Helen can't help herself. She asks, "Did Kate ask to see anyone else's work?"

"She did not."

"Margot Langley?"

"Nope. She complimented Ella, asked for Claudia's manuscript, and left."

Helen reaches out to touch the petals of one of the half-open roses. "Huh!" After she hangs up, she'll celebrate by having a glass of champagne. And by throwing out the letter she got from Margot Langley. She's finished with it, now.

thirty-five

"THIS IS GREAT," HELEN TELLS TESSA, SCRAPING THE LAST OF THE apple crisp from her bowl. "Where's it from?"

Tessa points to Jeff.

"*You* made it?" Helen says.

"Mom. Mom. Mom," Tessa says. "It's not 1950. Men cook. They do child care and housework. They even talk about their *feelings*." She gets up and starts clearing the paper plates from the table. Helen stands to help, and Tessa points a finger at her. "Sit *down*."

Almost all of Tessa's dishes are packed; one box has been left unsealed to accommodate those things that were used to make dinner. Tomorrow morning Tessa and Jeff will load the U-Haul and then head west. Helen offered to help with that and was instantly rejected; so this will be their last time together. "Excited to go?" she asks Jeff.

He looks over at Tessa. "I can't wait."

Tessa's head is bent, but Helen can see her smile.

"When are you going to come out and visit?" he asks.

"Oh, I'll be there."

"You're welcome to stay with us."

"She can stay with Tom," Tessa says, and then, seeing Helen's face, "What?"

"I don't think we're quite at that stage," Helen says.

Tessa looks at her watch, as though in half an hour she might be.

Helen excuses herself to go to the bathroom, where she stands looking into the mirror. This morning, talking to Midge on the phone, she wept about Tessa's leaving even as she said, "I know it's good. I know it is." Then she said, "But first Dan, then my dad, then Tessa . . . It just feels like a little too much."

"I know," Midge said. And then she told Helen about a retreat she had once gone to where there was a big discussion one night about how hard it was when your children grew up. A woman said, "Why can't they just stay those little people standing up in their cribs every morning, so happy to see you?" And there was a long silence, during which Midge supposed people—herself included—were visiting those memories of their children when they were young and when nearly everything they did delighted you. "But then," she said, "this other woman said, 'But what if it really did happen that way? Wouldn't it get boring? Wouldn't you get awfully tired of changing diapers and cutting up food into pea-size pieces? Wouldn't you walk into the nursery one day and say, *Why don't you just grow* up?' She said, 'I know it's trite, but isn't it really true that life is so beautiful because it's so fleeting and fragile?' And this one guy said, '*No!*' and everyone laughed. But it *is* true. You'll miss Tessa so much because you love her so much. Aren't you lucky?"

Helen hesitated, then said, "*No.*"

"I'll see you at the movies tomorrow," Midge said. "And let me just say now, if you yell at me about putting too much butter on our popcorn, I'm going to put on even more." Midge had suggested a double feature tomorrow: she knew Helen's heart would be heavy, and both of them believed in cinematherapy.

After she hung up with Midge, Helen went to her bedroom and sat in a chair, a quilt wrapped around her. Snow was predicted, and Helen decided maybe she'd take a cab to Tessa's, she really hated driving in snow anymore.

She stared at a painting on the wall, an abstract that Dan had bought when they spent one day looking at art galleries in Milwaukee. Every time she looked at it, she saw different things. This time, she saw the face of a girl, looking up. Storm clouds. A line of open boxes. A starless night. A canyon, wide at one end, but narrow at the other.

She sat upright and flung the quilt from her shoulders. An idea had suddenly come to her that was so obvious it made her laugh. She went to the phone and called Tom and left him a message. "I just made a decision I think you'll be happy about," she said. "I *hope* you will be. Call me."

Now Helen stares into Tessa's bathroom mirror, trying to think of the right way to make her announcement, and decides on the direct approach: less room for argument. She comes out of the bathroom, sits in a chair opposite the sofa where Jeff and Tessa sit, and puts her feet up on a box. "I wanted to let you know, I've found a buyer for the house in Marin."

"Who?" Tessa asks, and Helen says, "You."

At midnight, Helen closes the book of poetry and lays it flat against her stomach. Outside the flakes are falling furiously; there'll be a lot to shovel in the morning. She looks forward to it, in a way; she has begun to like the feeling of accomplishment shoveling brings, the way that a path is so quickly forged.

Tom called her back shortly after she got home from Tessa's and said he was delighted by her decision. He told her that if Tessa ever had any problems, she could call him and he'd help her—he knew the house inside and out, quite literally.

And then he told her something else. When he and Laura had

decided to get married, he'd been going to build a house for her—
one that just happened to look much like the one he'd built for
Helen. The artisan tile in the bathroom was one Laura had selected; it had been Laura's idea to put birth signs in tiny lights in
a bedroom ceiling. It was Laura who loved tree houses and it was
because of her that Tom suggested one to Dan.

Helen listened to him telling her this and realized that he built
that house not for Dan and her, but for Laura. He had a fine repu-
tation and was a generous man by nature, but what he had done
in that little house was over the top and she'd known it the minute
she saw it. Now she knew why. She knew, too, that it was possible
Tom would never get over Laura, and, truth be told, she understood and sympathized with that feeling. She'll stay open to spending time with Tom for as long as they're both interested, but
finding another man is not her priority now, and it might never be.
She can all but hear Midge telling her not to get all "Hello, Young
Lovers" on her—she said that to Helen before in the context of en-
couraging her to try to find another husband. "Dan would *want*
you to remarry," she'd said, and Helen had said perhaps that was
true. And at some point she may want to. Or she may get cozy
with the fact that she will live alone for the rest of her life, that she
will be like the two old friends she saw coming from the Steppen-
wolf Theatre after a matinee one day. One looked to be in her
eighties, the other in her sixties. They were both very well dressed
and made up. They held hands, helping each other along a sidewalk that had been indifferently cleared. They talked and laughed,
their heads close together, and went into a lovely restaurant, where
they were enthusiastically greeted and shown to a table by the window. Helen imagined them toasting each other with a complex red
wine, sharing an entrée, and then going home to small but ele-
gantly decorated apartments in art deco buildings, each with a
light in the window, each with real stationery in desk drawers,
written on with fountain pens, the ink peacock blue.

She told Midge this, and Midge stared at her, then said,

"Right. Or they might go home to their soulless new development condos and eat cat food for the rest of the week." Then she'd said, "Oh, I'm sorry. I don't mean to sully your pretty little fantasy. I just don't want you to be alone for the rest of your life. I want you to be all right."

Well, for now she is all right. She rests her hand over the volume of poetry and listens to the silence of the house, a blanket for her mind. The grandfather clock has wound down, the usual sound of airplanes is absent because of the snowstorm; all is so very still. She thinks of Tessa driving off tomorrow to the house her father commissioned, and then she thinks of how Dan has never been given the credit he was due for its creation. She thought of many of the ideas for the house, and for this she has received praise; Tom built the thing, and he, too, has had his efforts recognized. But what about the generosity of spirit that had Dan sacrifice his own heart's longing in order to make real a dream his wife described for him one lazy summer afternoon? Perhaps his daughter's joy in living in that house will be continual thanks for the gift he gave. And it will complete his mission. His intentions will be honored differently from what he had planned, but honored nonetheless. Helen imagines a grandson playing in the tree house boat, his eyes the color of Dan's.

She gets out of bed, goes to her bedroom closet, and pulls out the box with the sextant. She unwraps it and again admires its elegant construction. She will keep it until Tessa gets to California; then she'll send it to her daughter and ask her to put it where it belongs, in a boat cradled by the limbs of a live oak, where it sails the imagination.

She peers through the sextant's telescopic lens. She knows that this instrument is used to create an artificial horizon when the true one is not visible, because of fog, or on moonless nights, or in a calm. It comes to her that she can't see her own horizon, but then who can ever see that far ahead?

This is her intention: to keep her focus narrow and true. And to come back to love in whatever form it takes. Inside, it is as though something unhitches itself, and settles. She puts the sextant on her bedside table, its eye directed outward, toward the west.

So quiet. She climbs back into bed and turns off the light. She pulls the blanket up over her shoulder, breathes out slowly. She closes her eyes and an image comes to her, a woman walking to a bookstore on a foggy fall night. Beneath her open coat, she's wearing a purple sweater with a gravy stain on the inner aspect of the left sleeve. An ill-fitting black skirt and brown cowboy boots. She has on dangly turquoise earrings, and one is twisted off to the side, caught in the woman's scarf. She has black hair shot through with silver and it's coiled on top of her head and anchored with a child's barrette. She's wearing a lot of eyeliner, no other makeup. She looks up into the sky and there is a full moon, and she thinks, *Bomber's moon.*

Bomber's Moon. All the people hunkered down inside their houses, the blackout curtains drawn tightly, even while the sky is as light as day. What defense can ever be offered against the whims, the regularities and irregularities of nature?

Helen sits up. She feels a rush of longing so strong it is almost like nausea, and she keeps still for a moment, then slides her feet into her slippers and pulls on the robe she left lying across the bottom of the bed. She creeps into her study and turns her desk light on low, starts up her computer. The black-haired woman moves through the fog. Helen puts her fingers to the keys and begins to follow her. She knows what the woman had for supper: little red potatoes fried in butter, salt, and pepper. She sees her table, set for one: a plate, a glass, a knife, a fork, and a spoon, its little metal bowl reflecting whatever comes down to it, up. It is this image that will shape the way the woman will come into the bookstore, the way she will unknot her scarf and slide out of her coat, then begin walking the aisles, searching for something she is bound to find.

acknowledgments

I owe an enormous debt to a few people who saw the value of this book early on, when I couldn't. Thanks to Barbara Ascher, who told me about the metaphysical pleasures of sailing, and then referred me to William Steig's children's book *Amos & Boris,* so a mouse could tell me about it, too—and so succinctly! Phyllis Florin put in her two cents' worth, and her two cents are worth a million bucks. Cindy Kline read the entire manuscript in what seemed like five minutes and said, "What's the *problem?*" Judy Markey told me the ending gave her goose bumps. Jessica Treadway said, "*I* would publish this *proudly,*" and Jessica Treadway is a formidable talent. She also made specific suggestions that made the book blossom. Marianne Quasha told me all about tree houses and handkerchief linen and reminded me, as she always does, to keep the big picture in mind. She also told me she liked to put crayons up her nose and smell them, which made *that* day. My agent, Suzanne Gluck, makes me feel truly understood and appreciated, and my editor, Kate Medina, gets an A+ in knowing the best way to arrange pages and nurture writers. My writers' group offered wise and honest criticism, as always: yet another round of thanks to Veronica Chapa, Pam Todd, and Michele Weldon. I owe the biggest thanks of all to my daughter, Julie Krintzman, who planted the seed for this novel. When I was complaining that I felt like I couldn't write, she said, "Why don't you write about that?"

about the author

ELIZABETH BERG is the author of many bestselling novels as well as two works of nonfiction. *Open House* was an Oprah's Book Club selection, *Durable Goods* and *Joy School* were selected as ALA Best Books of the Year, and *Talk Before Sleep* was short-listed for an Abby Award. Her bestsellers also include *The Year of Pleasures, The Day I Ate Whatever I Wanted,* and *Dream When You're Feeling Blue.* Berg has been honored by both the Boston Public Library and the Chicago Public Library and is a popular speaker at venues around the country. She lives near Chicago.

about the type

This book was set in Sabon, a typeface designed by the well-known German typographer Jan Tschichold (1902–74). Sabon's design is based upon the original letter forms of Claude Garamond and was created specifically to be used for three sources: foundry type for hand composition, Linotype, and Monotype. Tschichold named his typeface for the famous Frankfurt typefounder Jacques Sabon, who died in 1580.